LOGAN Punished

New York Mafia Vengeance: Book 2

Alexandra Iff

Here's to new experiences and new worlds, may we uncover as many as we can in this lifetime!

CONTENTS

AUTHOR'S NOTE

LOGAN Punished is book 2 in the New York Mafia Vengeance series. It is a dark mafia, reverse harem romance that deals with mature themes. Trigger warnings include kidnap, white slavery, and reference to sexual/physical abuse.

CHAPTER 1

LOGAN

Life is not the same now. I hate to say it, but it's her. She's gone. In her absence, every moment stretches like a shadow at sunset. I often notice the pain in my chest, and I put my hand over it, clutching my broken heart.

We fought this war to get rid of Milan the Dog and be with her. To wake up next to Maisy, and live our lives with her by our side. Why the *fuck* did she get out of the car? It's on me. My fault. I should've been next to her, making sure she stayed inside and safe.

Dammit. I stop and take a breath.

"Come on, Mr. Terrence. Focus. I need you to kneel three times for me."

I got a new physiotherapist today, Marina. She came in Giovanni's place. He's got food poisoning, or so we've been told. So the agency sent this woman. Curves in the right places, blond hair, soft brown eyes, mid-forties. A total zero compared to my Maisy.

Uncle Jon sits in the corner, watching Marina. Since she's here under extremely shady circumstances, one small mistake and she's a dead woman. I mean, Giovanni did cancel his appointment literally twenty minutes before he was supposed to show up. Now she's telling me to kneel for her, which is unintentionally funny because she doesn't know that she's ordering around *the* Logan Vitali. Or maybe she does. Just in case, Uncle Jon gave me an alias, Mr. Terrence, which I know is not the best coverup and, for sure, wouldn't save me from intruders. Mr. Terrence dresses just like Logan, so no matter how hard my physio works me, I'm wearing the clothes I'm most comfortable in, my three-piece suit and shiny black shoes – with, of course, my trusted blades in my pocket.

I follow Marina's orders and kneel three times, then get up again with ease, throwing her a jokingly triumphant look.

She frowns. "Let's get you to do something harder. Can we try the stairs?"

I'm standing here alive, in my penthouse, thanks to the Delgados – thirteen weeks ago, one of them pulled me to safety and dropped me in front of Uncle Jon, who took me immediately to the hospital. Through the back door, of course. Although, with that many doctors on our payroll, I should've entered like a celebrity through the front entrance. And since I went to school with most of the doctors, everyone there knew me. Correction: everyone *feared* me.

And for the last three weeks, I've been stuck in my penthouse. I'm told it was Bobby who shot me in the knee, saying I should be happy I'm not dead. Like he did me a favor by not killing me, because I spared his life when I found out he was a snitch. He said next time, I'll be dead. *Me?* He should've killed me when he got the chance because he's gonna die the moment I lay eyes on him.

My knee is fucked. Actually, my knee is no more, gone. I now have a titanium knee replacement. That was bad in itself, but it was the bullet to the chest that nearly killed me. The doctors still wonder how I survived. But I know good old Uncle Jon. He probably threatened to kill every living relative of the doctors, maybe even their neighbors, if they didn't save me. My lung collapsed and filled with blood. Someone from the Delgados saw me and recognized a punctured lung, so the advice 'he needs a doctor in the next three minutes' did not go unnoticed. I didn't think much of the Delgados – apart from Kai, of course. I thought the rest of them were an uneducated horde. Clearly, I was wrong. I remember drifting in and out of consciousness and seeing tubes coming out of my ribs, both for air drainage and to inflate my lung. The good thing about being a doctor is being able to tell the doctors at the hospital were, in fact, trying to save my life.

And save me they did. Basically, I owe my life to the Delgados.

I was in hospital for ten weeks before I could come home. It could've been sooner, but we needed to vet the physiotherapist, Giovanni, because he'd have to come to my penthouse to continue working with me. I'm set on fully restoring my physical capabilities, so Giovanni's been working me real hard, with results.

My punctured lung is healed, and I need at least another week or so for my knee. After nearly three months of healing, my health is coming back to how it was.

Uncle Jon and I exchange glances at Marina's proposal. She's been cleared for any sign of weapons and doesn't exactly look like a threat, but suggesting anything out of the ordinary is a red flag in itself. Also, stairs are still kind of tricky for me. And she knows that.

"Sure. Over there." I point to the corner, at the staircase leading to my roof terrace. I'm focused on succeeding, not fearing.

Uncle Jon stands up, looking anxious. "Mr. Terrence, are you sure you can do that? Maybe you should wait for Giovanni."

Marina's quick to defend her suggestion. "It shouldn't matter who you're doing this with. If you want to get better, let's do it and not waste time." She's looking directly at me. Evidently, she can tell I'm the one making the decisions around here.

"I don't have time to waste, Uncle Jon." I start walking toward the staircase, with Marina following me.

I haven't heard from Kai or Orion in a little over three months and I still don't have any information on their whereabouts. If they were alive, they'd get in contact with me. But nothing, from either of them. Not even news of their death. Silence.

I'm hoping they've taken the road I have. None of my family knows what's going on with me. I'm up in my penthouse, and only Uncle Jon and the physiotherapists know I'm here. Everyone else coming and going in the building, cleaning, cooking, talking, having meetings – none of them know about my state. I could be dead as far as they know. Uncle Jon's keeping them under control. For the moment.

I remember the last thing I saw of Kai was him being dragged away to safety by his family, and of Orion, being mown down by bullets, and if that didn't stop him going after Maisy, that last hit to the head did. I hate having that image in my mind. It sticks around, no matter how hard I try to erase it. But had I not seen it, I wouldn't have had the vengeance in my blood to help me survive. I'm thirsty for Milan's death, him and every single Slav in his vicinity. As God is my witness...

A searing pain tears through my heart, one I've been trying to ignore all these weeks as I've been getting back to myself. It's been too long without hearing a word. My cell got lost that day, along with every phone number in it. But even with a new one, I don't know what I'm waiting on. Syncing my contacts with the cloud will get me one step closer to the truth, but I'm delaying what I might hear.

Everyone will get what they deserve. On that, I give my word to God.

And Maisy... My heart stings when I remember Maisy. Literally *stings*. That burning pain is still in the background and as my mind conjures Maisy's face, a new wound appears. It's my fault we lost Maisy. My chest constricts when I think of her and I stop walking to take a breath.

"Mr. Terrence?" Marina gently touches my elbow. "Are you okay?"

I wave her off. *Nonsense*. I don't get affected by pain. Time will heal everything. But fuck me if I don't get my revenge. We continue to the staircase, and the scent of cigars and whiskey reaches me. Uncle Jon is behind us, having moved his chair from the corner and positioned it right at the bottom of the stairs.

He eyes Marina suspiciously. "Don't mind me. I'd like to observe."

"Seriously, there's no need–" she objects, but seeing him sit down and lean back, she sighs. "Never mind. Let's get to it, Mr. Terrence."

I begin the climb, taking one slow step at a time, heading up the staircase with Marina following behind.

As we reach the top, her voice is a tad too loud. "Mr. Terrence, congratulations! It seems like you don't need me at all."

I turn to her and she grabs my hand, shaking it, pressing a small piece of paper into my palm.

"*Call Kai,*" she mouths as she takes a step backward. "Come on down, now."

Hearing Kai's name uttered by someone, anyone, makes me happy. But also: *How the fuck did she get in here?* She could've killed me. Plus, *Kai's alive.*

"Come on now, ten more steps," she urges.

"I swear, if this is a setup, I'll tear your heart out while you're still alive," I threaten quietly. I may be recovering, but my hands can still throw a blade and kill.

"He said you might say that," she responds coolly. "I'm a doctor, like you. I know it can be done, too."

We reach the bottom of the staircase and I immediately reach for my chair.

"Well done, Mr. Terrence!"

"That was challenging, Marina. But I'll try to do it more often from now on. I want to be one hundred percent ready when it's time to go back to work." I sit myself down. "You can go now. I can continue on my own. Thank you."

"Suit yourself, Mr. Terrence." She saunters back to the table where her bag and coat are. "Do call me again if your physiotherapist isn't available."

"Sure, sure." Uncle Jon cuts her off, already on his feet and breathing down her neck. He doesn't even allow her to put the coat on, just ushers her out. "Come on, I'll take you downstairs." Then they're gone, and the door behind them closes.

Fucking security. I'm going to have to do something about it. Vetting's the issue here. But anyway, if someone's playing me, I don't care. I'm going to check this out. It's been too long with no sign of either of them.

I take my new cell and carefully key in the number written on Marina's note. It rings a few times before I hear someone picking up.

"Please tell me this is who I think it is." Kai's familiar voice is low, desperate.

"Who were you expecting?" I grin so hard that the muscles in my face, having not been used in months, cause me actual pain. I want to embrace him hard enough that he'd squeal if I actually did it.

"You fucker! I thought you died on me." He's serious. Hushed. "Where the fuck were you all this time? They said you're still in hospital, breathing through tubes. A vegetable."

"I just about pulled through. One of yours saved me. Had to stay put 'til I healed. You?"

"It was touch and go for a few days 'til Marina and her team operated on me. They removed eight bullets. Eight *fucking* bullets, Logan! I saved them all for Milan."

"Goddamn, you're lucky! Can you ride yet?"

"Last week I rode for the first time since I got out of hospital. I drove by your penthouse, and then I went to Orion's. The road's slanted that way, you know." He takes a beat as his voice cracks. "The house was full. He's not there. Think he pulled through?"

I can't tell him what I saw – Orion being mown down. I don't say a word, and he continues.

"Well, anyway. We'll find out soon enough."

"How did you get through to me? I thought I was safe in my tower 'til Marina walked in. She was fully vetted, too."

"You are. You're safe. It took me a long time to get to you. But I had to use Marina herself, as she's a recognized doctor and your vetting would've had to succeed. She wanted to help, anyway. How hard were you hit?"

"Me? I got a collapsed lung, a new titanium knee, and still doing physio full-on, which I'm sure you're well aware of."

"Sorry, bro."

"Don't worry about me. Let's find Orion, or his resting place at least." I have to break it to him somehow. It hurts me too.

"He's alive," Kai insists. "Marina's working on finding him." My heart breaks for him. At some point I'll have to tell him. "I'll let you know if she comes up with anything."

"Kai…" I want to talk more. I want to talk about *her.*

And as if he knows, he sighs. "I'll find her too."

He didn't see what happened.

The phone line dies.

We were so mad at her that we left her vulnerable. I need to know where she's been taken. Buried.

KAI

Fucking lucky asshole! I *knew* Logan was alive, I just wasn't sure what condition he was in. He could've been a vegetable. I couldn't bring myself to tell him how much it meant to hear his voice, but I bet he knew.

If Logan's alive, Orion must be too. I *feel* it. I'm so close to finding out his whereabouts. It's really fucked up that the Cartes closed off all communication after the fight. It's been three months, and still not one of them has been in contact. I've wondered how they manage to stay so tight, and I only realized it last week, when I rode by Orion's house: they're all living there.

My cell vibrates in my hand again and Marina's name pops up on the screen. She's probably calling to report that she did the job as requested.

"Kai, I found him!" she huffs breathlessly, as if she's running. "He's at CityMD in East Brunswick! Urgent care!"

"Who is? Orion Carte?" I demand. "Marina? *Marina!*"

"Yes! And your message to Logan Vitali was delivered. Expect a call!" I hear the unlocking of a car, that familiar double beep, and some sort of commotion.

"What's going on? Where the hell are you, Marina?"

"Still at the Vitali tower. I was recognised by some of his men. I know them from the hospital, I've treated them for gunshot wounds before. They started asking me questions."

"And you're still there? Get the fuck out!"

"You don't think I'm doing that?" I hear the sound of a car revving up and pulling away. "I'll talk to you later!"

She cuts the line and leaves me to stew in the echo of my own words. She'll be fine. I'm not worried. Marina can handle herself. In fact, I think all that she's been doing lately is preparing for an inevitable face-off with Milan the Dog. Hatred oozes from her eyes when she talks about him – it's palpable. She's a true devotee to the cause of killing Milan.

Shortly after my father died, Milan the Dog killed her husband. The whole thing was gruesome and unforgiving but, at the time, I was dealing with the death of the great Mickey Delgado, and that was no small feat, considering he was my father. A few of my men insisted I should find out what was going on, but the only connection I could see was that Richard, Marina's husband, was the surgeon who'd tried to save my father before he passed away. That's all.

Of course, the only thing for me to do was show respect. I paid the funeral costs. Sent his wife, Marina, a card.

And three months ago, when they brought me to the hospital riddled with bullets, they told me she was the one who fought for me on the operating table. She wouldn't give up on me.

So I started asking questions. Took her under my wing. It took her no time to open up.

She wants to help me kill Milan, and the Slavs, in any way possible. She's not interested in mafia politics, families, or even taking sides. Her side is opposite the Slavs. Mine is too.

I checked her out, figured out how much she could be trusted. I bugged her house, her bed, her phone, her life, and she really was the most devoted person to me – actually, to hatred. And to killing Milan.

So I asked her to find Logan and Orion. She didn't even bat an eyelid. No judgment. No care. For her, it was easy; only a doctor would be able to find information on them, considering their condition.

I look through the window at the grey sky, expecting snow, but with the temperatures above zero, it's not going to happen any time soon. Winter has crept in so soon, and being in Orient Point, Long Island, finally making use of my beach house, I tend to be aware of the weather more than before. Especially in January, when I could get snowed in. Although for the moment all we've had is rain. Riding my motorbike in the rain is harder; in fact, I know I shouldn't ride when it's raining, let alone snowing, but it's the one thing that keeps me sane. And riding to East Brunswick will take me little more than three hours on my bike.

I press the last caller button and wait for Logan to answer, but he doesn't even wait for it to ring twice. "Kai?"

"We got him!" I exclaim. "Orion's at East Brunswick CityMD, urgent care!"

"What? Do you mean… alive?"

"Yes, alive! I'm going there now."

"Right now?"

"For fuck's sake, Logan, I just found you and you're getting on my nerves already."

"Dammit, I wanna come with you. But–"

"No. It's too dangerous being seen together. I'll call you once I get there."

"I'd slow you down, anyway. Ride safe, and call me the moment you find him, you hear? The very moment!"

"Will do," I chuckle, and cut the line.

I pull out my leather bike gear from the closet and throw it on the bed, including my trusted balaclava, the one specifically designed for winter rides. I've been staying at Orient Point to recover, to get away from everything and everyone and regroup. To think about the Delgados' future. We took a big hit. *Fucking Milan. Fucking Slavs.*

He's not only a dead man walking; I'm planning the ultimate punishment for him. Marina has one thing on her mind, but we're gonna have to share him for what I have planned.

CHAPTER 2

KAI

I've been observing the East Brunswick Urgent Care Hospital for some time now, but nothing much happens outside. There's no one from the Cartes covering the place. No snipers on the roof, no wary men shuffling about the entrance. It's strange he's all alone in there. If he really *is* in here.

An ambulance with the sirens on screeches to a halt in front of the entrance and a handful of nurses and doctors run outside. The back doors fly open and they surround the casualty, a biker who's been in an accident. *For fuck's sake!* These rookies ride to die when they get a bike. The first lesson in biking should be about riding in rain – it's dangerous because of the water and requires riding safely, not crazily. Young fuckers die every day because of this.

But this is my way in. I fire up my bike and ride up to the ambulance.

"Is he gonna be okay? Please tell me. He, h-he's my brother," I say, without much emotion. They don't care; nobody's paying much attention to me. They just want to help him.

"Park your bike and come through!" One of the nurses yells. She feels sorry for me. I'm not totally lying. One of my brothers *is* inside. Orion's the closest thing I have to a brother, or anything – a father or a mother. Logan too. My thoughts land on Maisy. Goddamn, I miss her like hell.

Having parked my bike in the bay, I remove my helmet and my balaclava and run to the poor mangled guy lying unconscious on the gurney as they wheel him inside.

"He's gonna pull through, right?" I try to put some urgency into my voice. He deserves that much. Whether he pulls through or not.

They exchange glances as they push him through the double doors. "Take this." A nurse passes me his bloodied leather jacket. "And stay here. It's better if you do."

The swinging doors swallow them up, and I wait a moment before I spin around, checking out the space. I don't want to look like an intruder in a hospital this small. With nothing happening, I decide to keep going. I push through the double doors, but instead of heading to the operating rooms I turn right and go up the stairs, reading the signage and trying to figure out where Orion could be.

A middle-aged couple are coming down the stairs. They glance at the helmet in my hand, the bloodied jacket in the other, and make space for me as I ascend. Usually they'd be afraid of me, the way I look, wide, tall, tattooed, but they aren't. Here, they feel sorry for me. Empathy does that to people. Wipes the preconceived judgments they have because ultimately, death catches up with us all.

I follow their cue and keep heading up. Not sure where they're sending me but I'm heading to the second floor.

I get to a large reception area, where the words *Coma Patients* are written above the open double doors. There are ten, maybe fifteen people around, but nobody's paying attention to me. Before I scout the second floor, I walk to the coffee machine and get myself one while I look around. I leave the bloodied jacket on the chair next to me and think, I must find a way to get into their computer system, look for a clue there. I'm checking out the space as I pick up the coffee and take a sip. It's passable for sure. I take another sip while my eyes roam around the room, eyeballing each person.

Right there, in the middle, I recognize Lisa. I try to call her name and swallow at the same time, which is never a good thing to do. The drink goes down the wrong way and I splutter and start coughing.

Everyone's eyes are on me now, including Lisa's.

She looks sad. Her shoulders are slumped, her eyes empty. Looking at me, she's considering her actions. She knows me. She knows Orion's like a brother to me. There's no need for her to be defensive.

I finish coughing, and without saying a word, I head to where she's standing. Her skin is pale and she's lost weight. As I get close she just falls into my arms, breaking down into sobs. She's *sobbing*. Lisa and I have had limited interaction, as Orion wanted it that way, but we know each other. She's brought food over many times. We laughed together only a few months ago. She knows about us, and that's why here, right now, she's crying in my arms. If she's been here for the last three months, no wonder she looks like this.

"It's okay, Lisa." I stroke her hair. "It's okay. Shhh."

She wipes her tears and sniffles. "He was fine. He was getting better every day. We were going to leave the hospital." The tears keep rolling down her cheeks and she swipes at them, like it's shameful to cry. She has Orion's pride.

"Where is he? Show me. Take me there." My arm's draped over her shoulders, and I wait for her to guide me.

"Last week, he started bleeding internally and they had to operate on him again. Now he's just lying in bed, looking like he did when they first brought him here."

I squeeze her shoulders in silent support as we pass two doorways and go through the third into what looks like the most remote room in the whole building, next to a closed-off fire escape.

"He'll pull through," I tell her. "I know he will. He's Orion, come on. Your big brother. Now, stop crying." It's a quiet order. She knows. We cry only for the dead, not for the living.

"Yeah." She nods. "Yeah, you're right."

Orion's lying on the bed, eyes closed, a small tube coming out of his nose and all sorts of drips going straight into the veins of both arms.

As much as it pains me to see him exposed and weak like this, I kill off every emotion I have right now. He stood tall and saved me from the rain of bullets that cut through me. And I'm gonna save him too.

"Hey, buddy." I punch his arm gently. "Long time." I sigh. I'd better keep talking. "I'm glad I found you. I found Logan today, too. He pulled through. Now we're just waiting on you, brother."

He makes a sound, a faint sound, but we both hear it. Lisa and I look at each other instantly.

"Is this normal?" I ask.

Lisa's voice is anxious. "Orion, can you hear me?"

We silently wait, not breathing, trying to listen in on every nuance of sound in the room.

There's nothing, and she continues. "Kai's here with me. You're still safe at East Brunswick, as you instructed. Nobody knows you're here except Kai. He found you, somehow."

"Of course I did!" I say. "Now come on, open your eyes. We got some ass-kicking to do." A single memory of that night crosses my mind and I know that we deserve to kill that motherfucker together. "That asshole fucked up our world, remember? It's payback time."

Another sound comes from Orion and the machines beep faster, and louder. His heartbeat speeds up, his eyes shift left and right under his lids, and finally, slowly and languidly, they open.

"Nurse, nurse!" Lisa yells, and a nurse runs into the room. "Something's happening!"

I grin and hug Lisa as she smiles through tears.

The nurse checks the machine, then his pulse. All the while, Orion's eyes slowly seem to focus. He's looking at me.

"Man, I would kiss you right now if you weren't this ugly!" I chuckle.

Lisa smiles, tears still rolling down her cheeks. Happy ones, for sure. Orion looks away. I know he's laughing inside.

The doctor walks in and together with the nurse, they check over his stats.

"How come he's here? With no protection?" I whisper. Lisa pulls me away from the doctor and the nurse hearing range.

"I had clear instructions in case something like this happened. None of the Cartes know where Orion is. I took him from the hospital in New York and brought him here using four different cars, all rented under four different aliases. No one was to know about this place 'til he recuperated. Or died. In any case, he wants to remain either a legend or as if nothing was wrong in the first place."

"That's smart." I watch the doctor closely. Everyone's suspicious in my world.

Lisa nods. "Yeah."

"And your daughter?"

"My friend's looking after her. Her daughter goes to the same school as Mya and I thought that was the best option, considering."

"Why's everyone at Orion's house, then?"

Lisa looks confused. "Who is?"

"That house was packed with people last week when I rode by. It's how I knew he wasn't there."

"Fucking idiots!" Lisa snaps. "Actually, no. I'm not gonna think about them right now."

"He's lucky he pulled through." The doctor turns, interrupting us. "A small pinhole in his lungs caused all this. It could've been much worse. As this was laparoscopic surgery, he should be up in no time."

"Thank fuck, doctor!" I exclaim, relieved.

He just looks at me, his eyes narrowing. "Sorry, and you are?"

"I'm his brother," I snap back. *Never question a Delgado.*

"Hmm." He regards me a moment longer and leaves us, the nurse following close behind. Lisa laughs, and only now do I see her severe frailty, as well as her hollow cheeks.

"When was the last time you ate anything, Lisa?"

"Can't remember. I'm not allowed to leave the hospital at all. Or order takeout. It's written in his instructions." She shrugs. "I've been surviving on hospital food."

"Come on, really?" I turn to Orion. "Look at her, she's lost fifteen pounds at least."

"Kai..."

Orion's trying to say something so I lean down, putting my ear to his lips to hear him better.

"... Fuck off."

I explode into laughter; I love annoying Orion. I pull out my cell to call Logan, and put him on speaker.

He barely lets it ring at all. "Kai, any news?"

"Logan, you're on speaker and, well, I can give you the bad news first. I found Orion and he's... still an asshole!"

"He's alive? Orion?"

"That's the good news!" I say, and bring the phone to Orion.

"Fuck off, Logan." Orion's clearly enjoying this.

"That's crazy, man, considering I saw you literally die in front of my eyes," Logan says.

"He was in fact dead for five minutes," Lisa says, "but the doctors kept resuscitating him. It's all in the instructions. At least twenty times, it says."

"Logan, you good?" Orion asks. It never ceases to amaze me how much he cares for us.

"Yeah, and with a titanium knee. I'm good as new. Ready to fucking peel the skin off every Slav out there."

"Yeah, me too," I bark. "Logan, I'll keep you posted."

ORION

Hell looms inside me. I should've been left to die at the hospital. Because now I'm the devil incarnate, ready to cause carnage wherever I go. And with Kai and Logan alive and kicking, I got that extra reason to get back on my feet. Maisy was taken away from me, from us, and I won't rest until Milan and every fucking Slav in New York is decimated.

After three full months in here, I'm finally leaving the hospital. Lisa tells me the Cartes don't have any indication that I'm alive, and that they've taken over my house. My uncles have made it their business HQ, back as it was in my father's days, when the house was used as the command center of the Cartes.

Lisa and Mya had to move back into Lisa's apartment. This makes me dangerously irritated. If any place should be safe for my sister, it should be my house. They took that from her.

I take a deep breath. I will not get riled. I got the all-clear from the doctors, but they also said I should relax, take it easy. Fuck, with the world I'm going back to, there's no taking anything easy.

Lisa's downstairs, waiting for me. She's called Leila to be ready for my call. My house needs deep cleaning for when I get there.

Dressed in an impeccable and comfortable three-piece suit, a long black winter overcoat, and leather gloves, I'm looking civilized enough, but underneath I can feel the demon inside, the crazed man who lost everything and seeks revenge.

I press the level-one button of the elevator and in the silence, my thoughts go to her. We had a good thing going with Maisy. She was perfect in so many ways and flawed in just as many. And the balance she kept in between was immaculate.

I dismiss her face from my mind as soon as the doors open. Lisa's waiting. She's doing everything to get me to appreciate that I'm alive but at the same time, she knows that's impossible. Especially now. She knows Maisy meant a lot to me, to us, and she hasn't asked me about her yet.

"Are we ready?" She smiles, keeping up the brave face for me. Underneath, I know she's suffering. And I know I made that happen.

I nod. "You've no idea how ready I am."

We exit the hospital and walk over to her car, a black Range Rover parked in the emergency bay, directly opposite the exit.

"Keys." I reach out with my hand and she has them ready for me.

We get inside in silence, but the moment I ignite the engine and pull away, she turns to me.

"Orion, I'm worried you could get yourself in trouble again. Why don't I call them, tell them you're coming home? At least they'll be warned." She looks anxious, and is obviously trying to placate me. She knows me too well.

"No. I wanna see their faces when they see me alive," I respond grimly.

"It's not wise if you kill anyone today."

"Who came to my house first, Uncle Leo or Uncle Colletti?"

"U-uncle Leo asked me for the keys."

"They're not even in my will. This is how they'll act if I get killed?" I snarl.

"I'm asking you for Mya's sake. She won't have an uncle if you do something stupid–"

I cut her off. "Do not bring Mya into this conversation."

"Well, how else do I get you to calm down?" she yells abruptly, her voice wobbly, which makes me slow the car down and regard her.

"Hey. You okay?" I ask quietly.

Lisa covers her face and starts crying.

This is unexpected. "Hey, hey, Lisa, what is it? Did something happen while I was at the hospital? I'll kill everyone that laid a finger on you!"

"No! Nothing happened, except you nearly *died!*" she sniffles. "And I had to look after you. I spent all my days here, worried if you'd pull through. I can't be doing that again, O-Ryon. I... I haven't seen my daughter at all. I'm just... I'm tired." She wipes her eyes. "I want to go home. And I won't have a home to go to if you do something stupid."

I press on the gas pedal and keep my eyes on the road, frowning. I'm considering my behavior for her sake. All I want is to crush someone's skull. I need that. I'm *owed* that, seeing as we lost the war with the Slavs. But I also owe it to her.

"Okay," I finally say.

"Okay, what?"

"Okay, I won't do anything stupid."

"Promise?" she asks through a stuffy nose, her voice child-like.

I remember that voice. It reminds me of when she'd come to my room each time she'd had a fight with our mother. Well, with Wendy, Lisa's mother. The worst possible excuse for a mother anyone could have. Whose manic manipulations made me who I am today, suspicious of every woman I meet. Luckily, I was there for Lisa. My room was her safe place. I promised I'd look after her, always.

"You don't have to ask. If I say it, I mean it."

She takes a deep breath and sighs, leaning back in her seat, the remnants of tears still on her cheeks.

"How's Mya?" I ask.

"Good. Better. Worried why I'm not with her."

"I'm sorry about that."

"Don't worry." Her hand lands on my arm. "I got your back. That's all. I love you, O-Ryon."

"I love you too, sis."

"Tell me what you're going to do."

"About what?"

"About the house."

We stop at stoplights and I turn to her. "I'll go inside and ask everyone, nicely, to leave my house and never come back without an invite from me and me only. From today, any work-related stuff can be handled at the boxing club, as it was before."

She flashes her teeth at me.

"Happy?" I chuckle.

"Yes. I am."

For the next half hour we ride in silence, up until the moment I remember Lisa got me a replacement SIM card and a new cell, which I didn't want to connect until I was certain I was heading back home. I turn it on and dial Kai's number. It rings as I connect it to the car's

Bluetooth, and Kai's voice booms out through the speakers.

"Are you at home yet?"

"Not yet. Heading there now."

"Is your house empty?"

"It will be the moment I arrive." I glance over at Lisa, who's scolding me with her eyes already.

"Don't look for any trouble, Orion. You're not fully healed."

Lisa's quick to agree, shouting so Kai can hear her. "I told him that, too!"

"Thank you, both of you. I can handle myself. Kai, once everyone's out, I want you at mine. We got a lot to plan. We must find Maisy's..." I stop. I cannot get myself to say *Maisy's grave*. They took her away from me. From my arms. They literally dragged her body away. "I'll tell you when it's safe to come. Make sure you call Logan too. Goodbye."

Why? Why the fuck did they do that? I grind my teeth, my jaw locking tight. I don't want to show rage in front of Lisa. It frightens her. She fears I'll end up dead one day because of my anger. Since they killed her husband, she worries too much for me. Rightly so, since I'm the only one she has for protection.

"Take a left here, you can drop me off at Elena's place. Mya's there. I don't want to be present when you face the Cartes."

I take the left turn and keep driving until she gives me further instructions. I know Elena, but I've no idea where she lives.

"Here, stop here." She raises her hand outside a two-story house. I stop the car, and as she reaches for the door handle, she turns back to me. "Don't do anything stupid. You promised." Without waiting on me to respond, she leaves and shuts the door.

Lisa's made up her mind. She told me what she needed to tell me and the rest is up to me. *Damn right it is.*

I nod to myself and drive off.

~

Seeing so much garbage outside my house gets me from zero to a million in an instant.

Jonathan, Darius, and Bao are smoking outside. They glance at the car and the three of them stop breathing, I can tell. Because who else would be driving Lisa's car?

I park in the driveway, exit the car, and deliberately walk around, checking out the scattered waste.

"Orion, *fuck* man – where've you been? Everyone thinks you died!" Jonathan's clearly shocked to see me. That's authentic behavior, which is good for him.

Darius and Bao are smirking and welcoming me back to the land of the living. But come on. They could do better than that. This is my world, my family, and I'm tired of untrustworthy people. They will have to go eventually.

I walk up the few steps and open the front door. A stomach-churning whiff of cigars hits me. Taking it in, I continue my approach and reach the kitchen, which is enveloped by a sudden silence when the people inside see me.

Five of them are playing poker at the table, including Uncle Leo. He has his back to me and, apparently struck by the sudden silence, turns around.

"Well, I'll be damned. Back from the dead, huh, Orion? Come sit, next to me." Trembling slightly, he turns to the person beside him. "Dean, get me a bottle of whiskey and a glass."

Dean, a middle-aged-looking man I've never seen in my life, proceeds to fetch him a glass and a bottle. "Here, Leo."

Uncle Leo keeps his cool as he pours. "Take it, Orion. Welcome back." He passes the glass to within my reach.

I don't take it. I'll let him stew over what my intentions are. I promised Lisa no trouble, but I can still be an asshole.

"I'll give you exactly five minutes" –I look at my watch– "to get your asses out, plus any shit you may have here, before I throw it away."

Uncle Leo is annoyed, he's always considered this house his when my father was alive.

"Don't worry, Orion, nobody's taken over. I didn't let anyone go upstairs. We kept the meetings in here, in the kitchen and the living room, as we weren't sure if you'd come back."

His arrogance is stirring the demon inside me. "*If* I'd come back?"

"We were waiting on Lisa for information on your whereabouts."

"While you took over my house?" Exasperated, I sigh. "Uncle Leo, please. You got three minutes left."

Everyone jumps into action, packing up their stuff. I get to see some of the Cartes and their questionable behaviors first-hand. They tend to bring women to where they work and I see a few being dragged out of the living room, half-drunk, half-drugged.

I pinch the bridge of my nose. I could murder Uncle Leo. He knows my triggers.

"Come on, everyone, stop dragging your feet, run! Get out!" he shouts.

Within four and a half minutes, the house is empty. I examine the mess, the trash, the filth left behind while I call Leila. She's expecting my call.

"Leila. I need you at the house."

I cut the line and for a brief moment, I imagine living a normal life in this house with a wife, with children, like any other man in New York does.

A sharp stab in my heart cuts that off, however, and I drain the glass unceremoniously. The bitter taste burns my insides and represses the demon inside me. For now.

CHAPTER 3

LOGAN

Kai mentioned I ought to be careful, in case some of the Cartes didn't get the message about Orion's house not being used as their headquarters any longer. I'm careful as I can be, arriving in a cab. It drops me outside Orion's and by this stage, if anyone's around, it's too late. I head for the front door, hoping it's unlocked. It is, which tells me the coast's clear and Orion's waiting.

I step inside and the strong scent of bleach attacks my nose. Bleach and other cleaning materials. His cleaner must be doing a damn good job if she's able to clean three months of filth, bodily fluids, and gunk in such a short time. The vultures took over the space as if Orion didn't exist. Luckily, I have my Uncle Jon to keep the Vitalis in line, although I wouldn't put it past him to immediately take over if I was gone.

I take off my coat, and peek inside the kitchen. The floor's almost dry, but the half-drunk whiskey bottle on the table, with two empty glasses next to it, invites me in. I get in and pour myself one. I know why Orion left it out. I leave my coat over one of the chairs, and with a glass in hand, I look for him in the living room, but he's not there either.

"Orion?"

My voice bounces off the walls. I know he's here, so I go back to the hallway and look up the stairs. We all know what's up there. Or *who* was up there, for some time. As if drawn by some force, I mosey up the stairs, straight to her room. Maisy's room. Now it has a name. I just want to take a peek before I search for Orion.

The door's open and I lean against the frame, my eyes landing on Orion, lying on her bed. *Her bed.*

He's propped up on the pillows, one leg bent at the knee, the whiskey glass resting on it with his support, his mind clearly miles away. The moment he sees me, he jumps up. "Logan."

His arms open as he runs to me. I embrace him with all my might. Two grown-ass adults, mafia heads no less, holding onto each other for dear life. We got annihilated that day. The closest we ever came to dying. Almost lost our lives. Which is quite unlucky for the Slavs, who will now see true demise falling upon them.

We embrace each other as family, brothers, friends with a bond no one can break. It lasts longer than usual, and it's tighter. No awkwardness. We are one.

A knock on the open door brings me back, together with Kai's joyful voice. "Get a room, you two."

We turn to him and laugh. He's in leather as usual, with extra padding because of the weather.

"Kai, you lucky fucker!" Orion heartily embraces him, and I wait my turn to give my love to Kai, who came through for us.

"Glad you're alive, man," I grin, and slam a kiss on his cheek.

"Hey!" he protests, wiping his face. "I'm glad you're alive too, but keep your hands to yourself, okay?" He pats my shoulder.

"You're both good?" Orion sounds affectionate, which is unlike him.

"Yes. And you?" Kai asks him.

"Yeah. Considering." He looks over at Maisy's bed.

There it is again. Maisy's bed. Instantly, the energy drains from me. I'm happy we're all alive, but we're without Maisy. *I didn't keep my word.*

Kai pushes between us and takes her pillow, pressing it over his face and inhaling. "Mmm, I can smell her." He lies on her bed, holding it tightly to his chest.

Orion's jaw is tight. "That won't do you any good, Kai. Leave it."

I frown at him. "*You* were in her bed a minute ago. Let him grieve as he wants."

Orion regards me and shakes his head, looking frustrated with himself. "You're right." He sits in the chair opposite the bed. "I'm sorry, man. I don't know… I don't know what to say."

Kai shakes his head. "I'm not grieving, anyway. Maisy's alive."

His optimism gives me so much redundant hope. But Orion and I know the truth, so we don't even flinch.

"Okay, Kai." I'll play along. The least I can do for the moment.

"I have people searching for her," he continues. "You know, killing every Delgado snitch worked in my favor. My people saved me, made sure I survived, so I trust all of them with my life at this moment. They found both of you, remember? And now they'll help me find Maisy."

"You know what the last thing I said to her was?" Orion's miles away, not listening to Kai at all. "*I don't wanna see you leave the car.* Yet again, she didn't listen to me." He looks up at both of us, looking torn up with guilt. "How are you supposed to protect someone who doesn't listen to you? Tell me that."

"Orion, come on. She–" I start, but he cuts me off.

"Don't say she got what she deserved!"

"I wasn't going to. I was gonna say, she always did what she wanted. Whether we liked it or not."

"You know, we should've seen the signs." Orion continues. "That night she hardly slept, and in the morning, she woke up crying."

Kai nods. "Uh-huh, she did. She was so fragile when she cried."

"I lied to her," Orion says sadly.

"You? When?" I ask.

"In the car, on the way there, when she asked if the name Rebecca Trellis meant anything to us? And we said no. Well, I lied. That's the name of the woman on my birth certificate. My mother, apparently. The person who gave me my middle name – 'death.'"

I try to make sense of this. "Maybe Maisy knew about her?"

Orion nods. "Oh, she did. She knew a lot about everyone. That's why she always had the upper hand."

"What was she trying to tell you?" Kai asks, seemingly engrossed by this new mystery.

"Us... What was she trying to tell *us*, Kai?"

"Why 'us?'"

"Maisy mentioned an article about Rebecca Trellis. I already called my PI to see what he can find on her."

I'm puzzled. "What d'you think he'll find?"

"Logan, you found your birth certificate, but your mother's name's been crossed out, right?"

"Yeah," I recall. "I could just about make out a few letters of her first name, e-b-e."

"It's far-fetched, but if you think about it, those letters are in *Rebecca*."

I raise my hand. "You're crazy! Have you lost your mind? My father hated your father's guts! You're a Carte! There's no way, no *way* it's this easy. I've been looking for her all this time and if this is the case, and Maisy knew, she could've said something. She *would've* said something!"

"That's the only way it makes sense in my head."

"Look, Logan, your middle name's Moros, which means impending doom," Kai says. "And it kind of goes in line with Orion's: death."

"Oh, but not yours?" Orion scoffs.

Kai's cockiness shines through his ass. "Mine means destruction. Not death or doom."

"You think that's somehow different?" I rib him, and as though a day hasn't passed between us, we end up laughing at our own stupidity. But this time, as the laughter subsides, the idea lingers.

"Wouldn't be the craziest thing if we're brothers, huh?" Orion chuckles.

"Keep us posted on that PI report," I concede, "but don't get your hopes up."

"Meanwhile, we could ask Maisy herself." Kai's eyeing us with glee. "I'm waiting on a call from my doctor, Marina. Your physio, Logan. She knows everything and everyone. And she hasn't seen Maisy's body anywhere yet. I'm certain she's alive."

"Kai–" I start, but his cell ringing interrupts me and he raises his palm to me.

"This must be the call I've been waiting for." *Cocky asshole.* "Doctor." Someone talks to him on the other end, and slowly Kai's face stretches into a smile. "Yeah, okay. Got it. Send me the info. I'll try to find out. Thank you." He cuts the line and looks at us.

I don't even know why I'm holding my breath. Maybe I'm holding on to the speck of hope he insists on offering.

"Are you gonna say something or should we beat it out of you?" Orion demands, but Kai confidently flashes a grin at us. That cocky smile makes me want to punch him too.

"Maisy's alive," he announces, lifting his chin like he just saved the world.

"Kai, you'd better be serious." I take a step toward him, as if it'll get me closer to Maisy.

"I am."

"Is your source trustworthy?" Orion's the calm one, asking the right questions.

"She found you two," Kai points out.

"Where is she?"

"We don't know."

"How do you know she's alive, then?" Orion asks.

"She's been taken abroad. Marina thinks she was sold."

"What the *fuck*, Kai?!" I yell. That's unacceptable, in every possible sense.

"Look, it sounds worse than it is, considering you thought she was dead a moment ago." The certainty in his voice appeases me. "She's alive. We'll find her and bring her home."

"This is big. Fuck, I need another drink." Orion stands up and leaves the room. We follow him.

MAISY

The beep of the medical equipment bounces around the room and I hear my heart rate. I'm numb, I think. I barely feel anything and yet, when I try to move, a startling pain zings throughout my body, like every little bone in it is broken and screaming at me to stop.

How did I get here? I struggle to recall. My blood pounding in my head is the one thing I feel. *Try to remember, Maisy! Remember!* My eyelids seem to be glued shut and it takes me a while to force them open. Once I see light, my blurry vision gradually crystallizes.

A grand chandelier hangs above me, looking familiar for some reason. My vision sharpens and I see the tubes coming out of my mouth and nose, an air compressor rising and falling, and a screen with a wiggly line going up and down. I'm surrounded by a lot of medical equipment, but this is not a hospital. It's someone's house.

I raise my head to look around, and as I do my eyes land on my wrists. I'm handcuffed to something. A metal frame. *Why am I cuffed?*

I'm drawing a blank. I knew everything and anything, and more. My head was always buzzing with stupid nonsense, and now it's at a total and absolute standstill. *How come?*

But the fleeting amnesia is gone with the sound of a door slamming behind me, and in a painful flash, I remember. Shooting, crying, grief, anguish. The *pain…* The pain in my heart is bigger than any my physical body can endure. I remember everything. That animal made me betray the men who did everything to protect me, even when I did nothing to earn their loyalty or protection.

The men I saw dying in front of me. My eyes fill with tears that roll down my face, and the machine beeps faster and louder, exposing my weak state.

All of a sudden, there's a stir. "She's awake!" A voice, vile and menacing, grabs my attention. Too familiar to ignore. I turn, searching for that abomination of a man, but he's standing in shadow.

"After only a month? Can't be." Someone else is here too.

"See for yourself." A man in a white coat pulls at my chin and shines a light into my eye. It hurts like hell.

"God almighty. She *did* pull through." This one sounds disappointed.

"And you wanted to leave her there. Asshole. I knew she'd live. I just knew it."

Why didn't I just die?

The last thing I remember seeing is Orion's panicked face. Bullets razed through my body as I watched him go through unimaginable anguish, right there before my eyes. Was that because I was dying? I'm not sure. But if me falling saved them, I'm happy that it happened. *Please God, I hope they survived.*

Because I'd be happy to serve Milan forever if it means they're alive, since this is Milan's house, I'm back under his control, and will end up doing his dirty deeds again, for sure.

"Maisy."

I hear Rosey's hushed voice. I'm sure it's her. But it can't be. Orion said my sister killed herself. Another stab at my heart. *Milan lied to me. She's here with him. God, I wish I did things differently.*

I squeeze my eyes shut, expelling the remaining tears from them. I cannot face him. I *will* not face him and, when I have the chance, I'll kill myself. I tried getting away from him, this monster, but I end up in his filthy hands each time. Well, no more. Not this time.

"Maisy." Someone jabs my arm. "Maisy, I know you're listening to me, sweetie. Remember what I said if I see you holding a gun again? When are you gonna get it in your smart head that I own you? Remember? I *own* you. Now, get better, because you're flying to Riyadh soon. You're going to learn what obedience looks like before we have our way with you."

My body tightens, and my heart betrays me by speeding up, the beep of the monitor going off the scale.

"She's going into cardiac arrest. Move!"

Their hurried, anxious voices contrast with my body, which has already given up, and I find myself sluggishly drowning in silence.

ORION

Sold? Sold? She'd better not be sold!

With our glasses filled to the brim, we head up the second flight of stairs toward the attic, my security room. The third and last staircase is narrow and steep, and we walk one behind the other.

I've held my anger inside me as long as I could, but I can't anymore. My mind will explode. I turn to Logan. "How the *fuck* can she be sold? And you saw her dying, right? Even if she didn't die, she wouldn't have recovered by now."

Logan nods. "I saw bullets raining down on her body. I saw her falling. Just as I saw you die, too. I thought—"

"Can we talk upstairs, please?" Kai sounds irritated, last in our line of three in this narrow space.

I climb the last few steps and wait for both of them to join me before I turn the light on and put a hand on Kai's shoulder. "Look, she can't be alive. Trust me. I want to believe it as much as you, but it's just not possible."

Logan's eye starts to twitch. Maisy's death hit us all hard, and none of us will get over it. The good thing to come out of this agony is that he's now ready to slay every Slav out there. I am too. Saying that, if it turns out that Maisy is in fact alive, the mere thought of her being sold boils my blood. I'll be certain for Milan the Dog's last days on earth to be a warning to everyone out there who dares take something of mine. There won't be anyone saving him from my wrath. I hate to say it, and I don't want to think it, but it's better if she's dead. Better dead than sold.

"What if I'd taken the word of my family, who said both of you died that day? What then? Look, Marina found you two." Kai jabs at my chest with a forefinger. "Even with your stupid off-the-chart security. Marina wouldn't just say Maisy's alive. She has her sources. And people trust her. *I* trust her. If Marina says Maisy's not in the States, I believe her."

Kai has a point.

A sound pings on his cell and he pulls it out. Logan and I look at it too.

"Marina sent me a photo."

We wait for an excruciating few seconds for the attachment to open until, finally, there it is. A grainy, pixelated image taken from a street security camera. There's a van, four men with guns standing around it, someone on a gurney halfway inside the van, and two men in white coats. They're outside a light-colored, two-story house, seemingly atop a hill, as there are no more houses in the background.

A fat, round man, to me the very image of Milan the Dog, stands at the side, watching the person on the gurney.

"Is this Maisy?" Logan takes Kai's cell and enlarges the photo. "Dammit, everyone's too blurry."

"That's fucking *Milan*. I'd recognize that scumbag from miles away," I growl. "Let me see." I take the cell and start moving the enlarged image on the screen to investigate other elements of the scene.

"What the hell are you looking at?" Kai demands. "Check the faces, not the street."

"Send me the photo. I'll run it through the software. Let's see it better."

"Oh, right. right." He takes back his cell and sends the photo over to me.

I make myself comfortable in front of the screens that show the security camera feeds of the house. I often came here when Maisy was staying with me. My state-of-the-art security nook. I watched her sleep. I sometimes went through the feed to see what I'd missed. Like the day Maisy ran to Logan's club, or when... *Fuck.* How could I have missed Milan coming to my home? *My home!*

I found Uncle Leo was right when I checked the feed: nobody had dared go anywhere in my house apart from the first floor. Everything was left as it was, including my trusted MacBook in the attic, which is right now keenly awaiting Kai's email, still sitting on the desk here as it has been since my father's days. The light oak wooden floors and exposed brick walls are the same, too. The only thing new is the chair, leather – a much better one than he had.

I helped my father in here while he was alive, although nobody from the Cartes knew of my knowledge of cybersecurity. I'm not a hacker, but a lawyer, though I'm an excellent lawyer because I'm able to confirm things myself. *Trust no one*, my father told me. And I haven't. Logan and Kai are the only ones who know about it.

Kai's image comes through to my cloud just as I'm logging in to the best software the States offers for sharpening up images with a few clicks. As I search for the image, all of my photos populate the screen, and I know it'll take a few seconds for me to find it.

Logan stares at the screen, his eyes almost popping out. "Whoa! Is that... Is that Maisy?" His index finger points at a photo thumbnail.

Seeing it, I remember. I forgot I have it. "I took this when she wore heels for me. I knew you'd appreciate it." My cock twitches, reminding me of just how bad I still crave her cunt.

"And look, here." Kai points to the photos we took the day before we lost her. When all of us had her. I try to etch the memories into my mind. She was perfect. In every sense of the word.

I finally see Kai's image on the screen. "Let's look at this." I run it through the software and in less than a minute, a less pixelated version comes back.

All I want to see is if it's Maisy. I enlarge the photo as much as possible and it's there, on the screen, my worst nightmare. Death is not a nightmare. This is. Maisy's face is contorted. She's tied to the gurney, crying, as she's taken inside the van by the men in white coats.

"Give me your cell, Kai."

He passes it to me. "Why?"

I snap a picture of the doctors. "Here, send this to your doctor, Marina or whatever her name is. See if she recognizes them. I need their names."

"Sure."

I move the enlarged picture around, looking for any clues, and there it is, right in front of me: *Greenwich Avenue*, clearly written on a sign at the side of the road.

Logan's standing annoyingly close to me, staring at the picture. "This doesn't look like New York."

I start searching for all Greenwich Avenues in the vicinity of New York with light-colored two-story houses, with a condition that it's situated on a hill. In seconds, I have it. Greenwich Avenue, Central Valley, NY.

I upload the properties on that street into the program and run them against the photo. Another few seconds later, we have it.

The number blinks on the screen. *33 Greenwich Avenue.*

I look at Logan. This is it.

Having texted the photo to the doctor, Kai leans on the desk too. "When are we going?"

I'd love to tear that house to the ground, brick by brick, but we must stay focused and not get distracted. We weren't really seeing the full picture of Milan when we were balls-deep in Maisy. But not this time.

Logan jabs my shoulder. "Yeah, Orion, when?"

"Patience." I open Google Maps and check out the street view. I follow the road and the houses methodically, one by one. The apps are side by side and I compare the images until I'm certain I have the right house. Number 33, Greenwich Avenue. The house where Maisy was taken to. With nothing but anger and pain filling me, I struggle to control myself. I too want to kill someone tonight, but it would be too soon.

I stand up just as Kai's cell pings again. Logan and I wait with bated breath as he checks it.

"It's from Marina. She says, *The one on the left spilled the beans on your girl. Do not approach. He trusts me.*"

"Fuck," I mutter.

"Yeah. Fuck," Kai echoes. "Look, I trust Marina. Milan killed her husband and I think she's running a personal vendetta against him. That's why she joined us. If we don't get him, she will, I bet."

"We–are–going–to–get–him." Logan enunciates each word through his teeth.

"It was a figure of speech, Logan, for fuck's sake!" Kai snaps back.

"Let me check one more thing." I ignore their stupid spat and lean back in my chair as I scan the license plate of the van. I email it to a buddy of mine at the DMV and follow up with a personal text: *I sent you something. It's urgent.* "This shouldn't take long. He's usually fast," I tell them.

"This doctor, Marina, how well d'you know her?" Logan asks Kai.

"Marina Connely. I looked her up when she came to me. She's in her mid-forties. Her husband was a surgeon, killed by Milan. I like her. She's extremely efficient. Currently much better than any of the Delgados."

"Where does she work?"

"At the hospital. That's how we met."

My cell pings with a message. My contact came through. "The van's registered to the Embassy of Saudi Arabia, to a man called Hazim Taher. Left the States two months ago." I look up at them. "We got his address in Riyadh."

"I'm gonna peel his skin slowly – literally, peel his skin off – if he's laid one finger on her," Logan announces darkly.

"I'm gonna cut his dick off," Kai says. "I know that's your thing, Logan, but fuck it, I'm doing it."

"Do that. I'm happy with his skin."

"Right." I stand up. "Let me talk to a few of my contacts. If it all works out, we should be able to fly out tonight. Meanwhile, go get your passports and tell your people the war with the Slavs continues. If they don't like it, shoot them. No more lenience."

"Works for me," Kai says.

Logan's jaw is set. "I got contacts in Riyadh. I'll reach out too."

I nod in approval. "Kai, get a suit. We don't wanna stand out in a crowd." This is something I'd never ask from him because I know he wouldn't do it – not for me, or anyone – but I also know Maisy isn't anyone, and that it'd be dangerous to go there in biker leathers looking like a New York mafia member.

He starts shaking his head, but then concedes. "For Maisy. I'm doing this for Maisy."

"I know."

CHAPTER 4

KAI

"You can't take your blades through airport security, so don't. Orion and I will leave our guns on the plane, too," I tell Logan.

"Don't you worry about that. I got a contact who's gonna supply me with enough blades to cut someone in half if I want to. And I do." He stares through the window of the Challenger 650 Jet that Orion managed to arrange in an hour. It's the whole shebang: a jet, a pilot, and a flight attendant. Ready to take us to Riyadh and back.

Sometimes I think Orion's too powerful. Not that I couldn't find a private jet to take me to Saudi, but it'd probably take me more than an hour.

I'm suited perfectly well too, just like Logan and Orion, including the long winter overcoat. That was my father's thing. He thought he looked intimidating in it. I just think it's nice and warm. The downside is that I had to take a cab to the airport, and not ride my bike.

"Here you are." The flight attendant, Francesca, with a blond bun tied at the top of her head and clothes far too tight for her, hands me a glass of whiskey with a smile. She introduced herself when we boarded the jet. *How very polite.* I wonder if she knows who we are.

I take it, drink it in one, and put the glass back on her tray. "One more."

This is not me, enjoying luxury in beige leather seating. The inside of the jet looks more like a hotel lounge than an airplane. And the black three-piece suit and tie I'm wearing are fucking constricting. *It's a good look on me, though. Can't lie.*

"Sure. Anyone else need anything?" Francesca looks over at Orion and Logan, who both look lost in their own thoughts. Orion glances at her, but says nothing.

"The flight's nearly fourteen hours, so feel free to get comfortable. We'll get there at around four PM. If you check on your left-hand side, you'll find a lever, and if you pull it, it turns your chair into a fully functional bed. Let me know if you need anything else." She turns and saunters off behind the door, into her own space.

Once the coast's clear, Orion leans in. "We're in and out of there in an hour. Logan's contact will have a car waiting for us at the airport and will take us straight there. By the time we're back, the plane will be refueled and waiting for us."

"So, no plan whatsoever?" I frown at him. This is Saudi Arabia, one of the worst countries to get stuck in. "Guns?"

"The guns will be in the car. As will a passport for Maisy," Logan confirms. "It's not hers, but they won't check over there. She'll be wearing a burqa."

"Fucking hell," Orion growls.

The flight attendant strolls back in with my whiskey and leaves the tray on the table. She pulls open a side cabinet and takes out pillows and blankets.

"If you need anything else, let me know. I'll be at the front of the plane. Food will be served" –she looks at her watch– "in about ten hours, a few hours before we land."

Orion nods. "Thank you, Francesca." He pulls the lever on the side and his chair flattens into a bed. Logan goes to do the same but his phone pings, and both Orion and I stop to look at him.

He reads the message on his cell. "*I got more on Hazim's house. It's a harem.*" He looks at us. "He doesn't live there. It's where his wives live."

"Wives?" I grimace in disgust and Orion puts his hand on my shoulder. I don't know how he does it, keep his cool.

"Good news..." Logan continues reading. "She could be there. There's been a doctor attending that house for the past few months. Hazim will be at the house today, celebrating his latest marriage."

"He better not have fucked her yet," Orion says through his teeth.

I don't say anything. Inside my chest a black fire burns, one reserved for the worst kind of killing. I just flatten my chair, take a pillow, and lie down. Logan does the same.

"We take Maisy. In and out. Make sure we kill that asshole if he's there, then leave," Orion states before he lies down, too.

"Got it," I say.

Logan nods. "Understood."

LOGAN

I'm in a living nightmare. And usually, I wouldn't mind being in one, because that's how my life is. I've accepted it. But with Maisy at stake, it feels different. I can't wait to wake up.

How lucky it is that I've got Ajmal in Riyadh. He left New York – and my father's syndicate – five years ago, and it's good that he did, because he'd have probably ended up dead in some turf war. Got married, has kids now. When I reached out he was only too happy to talk to me. He said he heard about my father dying; he's keen to find his killer and have his way with him. He misses New York. The life.

If this works out, I'll arrange for him to come back. I told him about the Slavs, and Milan the Dog, that all of us now work together to exterminate them from New York. I had to. I'm certain he recognized Orion and Kai when I introduced them. He didn't say anything, though. Didn't think it was his place. Which tells me he's loyal. That's the type of people I need, not the assholes that snitch and repeatedly question their leader.

"Logan, eyes up!" Orion snaps at me. With the machine gun in his hands, he gestures at the open window on the second floor.

We've climbed over the security walls, and right now we're in the tropical garden of Hazim's harem, in the late evening, searching for a way into the house. Lots of trees surround it, but according to Ajmal, trees are how we get inside. I nod at Orion and Kai. The window looks like easy access.

Looking at them, I wonder if we've thought this through. We're wearing our suits, the three of us, and we each have a machine gun in our hands. It's good that we didn't need our winter coats in here.

Ajmal said the security of this place is minimal; there are two bodyguards with machine guns at the entrance, who we saw, and very few security cameras. Hazim is certain his wives are safe. Cocky, I'd call him. Of course, if we're seen, we may not live, but if Maisy really is here, goddamnit, we're taking her back.

I check all the other windows. The lights inside the house are off except one on the second floor, a dim light coming through the drapes together with some faint Arabic music. The open window Orion pointed to is adjacent to it.

Beyond the walls, distant noise can be heard from the city, enough to distract from any sound we may make as we get to the room. Kai nods at us, slings his machine gun on its strap over his shoulder, and shimmies up the tree. You can tell suits are not his forte; at this very moment his is all crinkled, and he's struggling not to rip it as he scales the tree like a monkey.

Come to think of it, all our suits are crinkled after a fourteen-hour flight, but they'll be much needed when we leave the house through the front door. Because no matter how many plans we come up with, we can't expect Maisy to climb down a tree, especially if she's not in a physical condition to do so.

This is it for us. We're stuck here. Either we succeed or die trying. Taking more people with us to Riyadh was an option but a dangerous one, as we'd have looked even more out of place.

Kai reaches the window ledge and jumps inside. Those few seconds before he pops his head back out feel like eternity, because both Orion and I know Kai and his explosive nature.

In a few moments, he reappears and motions for us to climb up.

We quickly follow his path up the tree, the foliage providing essential cover. Kai helps me get inside the window, and we both help Orion.

We appear to be in a short, dark hallway. The Arabic music is coming through the slightly open door in front of us.

Ajmal got us the blueprints of the house, as well as providing us with a black burqa, an enveloping outer garment worn by Muslim women in Riyadh to fully cover the body and face. To cover Maisy.

Standing in darkness, it's easy to see through the gap of the open door. I'm looking into the master bedroom, which connects through double doors to a large bathroom. The doors are open and I can just about see a small pool and five or six women, all of them pampering one other, who's sitting on a chair in the middle. I'm trying to find Maisy among the women, but it's hard; they're too far away and they wear different-colored veils over their faces. They're all wearing the same outfit: a beaded bra, a low, sequined belt, and a flowing skirt. It's as if they'll start belly dancing at any minute.

"It's impossible to see if she's in there," I whisper.

"Hmm," Orion agrees, still squinting to see her among the women.

I glance at Kai, and by the way he's standing, I think he's stopped breathing. I follow the direction of his stare – he's looking at the woman in the middle. She's being massaged with oils and shiny ointments on her arms and body.

"Kai, that's not her." I'm sure of it. Her posture, her empty stare from under the veil – that's not her.

"Wait, wait, they're removing her veil."

Two women carefully detach her veil and as they put it aside, a clear view of her appears. I stop breathing. *Maisy*. But half-dead. Alive, but like an apparition, an empty, hollow shell of a human.

The women help her get up. Like a doll, she follows their lead as they take her to the double doors leading to Hazim's bedroom, toward us.

I'm absorbed by her, trying to see some trace of our girl inside the shadow in front of us.

Kai enters my peripheral vision, stepping forward, but Orion stops him by slamming his palm into his chest, his lips drawn back in a snarl. "Wait!"

The double doors behind Maisy close and she's left inside the bedroom, in darkness. My eyes gradually adjust to see a shadow, Hazim probably, showing up out of nowhere. He must've been in the bedroom all this time. He approaches Maisy, his back to us.

"We don't have much time," Orion mutters. "Aim for his throat, but not the jugular. We don't want mess."

I nod. "Now?"

"Now."

I silently push the door fully open, hoping for the element of surprise, but the floorboards underneath my foot squeak and his head snaps toward me. So much for that. Before he can make a sound, I fling my blade in his direction. The blades Ajmal gave me are bigger, heavier, and they do the job fast.

He drops to the floor with a thud, and he's bleeding to death by the time the three of us are next to Maisy.

Her eyes fall to Hazim's body, and she doesn't raise them to any of us. *She's afraid. She's given up.*

"Maisy," I whisper. I take her hand and lift it to my lips, kissing her softly.

Kai takes her other hand. "Maisy."

"We've come to take you home, darling." Orion's voice is deeper, firmer. He makes it clear she has no choice.

Something appears to get through to her, thankfully, and she raises her head, staring blankly at Orion. Her eyes land on Kai, then me. Sadness clouds her beautiful features.

"Hey, sweetheart." I speak gently, hushed. I don't want to scare her.

In the darkness of the night, all I can see is the dark pools of her eyes, staring, getting glossier. They brim with tears as recognition dawns on her face. As if she's trying to see better, she scans our faces frantically as tears roll down her cheeks.

"This isn't real. I want you all here, but you're not real." She sobs and falls to the floor. "I killed you."

We kneel next to her. "Hey! We're here, baby girl," Kai says. "Look, here's Logan, and Orion. We came to take you home."

A beat passes before she starts anxiously touching us, one by one. She looks up at us, grinning through tears. But all of a sudden, terror overtakes her face. Her eyes grow wide. "If they see you, you'll die."

They've broken her. It kills me to see her like this.

"Maisy, will you let the doctor take you away from here?" I ask.

Still looking fearful, she nods quickly, as if I'll change my mind. She looks at me with those wide doe eyes. "Yes. I will."

Orion produces the black burqa from his bag. "Darling, you're gonna have to put this on and walk with us. Do you think you can do that?"

Her eyes land on him and it's as if she's only now recognizing him. Her brows knit and her forehead creases as her face contorts into a silent sob.

Orion pinches her cheek softly. "Shh, Maisy, please. We must be quiet if we want to get out of here." He strokes her hair. "Come on, darling. For me. Would you put this on?"

She nods, but I don't know how much she's aware of what's going on.

Kai kisses her head. "Baby girl, we got you."

I lean closer to Orion, making sure she doesn't hear me. "Maybe she's drugged."

He nods as he helps her with the burqa, lifting her to her feet and covering her body and face. "Ready?" He peers at her eyes, like he'll find some kind of recognition.

"Kai, help me here." I point at Hazim's body. Kai grabs his legs and we push him under the bed. "Your gun. Stick it under there too." I put mine under the bed. Orion passes me his and I do the same. "Let's go." I straighten up, then nod at Kai. "Tuck your shirt in."

The three of us are ready, and with Maisy in the burqa between us, we leave the room. According to the blueprints, this hallway takes us down the stairs, around a corner, and directly to the main entrance, so we head there.

As we turn the corner, we immediately see two security guards beside the main doors.

"Shit," Kai mutters under his breath.

Shit indeed. We didn't know there were men inside the house.

Cool as he can be, Orion leads us as per the plan. We reach the lobby and he nods to one of the guards. He doesn't question us, just nods at the other guard, and they open the doors.

Outside are the bodyguards with machine guns, the ones we knew about, but they too step back for us to pass. We exit calmly and head straight to Ajmal's car, waiting for us on the street. Like in a movie. We're calm, but ready to die trying to save Maisy.

What she's done to me, I can't put into words. I know that with every breath she draws me in, just like the moon does to the tide.

We climb into Ajmal's car, sit Maisy between us, and pull away. "Ajmal, the airport, please. As fast as you can, but stick to the speed limit," I tell him.

"Of course, Logan."

Ajmal watches the road for the whole trip, uninterested in what's going on in the back of the car. I asked him to help with one particular element of our plan and he did, no questions asked. Professional as ever. No wonder my father liked him.

The drive to the airport is without issue. Once we get there, thanks to Ajmal's connections, we get through security and onto the jet with no glitch. He couldn't go through security, but sent one of the guards with us to make sure we got on the plane as promised. If this works out, I'll be in his debt forever.

This whole time, Maisy hasn't said a peep. I wonder if she can see through the burqa. Pliable, submissive, she does what she's asked.

"Are we ready to take off?" Orion asks Francesca as he secures Maisy's seatbelt.

"We sure are. We've been waiting for you. I'll tell the captain."

"Hurry," Kai says, buckling himself into the seat opposite Maisy.

I sit next to Maisy and, wanting to make her comfortable and end this nightmare for her, I move to pull up her burqa.

"Leave it." Orion nods at the window. The security guard's still on the tarmac, eyeing us warily.

I nod and lean back, buckling myself in as Orion sits on the other side of Maisy.

The engines come on, sending vibrations through the plane. We begin barreling down the runway, slowly accelerating. I know it's fast, but everything feels like it's happening in slow motion. At least, in my mind it is, until finally we take off, the noise pulsing even harder in my head.

I turn to Maisy. All I see through the tiny slit of the burqa is her wide eyes, watching us.

Orion nods at Kai. "Ask Francesca for some clothes. She must have some." He turns to me. "Help me take this off her." I unbuckle her seatbelt and both of us pull the black material above her head.

"We're used to seeing you in a cami and panties, darling." Orion chuckles and drops the burqa to the floor. He studies her face and shakes his head, his mouth curving into a smile as a flicker of recognition appears in her eyes. "There's our girl."

The color slowly returns to her cheeks, and her eyes wander all over the plane. She's checking out her surroundings. Just like she did when I first saw her at Orion's house.

"Hey, sweetheart," I say. She studies my face for a few seconds longer, as if she's recalling.

"Hey," she eventually breathes in her sweet voice.

"Remember us?"

Tears instantly brim at her lashes. She nods as Orion wipes away one of the tears that rolls down her face. "Why?" she whispers. "Why are you doing this?"

"Oh, sweetheart," I say. "You belong with us. Nowhere else." It's a vow.

She starts sobbing and throws herself into my arms.

I embrace her tightly. I want to protect her. We're not letting her go anywhere ever again. But she needs to cry, to expel the trauma of the past three months. She's numb, and I know crying will get rid of some of the stress and make her feel better. That's what Rosa used to say.

Rosa... I haven't thought of her in years. She used to take me to school when I was young. I never really had anyone I called Mother, except the full-time employees of my father's strip club. In a way, they all acted as my surrogate mothers.

Orion has found a blanket. He covers her with it and rubs her back.

There's nothing left for us to do now. She cries in my arms as the three of us eye each other, concerned for her, yet relieved at the outcome.

CHAPTER 5

ORION

The plane ride was the easy part. Facing a dangerous world with her exposed and vulnerable will be harder.

I slept as much as I could on the journey back. Maisy cried a lot in her sleep and, of course, we couldn't ignore that. We made sure she was comfortable, the three of us taking turns as she had to be held close. I could've taken a shower, freshened up after Riyadh, but I didn't. Holding Maisy was extraordinarily calming, especially after my memory of her 'dying.' It was surreal.

As I held her, she was calm at first, but the deeper she slept the more restless she became. It reminded me of our last night, when she knew she was about to take us straight into a trap. I knew back then something was wrong. And now I'm thinking the same thing, even though I dare not say it out loud. My attorney's mind is trying to see everyone's point of view, to find the truth. *Is* something wrong now? Apart from us taking her out of Riyadh, taking back what is rightfully ours, and, maybe, her having endured an ordeal of the worst kind? What else hasn't she told us? I can't ask her all that now, Kai and Logan won't stand for it. But I have so many questions. *Too* many. Still, I kept her in my embrace and whispered in her ear words that soothed her. She stopped crying and moving restlessly, and a few times, she seemed to get some decent sleep. Her even breathing warming my chest brought me some peace. The kind that I find with her, and she finds with me. But it was always short-lived. She'd suddenly start whimpering like a puppy and I had to stroke her back, her head, kiss her cheek and hold her closer, tell her she was safe, that she was with us.

Over breakfast, while she slept or tried to, Kai, Logan, and I debated where we should take her.

"This is not up for discussion," I said sternly. Though considering Maisy was still in my arms, I don't think I made my point as strongly as I wanted to.

Also, Kai was being very logical. Being with Maisy has done something to him and he's grown, the fucker. Apparently, my house is out of the question because that's where Milan got to her. "Milan knew the ins and outs of your place and unless we babysit Maisy like a child, we can't take her there," he insisted.

Which got me seriously riled. Everything that happened to Maisy, and us, was because Milan managed to get inside my house. I'm not sure I can ever forgive myself for that. Unless I give Milan one more chance to visit my house, specifically my special treatment room in the basement. Only then will I be exonerated.

Logan insisted his penthouse is the perfect safety net for Maisy, being so high up, on the tenth floor. The first floor of the building is their strip club together with the Vitali HQ, and his family members live in the apartments throughout the building, so Maisy couldn't be safer.

Kai insisted Maisy would be kept safe by his people, seeing as she helped them identify his father's killer. She also helped unpick quite a few disturbances the Slavs made for them. "My guys have a newfound respect for Maisy. They wanna apologize to her about what happened, and I bet they'd be more than happy to act as her bodyguards 24/7."

She'd stay with him in his condo in midtown. Which I think is ridiculous, because that condo's for bachelors and is always full of people. Once, only once we've been there, after he assured us it was safe, and we almost got caught that night.

As we were landing, Francesca informed me of the full five-star service my goodwill client provided for me, which meant a limo was available to take us wherever we wanted. I had hold of Maisy, the most important item in our cargo, and together with the rest of the stuff, which was mainly guns and Logan's blades, we offboarded the plane, still discussing where Maisy would be staying.

That was until we were in the limo. I could easily have said "Take us to my house," but Kai was right. I wasn't gonna just hand Maisy over on a plate, not again. She was frail enough.

Then, Kai took over. Which is not something Logan and I are used to seeing. "Take us to Orient Point, Long Island." Kai's house, that none of us have been to. In fact, I don't think any of his family know where it is. It actually seemed like the best place to take her. For the moment.

Maisy's still in my arms, covered with a thick blanket. Underneath, Francesca's baggy jeans and white jumper fit her well, though while Francesca was more than happy to part with her clothing, Maisy didn't like them. What has shocked all of us the most is the amount of weight she's lost.

I stroke her head under the blanket, something I do each time rage overwhelms me, when I think of how helpless she was, and she surprises me when she peeks out from under it. She's craning her neck to look up at me through doe eyes circled with black eyeliner.

"Why can't I go to your house?" she breathes. Her voice is faint but all three of us can hear it. Suddenly, there's no more bickering in the limo; our attention is on her.

Shrouded by the blanket, she's studying my face for an answer. I press her closer to my body, tightening my embrace. I wish I never had to let go of her, and at the same time, I want to spank her so badly because she's been a very, very bad girl.

Her lashes flutter and her eyes widen. "Hmm?"

"Because, my sweet darling, we've established that my house isn't safe." It kills me to say it, but there it is. The bare truth. One that means I failed to protect the one thing I promised I would. Still, my response is soft. Honest. A little sad. If Milan managed to get to her, she was not safe at my house. No point lying to myself about it.

"Why not?"

"Because Mil... Because I'm still updating my security after what happened." Technically, I'm not lying. I am going to do it, but I haven't started yet. I only just got back from the hospital, and immediately had to fly across the globe to take back what was mine. This gemstone in my arms.

"I want to stay with you."

"Wherever you go, I'll be there. I promise." I kiss her forehead lightly.

Her eyes well up; she chews on her bottom lip and looks away. She's trying not to show she's crying, but tears roll down her cheeks.

"Every time I leave your house, something terrible happens to me." A sob escapes her throat and she pushes her face into my chest, her shoulders shaking as she weeps. "I wanna go to your house." She's sobbing and pleading, her words barely distinguishable.

"Shh, Maisy. Stop that. Stop crying. We're here. All of us. Look." I pull back slightly so she can see me. "We're gonna take care of you no matter what. Wherever we take you, you gotta know it's because it's the safest place for you for the time being."

Her red, puffy eyes are filled with tears, and still she frowns up at me. Then she peeks through the blanket at Logan and Kai, who are stroking her back. Her lower lip trembles. "What if something bad happens?"

"Nothing will happen, sweetheart. I promise you. We got you," Logan croons.

Her eyes bore into Kai, demanding a response.

"Come on, baby girl, do you really doubt us? We kept you safe, 'til..."

Fuck. Kai seriously doesn't have a filter. But surely he must know, with women, especially Maisy, you don't just say things. She's been through fuck knows what with that asshole.

Another sob escapes her and her shoulders begin to jerk again, but she doesn't hide it this time. "I'm sorry, I'm so sorry. I'm sorry. I went over that day in my head too many times and this, what you're doing for me right now, I don't deserve. You should've left me in Riyadh, at least I'd have atoned in some way. Milan had me... He had me cornered."

"Maisy, please, don't think about that." I pull her into my chest as she cries. "Everything that happened that day is on me. And my security." I glance over at Logan, who shakes his head. He doesn't agree with me, but really? Who else is at fault? Had my house been more secure, we'd be elsewhere right now.

"Orion, that's absurd," Kai argues. "You know Milan would've found a way somehow or other. He always did, the fucker." He mutters the last words darkly.

"Maisy, look at me," I say. I'm going to find out one thing that's been driving me crazy me all this time.

She sniffles and turns her head toward me. Her eyes are puffy, swollen, and her hair's stuck damply to her face. Still, she glows.

"Can you tell me... us, I mean... Has he..." *The fuck is wrong with me?* I'm not usually lost for words, but this is sensitive and must be broached delicately. Not because of her, but because of how it will affect us.

I clear my throat and glance at Kai and Logan, who know very well what I'm asking, but keep quiet like the pussies they are. *Fuckers.* I frown at Maisy. This is just like being in court. Questioning the witness, no emotions involved. But fuck me, it's hard. If she says yes,

I may kill the driver because I'll be furious enough to do anything. "Has Milan, or anyone else, raped you? Or taken advantage of you in any way?"

Her eyes close and she leans into my chest again. Kai and Logan hold their breath. As do I. Her crying stops. After a while, her head shakes slightly. I hope that's what I see, because a whole world of worry drops from my shoulders. I may even be merciful with Milan. I'll let him die after twelve hours of torture, not the twenty-four I was planning. "Is that a no?"

She nods. "But–"

"But what?" Logan's impatient. "Maisy, we must know."

I glare at him as I stroke her head, waiting on her to continue.

"After they operated on me in New York I was in and out of consciousness, but I remember waking up a few times and he was there. I... I couldn't do anything." Her eyes fill with tears again. She looks at me and whispers, "I *couldn't*."

A loud bang startles her in my arms, and all of us for that matter. Logan and I glare at Kai, who's punched the padded leather door next to him.

Maisy lifts her head. "What was that?"

"It was me. I was practicing taking out the soul of that bastard. I didn't mean to frighten you."

"What about in Riyadh?" I ask, too aware I'm gritting my teeth. I need to know every fucking detail before I remove the heart out of Milan's chest.

"I was still recovering when I arrived there. They really looked after me. The women were good. I had a doctor checking up on me twice a day." Sadness clouds her beautiful eyes. "Nothing happened there. It was going to happen last night, when you came."

Logan continues on my line of questioning. "Do you know if Milan tried to, um, to have sex with you when you were sleeping?"

She shrugs. "I don't think so. If he did, I was out of it. They gave me lots of Valium."

The mere words cause my index finger to twitch, the one I'll use to end Milan's life after I bring hell to his door.

"Why are you doing this for me? After everything I've done to you, I... I don't deserve you," she whispers.

Kai soothes her. "Maisy, we're here to protect you, baby girl. You're ours to protect."

"Everyone would've done what you did if they were in your place. Can't you see?" Logan asks.

She shakes her head and her brows draw together.

"Maisy, look at me." I lift her chin. "You're here, with us, and nothing else matters. Okay, darling?" I could get lost in her dark eyes, a sky without stars. I tuck her hair behind her ear. "Yeah? Is that okay?"

She nods and glances at Kai, then Logan. She reaches for Logan's arms and he pulls her into his lap, kissing her head before she rests it in the crook of his neck.

Kai's face lights up as he peers through the window. "We're almost there."

We're looking through the windshield, searching for Kai's house, when Maisy chooses to speak again.

"I saw Rosey. She's alive."

Breathe. I don't have the eye twitch Logan has, but if anyone could see the sudden war raging inside me, one side against Maisy and one for, they'd section me. She got in so much trouble because of her sister, about whom we saw a note stating that she'd died. Was that Milan's malicious plan? Fuck if I know, but it's clear now that Milan knows her inside and out.

Kai's staring at her in disbelief. "Your sister?"

"Are you sure?" Logan's crooning again. His tone verges on condescending and she sees right through it.

"Yes. She was with Milan. They thought I was unconscious, but I heard her." Her chin's starting to shake.

Logan prods for more information. "Maisy, you said you were on Valium. It can make you hallucinate. Are you *sure* you heard Rosey?"

She nods against Logan's chest and her shoulders shake again. She's crying silently. This girl has been through so much alone, and now she's lost the only family member she lived for. The rage inside me is gone and now all I want to do is protect her.

The car comes to a stop. "Baby girl, we're your family now," Kai says, reading my mind. "Come on, I wanna show you my house."

Maisy reluctantly unglues herself from Logan and reaches for Kai's open arms. He takes her into his lap just as the driver opens the door.

"Wait." I throw the blanket over Maisy, she doesn't have a coat and I don't want her catching a cold now that we got her back.

Kai secures it in place, and kisses her cheek. "Let's get you home, Maisy."

MAISY

Is it possible that my miserable life still continues? I've wished to die so many times. I've wished I was brave enough to take my own life, but I wasn't. I couldn't. There was this one speck of hope inside me, wishing I was wrong about Rosey.

That I didn't hear her talking. That I didn't hear her laughing with *him*. How could she? But then again, how could I have done to my boys what I did? I should be hanged for that. So many lives were lost. I heard Milan talking on the phone. Every family lost at least twenty people. Milan lost forty men. All in all, one hundred men died because of me. *Me*. The last person on earth that anyone should save. I don't deserve to live.

In fact, I died. I know I died that day. Why the fuck would anyone bother saving me?

I saw Kai lying on the ground, Logan too, and Orion – he got mown down with bullets as he was running to me. So why aren't we all dead? We'd be happy living in heaven, without all the heartache and pain. But oh, no. For some unfathomable reason I'm still alive, and not only that, but saved and brought back home.

They sold me. Milan and Rosey *sold* me. Like a piece of meat.

And yet that was the better of two evils, better than being anywhere with Milan, being woken at night by the most repulsive odor, his hands on me. I couldn't eat anymore. My body rejected the food. I'm lucky that in Riyadh, they fed me through a tube. They brought me back to life.

Still, over there I was alive, but dead. A hollow body, for months, until I saw them right in front of me. My boys. I couldn't believe my eyes. They just showed up and took me away. No questions asked. Just like that.

I still don't understand how it is that the people I hurt most are the ones who rescued me. Can I ever repay them? *I know I can.*

My body healed fast while I was in Riyadh. That place was going to be my tomb, one I was willing to stay in until death called me forth. Life was not worth living any longer. But it turned out, the women there knew how to look after me. They spread some sort of goop on my wounds that got me better, fast. I remember hearing the doctor in New York; he didn't think I'd survive with so much blood loss and so many bullets having riddled my body. He was genuinely shocked that I did. But Milan knew I'd stay alive. He sent me to Riyadh to learn my lesson. He hoped I'd be alone, raped over and over, learning my place. Or maybe he thought it would kill me. That would teach me a lesson for sure.

But boy, was he wrong. Here I am instead, in the arms of the most feared and ruthless men, those who vowed to me months ago that they'd keep me safe. They promised. And here they are.

"Put me down, Kai." I push away the damp hair from my face. I've cried too much in the past twelve hours, but now I want to plant my feet on the ground and feel my freedom. Feel my strength.

It was okay being held on the plane; their arms around me helped me sleep, gave me security and peace, but now, on US ground, I want to be free.

"It's cold. You've got no proper shoes on." Logan objects.

"I'll be fine, please, put me down."

"As you wish, baby girl."

"Don't let her go fully, she might–" Orion stops himself mid-sentence. I set my feet down and frown at him. He's always too protective.

"Hmm." He observes me skeptically and I smile tentatively. I forgot how tall and all-consuming he is.

Just as he's about to take a step in my direction, Logan sweeps me off my feet and lifts me in his arms. "There she is, my gorgeous girl!"

I shriek and, despite my blocked nose, manage to let out a chortle. I've cried enough. I wipe the remaining tears from my eyes and somehow, I'm lighter. I never thought I'd smile again in my life. "Put me down, Logan, I want to walk. I'm okay."

"You've lost so much weight," Orion remarks. "You must eat something."

"He's right, actually, you are very light," Logan confirms.

"Would you put me down if I tell you I'm hungry?"

"You are?" Logan slowly lowers me to the ground.

"I am."

"Well, you're in luck, because I have the best takeout menus you can think of," Kai chuckles as he unlocks the front door. This I believe is his beach house, the one he promised to take me to. From the look of it, it's bigger than a regular beach house. The sea must be on the other side as I can hear the waves crashing. January is the cold and windy month. We could have snow, too.

"I just want soup," I tell him.

"I'll make you a soup, sweetheart," Logan says sweetly, and takes off his long overcoat, even before we enter the house. "Kai, show me to your kitchen."

"Follow me. But wait. First..." Kai turns to me and lifts me off my feet again.

I squeal as he takes me over the threshold into his house. "Put me down, Kai! I can walk!"

"You are officially my family now!" He lowers me onto my feet as Logan laughs.

He follows us inside. "For that you have to marry her, you idiot!"

"Now I can show you the kitchen," Kai says, then turns to me. "Ignore him, please."

Kai leads Logan to what I'm presuming is the kitchen while I stand alone in the hallway.

I get a sense of coastal warmth and rustic charm from this house. The wooden flooring, bearing the marks of time, is polished to a sheen. The foyer is illuminated by natural light filtering through from above. I look up to see a wooden staircase ascending to the second floor where the glass dome of a skylight can be partly seen, with the landing up there overlooking the front entrance.

It's an open-plan space, and I can see the living room in the distance, ending with large windows on either side of the back door that allow the sunlight in. I check to see where Orion is. Just as I thought, he's standing outside, in his smart long overcoat, fixated on me.

"Aren't you coming in?"

He saunters inside and wraps his arms around my waist, pulling me flush against his body. "I intend to. Many times." *That sounds like a promise.* He leans down and nuzzles the crook of my neck as he breathes in my scent. "Fuck, I missed you."

I embrace his bulky body and run my fingers through his hair. "Why?" I whisper. "Why did you save me?"

He raises his head. I forgot the effect his onyx eyes have on me. He pulls me inside them and I'm lost instantly. Nothing makes sense, yet being with him is soothing. I feel protected, peaceful.

His voice is somber, threatening almost. "Because you're ours. And nobody takes what's ours."

Theirs. I like the idea... But surely I'm mine, too? At what point will I become fully mine?

"Now, how tired are you?" he asks.

"A little. I think I slept through a lot of the flight. You?"

"I'm fine, don't worry about me." His voice is deep, confident. Almost cold.

"But you were up all night. You must be tired. All of you."

"I'm not. Come, let's see what Logan's making for you." He wraps an arm around my shoulders and guides me toward the kitchen.

I crane my neck to look at him and catch a wince and an inward groan. I stop. "O-Ryon, what's wrong?"

"Nothing's wrong." There it is again, the way he cuts me off, never allowing me to care for him.

"*Something's* wrong." I stare at him. I know what I saw.

"I'm not fully recovered, I think," he says matter-of-factly. "I was released from the hospital two days ago and flew for twenty-eight hours straight."

"Oh god, Orion, I... I'm so sorry." While I was sound asleep, he was hurting. I start to fret, trying to think of a way to help him as tears well in my eyes.

He pinches my chin, pulling my face to him. "Darling, this is what we do. I told you before, don't think it's because of you. This is our life. Which you're now part of."

Kai's in the kitchen doorway, listening to our conversation. "Part of what?"

"She better know now rather than later. All of us got hurt, Maisy. Logan blew out his knee among other injuries, and you, Kai..." Orion turns to him. "You died and were brought back to life by that doctor of yours."

His eyes are back on me. "This is our life, Maisy. You may have been sheltered from it while you stayed at my house and had fun, but the truth is, this is what life is with us. It's uncomfortable, because there's always someone dying in our circle."

"But you're gonna change that. Right, Orion?" Logan's been listening in, joining Kai in the kitchen doorway.

"Right. That's the plan. Or *was* the plan." Orion's disappointed voice is strange to hear.

"That's the plan, for sure," Kai says firmly. "Logan, back in the kitchen. Orion, grab some wood, we need to light up the fireplace."

Orion's dark eyes shoot me a fleeting look before he turns. "Sure."

"I want to be a part of it," I insist. "I do remember. I saw you all getting hurt. You all died as far as I knew, and I mourned you. I never thought I'd see you alive again. I wanted to die too. God, so many times I wanted to take my life. It's killing me that I caused so much pain and suffering, and if I could, I'd die for what I did. But at the same time, seeing you alive feels like someone giving me oxygen to breathe in a room where everything's dead. Giving me hope. You brought me to life, you kept me alive. And I'll choose this over any life I'm given."

I'm not sure if he believes me. He waves his hand dismissively as he heads out.

"Do you hear me, Orion?" I call after him. "What's changed with you? Why are you different?"

I turn to Kai, wondering what just happened.

"Let him be. He has a different way of processing emotions," Kai tells me. "Right now, I want you to eat and then rest. That's all we're gonna do while we're here. In my paradise."

ORION

Why am I different? I did wonder that, for days, while I was lying in bed in the hospital in East Brunswick. And my conclusion was that I became weak. I've been weak ever since I met her. And Milan used her against us. Right now, we're preparing to raise hell, and the more dust we lift, the harder it will fall on us and Maisy. I will never forgive myself if I get her killed.

Having gotten the kindling from the shed outside, I go back into the house and sit in front of the fireplace, trying to light it, ignoring Maisy and Kai who sit behind me.

"I like you in a suit," she tells him, giggling.

"I'm gonna have to wear suits more often, then," Kai responds.

"I like you in leather too." *Flirty little slut*. I feel my lips curl up at the corner.

"That, I know." They chuckle while I try to remember how to light the fire. I've done this before; my father taught me quite a lot of things in my life. As cruel as he was, he got me ready for life. He also told me about women. *They make you weak*, he said. *If you fall for one, you're vulnerable*. I try to suppress the words swimming in my head as I continue with what I'm doing. I open the damper, the movable plate inside the flue, to make sure the smoke and ash travel safely up the chimney.

I grab the metal poker and start positioning large pieces of wood in the bottom of the fireplace in one row, then take mid-sized pieces and stack four or five rows on top of the base layer. Lastly, I take the smallest pieces of wood and pile them on top.

I have a feeling Maisy and Kai are watching me, though I may be totally wrong. Right now, I'm in my head, which is never a good place to be. I hate how much I need her. This is it for me, I guess. My fall. Brought on by a woman. I light the top of the stack with a single match and watch the fire travel down, igniting the pieces underneath.

I stand up and turn around to see Maisy nestled under Kai's arm, giggling with him as he whispers something in her ear. She's irresistible. And yet, deadly. How is one to live with so much temptation?

Kai pulls me out of my destructive stupor. "Don't just stand there, Orion, come here. Sit."

I take off my overcoat first, leave it hanging by the entrance, and sit on the chair next to the couch. I'm sure Logan will come out of the kitchen any time now. He wants to enjoy her too.

"Who's ready for some chicken soup?" Logan zooms into the lounge carrying a tray holding a bowl of soup, a spoon, and bread.

"I am!" Maisy breathes happily. She loves to be taken care of.

Logan plants his ass on the seat next to her – of course he does – and leaves the tray on the coffee table. He picks up the bowl and the spoon and turns to her. "It's a little hot, so you'll have to blow on it." He takes a spoonful of liquid and lifts it to her lips. All movement in the room stops while she softly blows on it, then takes the spoon inside her mouth.

I'm watching without breathing. *Fuck, I need her.* And from what I can see by their drooped eyelids and distended crotches, Logan and Kai need her too.

"Good girl, Maisy," Logan chuckles.

"Mmm, this is good. More, please." Maisy opens her mouth for a second spoonful, but my mind is telling me to slam my cock inside it. She must be doing it on purpose, because I cannot be turned on so fast and so hard just by watching her eat soup.

"Baby girl, the way you're taking that spoon... Stop giving me ideas," Kai says.

She's on her second spoonful and with it still in her mouth, her eyes dart to Kai, then to me. Instantly, her lips curve into a smile. She licks the spoon clean and releases it for Logan. Her teeth flash with a grin. "I am?"

"And nothing's gonna happen 'til you finish your food," I say, cutting off Kai's perverted thoughts. Mine too. I stand up. "Kai, come on, show me around the house. I need to see the security you have in this place. Maisy, try to eat in peace. Logan, we trust you you'll feed her properly."

"I sure will." Logan chuckles. "Come on, Maisy, say aah for the doctor."

I'm not looking at them any longer. I can't. My pants will explode.

Apparently, Kai doesn't want to take one step away from Maisy. "We're safe. Trust me."

"Actually, why don't you show me my room? I need a shower and a change of clothes, if you have any to lend me."

Reluctantly, Kai stands up and rolls his eyes. "Very well. Follow me."

He leads me out and up the stairs. "All I have is fresh socks, jeans and a turtleneck sweater," he says.

"That's fine for the time being. I'll send for my suit to get dry cleaned."

"We're at the far end of a very long island, Orion. There's no one to send. But don't worry, I'll take it to the cleaner's later."

"I noticed. You'd better have a boat here, Kai." I squint through the window beside the staircase. "Security's important. If we're under attack, we won't have any place to run except to the sea."

"In the garage."

I nod. "Good."

We reach the landing and in front of us opens up a large space with four doors leading from it. The landing is light and inviting. The walls are white, the carpet beige, and above us is a skylight, the brightness shining down and making the area cozy and separate from downstairs. A large beige couch is placed against the railings, directly overlooking the front door and making the whole space feel like one welcoming room.

"You can see the front door from here. Cool. It gives you an advantage," I observe.

Kai smirks self-assuredly. "Yeah, that's what I love about it."

"Any security cameras?"

"The panel's in my room."

"The perimeter?"

"About halfway up the island."

Satisfied by his answers, I relax somewhat, and nod.

"I've learned from the best, Orion." He pats my back reassuringly. "Come on, this is your room." He guides me through the first door on the left, a decent-sized beige room. The bed's made up just like in a hotel. There's a closet and an ensuite bathroom too. "Although you can always stay in the master bedroom with us."

I frown at him. "Us?"

"I'll give Maisy my room, and, well, I'm gonna sleep in there too." Kai snickers. "We'll share my bedroom." His toothy smile couldn't be bigger. He's thrilled we found her. She has the power to destroy us, and at the same time, to bring something out of us that even we didn't know existed.

"For the time being," I remind him. I'm not sure she's safe here yet. Or even if *we* are. But it's a good place to regroup.

"Yeah. For the time being. Let me grab the clothes for you."

"Sure."

Kai leaves my room and I don't wait to head for the shower. I remove my suit and pants, shrug out of my ruined shirt, and fold it and put it on the side. It'll have to be dry cleaned as soon as possible. It's grimy, sweaty, and crumpled. There'd better be a good dry cleaner's out here because I love this suit. And it cost a fortune, too.

I step into the shower and turn the water hot, accepting the fact that I will suffer under it. My wounds are healed but the skin's tender and reacts under the spray. I don't get how I can be with her and be myself. As I lather up my body, my fingers run over my bullet wounds and I'm reminded that this is all because of her. *This one, and this one, and this one.* I search for all the scars. There are too many.

I forgave her, but forgetting is going to be the hard part, especially with so many reminders. There'll always be doubt. Damn my wary mind.

Kai knocks on my bathroom door and shouts, stirring me from my downward spiral. "Your jeans and the sweater are on the bed! Come downstairs when you're ready."

"All right, man. Thanks."

CHAPTER 6

KAI

"I ordered us pizza and Chinese takeout. It should be here in a half hour." I'm starving, and everyone else must be too. Even Maisy, though she did have a bowl of soup.

Logan and Maisy are still on the couch in front of the fireplace, the empty bowl on the coffee table in front of them.

I haven't played host to Orion and Logan before, except that one time when I nearly fucked everything up, and I want to show them that I, too, can do it. With Maisy here, I'll bend over backward just so she falls in love with my place.

"And the soup I made?" Logan protests.

"Since when is soup a substantial meal?" I wink at Maisy, making her giggle.

She sweetly defends Logan, though. "The soup was great, Kai. You should try it before judging."

Logan kisses her hand. "Let him be, Maisy. He doesn't know what he's missing."

"Are you ready to be shown to your rooms, ladies and gentlemen?" I put on an English accent, making them laugh. I'm definitely more of a gangster than an aristocrat.

"I thought you'd never ask," Logan chuckles, mimicking me, but breaks character immediately. "In other words, please get me to a shower so I can get out of this suit. I can smell today on me."

"Come on, I'll take you two to your rooms." I help Maisy up by wrapping my arm around her waist, and lead her up the stairs.

As we reach the landing, I see her eyes wandering about, taking in her surroundings.

"Wow! This is so beautiful. So bright, especially under the glass dome," she purrs, sitting on the couch and looking up.

With the brightness of the day falling on her, she looks like a goddess. She always has. Even in Francesca's baggy jeans and white jumper, her body contours are visible, and her breasts, even though she lost weight, are still ample like before, prominent under her top. Her hair has grown, now falling beyond her shoulders.

"Cool, you can see the front door from here." Logan notices the same thing Orion did. I'm glad they're on top of their game.

"My beach house has the perfect security in place," I boast, puffing out my chest. I want Maisy to stay here with me, and I'm gonna showcase every security detail I have so they agree.

"Logan, this is you." I open the door next to Orion's room. "I left a pair of socks, jeans and a crew neck sweater for you. If you want your suit dry cleaned, bring it down and I'll take it later."

"Thanks. And Maisy?"

"She's taking the master bedroom. Over there, Maisy." I point to the door opposite Logan's. "Go and freshen up, take a shower if you want. Take that makeup off your face. I don't have any clothes for you I'm afraid, but we'll get something later."

"That's okay. These are good. Thank you." She smiles sweetly and walks into the master bedroom.

Logan narrows his eyes at me. "And you?"

He knows. I know. I'm trying to keep a straight face. "This is my house, Logan. The master bedroom is *my* bedroom." I snigger and follow Maisy.

"Dickhead. She should rest!" he yells as I close the door on him.

"I'll make sure of it," I laugh.

Maisy's laughing too. "Why are you teasing Logan?"

"Let him think he's missing out. He gets so mad," I grin. "Come over here, baby girl." I burrow my face into the crook of her neck and smell her skin. It gets me going, and I bite the muscle between her shoulder and her neck.

"Ohhh!"

"Did that hurt?" I mutter. I know I didn't bite her hard. "Or something else?"

"That was hot, Kai," she grins.

Our laughter is interrupted by a knock on the door. We look at each other and burst out laughing again.

"Now what, Logan?" I open the door and instead of Logan, it's Orion standing there. Looking oddly casual. I'm not used to seeing him without his suit, unless we have a job in the middle of the night, when he wears black sweats. I doubted I'd ever see him in jeans. And here he is, in jeans and a black turtleneck sweater, with wet hair sleeked back. He looks like a real-life assassin in these clothes. "Orion! Everything okay?"

"I need to talk to you. Come on, let her shower by herself."

Maisy's peeking around me, staring at Orion. He's a sight to behold for sure. "You gonna be okay showering by yourself, Maisy?" I beg her with my eyes to say, "*Please Kai, come and help me,*" but she's engrossed in Orion, her lashes fluttering, her bottom lip between her teeth. The fucker. *The cockblocker.*

"Sure." She laughs shyly.

I groan. "Okay, I won't be long." I walk out and close the door behind me.

"What is it, Orion?" I ask impatiently. I want to spend all my time with Maisy and I think he's being immature taking me away from her.

"We need to talk," he says, and heads downstairs.

The words are said with such weight that I know something's up. I follow him in silence down to the lounge, where he's waiting for me.

"Call your doctor. Marina, was it? If you trust her. Maisy must be checked. We don't know what they've done to her. You don't want to have sex with her if she's been raped."

"She said she wasn't," I protest. "Don't we believe her?"

"She also said she would wake up and Milan would be there groping her. Who knows what that Slav's capable of." His eyes darken, his jaw clenched.

The mere thought of that man doing something to her, again, makes my hands curl into fists. "Right. Sorry." I didn't think of that. I'm back to thinking with my cock again. *Ugh.* "I'll give Marina a call now. She can be here in a few hours."

Orion nods. "The three of us need to talk about exterminating the Slavs once and for all. Totally annihilating them. Our families must be on board, too. And this time, Maisy's not gonna be involved. In *anything.*"

"Got it," I agree.

"Now, who else knows about this house?"

"No one. My father, some of his associates, all now dead. We should be able to chill for a couple of days and make a plan before heading back to the real world."

"Sure. I'll call Lisa, tell her to keep an eye on the house. Those bastards better not go back." Orion turns and walks outside, to the porch.

I pull my cell from my pocket and text Marina. *Can you talk?*

She responds immediately. *Yes.*

I call her and it rings only once before she picks up. "Hello?" Her voice is deep, strong, giving me the notion that she can take care of any and all shit I send her way.

"Marina, I need you to check on a patient. She's with me right now."

"You found her – Maisy Roy?"

Two days ago she gave me the information on Maisy, that she was in Saudi.

"Yes, I did. I need you here to check if she's okay."

"Can't Logan do that?"

"No. We need a woman."

"What's wrong with her?"

"Nothing. But I need assurance, from a doctor."

"Where do you want me to come?"

"I'm in Long Island. Um, Marina? I'm trusting you with the only safe place I have."

"Kai, you know why I'm with you."

I nod, as if she can see me. "Sound View Road, Orient Point. Make sure you're not followed. Oh, and please bring a few changes of warm clothes for her. She's a size six, I think. Shoe size seven."

"Sure. Give me a couple of hours," she says, and the line goes dead.

I look up in time to see Logan coming downstairs, when the doorbell chimes and he freezes. Panic overwhelms me, as it always does in these scenarios. We look at each other, then at Orion, who's regarding us from the porch through the glass door.

"Check if it's the takeout," I say to Logan.

Logan walks up the stairs stealthily and, from the landing, yells, "Takeout! I'll get it!" He runs downstairs again, thundering like a giant this time, and opens the door and takes the food. "Kai, you got twenty dollars?"

"I gave him fifty when I ordered. Tell him that, unless he wants me to come and remind him *my* way!" I yell, annoyed.

Logan gives the delivery guy some scary spiel and closes the door. He carries the food bags inside and sets them on the coffee table. "Who was that on the phone?" he asks.

"Marina. She's coming to check on Maisy."

"Here? Is it safe?"

"Yes. She'll be here in a couple of hours."

"Great. Let's dig in, I'm starving." He opens his pizza box and takes the biggest slice. He always has the same spicy pizza wherever we go.

I take the box of Chinese noodles and the chopsticks. "Orion said we got to talk to our families about getting rid of the Slavs. But this time he doesn't want Maisy involved."

Logan nods as he chews. "Good idea." He swallows. "Which is why I keep saying that Maisy should be staying with me. She'll be at my penthouse, the top of the tower, and my people will protect her. Getting to her would be impossible and she'd be out of everyone's way."

"I hate to be the one saying it, but it makes sense," I admit.

He nods again. "It does."

"There's just one downside to that," I say as I watch Orion approach and join us.

"What's that?" Logan asks.

"Orion and I won't be able to see her, let alone fuck her. What do you say to that?"

"Sacrifices must be made." Logan grins and takes another bite of pizza.

"Nuh-uh. It's a no. It makes sense, but you don't get my vote," I insist. *There's no way.*

Orion picks up a box of sweet and sour chicken and some chopsticks. "We're gonna be working together. I don't fucking care if your men have an issue working alongside a Carte or a Delgado or a Vitali. We *will* be working together. And we *will* be having meetings at Logan's penthouse." He picks up a piece of chicken with the chopsticks and brings it to his mouth.

"So Maisy can stay with me?" Logan's eyes go wide, like he's a kid being told his best friend can come for a sleepover.

Orion shrugs. "If we want her out of the way, she has to be somewhere nobody can get to. And at the moment, your penthouse looks like the best place. What do you think, Kai?"

"I want her to stay with me. But I get what you're saying. We need her out of this war," I concede.

"Agreed." Orion nods and points his chopsticks at Logan. "You better keep her safe, Logan."

"I will. You know I will."

"You will, what?" Maisy's saintly face makes an appearance from the landing. Logan and I have our backs to her, but Orion must've seen her coming.

The dark eyeliner around her eyes is gone, and she blow dried her hair.

"You'll be staying with me at my penthouse 'til we finish this war with the Slavs," Logan tells her. "I'll keep you safe there."

"Your penthouse? Will I be able to leave?" she asks innocently.

"Not 'til we get the Slavs, and revenge on those scumbags," Orion replies.

Her shoulders slump. "So it's gonna be the same as before, then."

"Sweetheart, come here." Logan reaches for her hand, and upon taking it, she climbs gracefully into his lap. "We don't want anything to happen to you."

"I want my revenge, too," she declares. "I want to stick a knife through Milan's heart and look in his eyes as he slowly dies, and then twist the knife just so I can keep him alive for a split second more, that painful moment when he knows it's the last beat of his heart."

"Who are you and what've you done to Maisy?" I ask, shocked. I'm not grossed out, because that's exactly how she *should* kill him. I'm just shocked it came from her.

"That Maisy is gone. I'm ready to fight my own battles and not hide anymore." Sitting in Logan's lap, she looks so cute. She even lifts her chin when she finishes her speech.

"It's gonna be hard doing that from the penthouse," Orion points out, observing her reaction.

This is no joke anymore. We don't want her out on the streets while this war against the Slavs is raging. Besides, for some reason, Milan has it in for her.

"I don't want to hide again," she protests.

"Sweetheart, it's only for a little while. I promise you." Logan passes her a slice of his pizza and smirks. "Care for something hot?"

She regards all three of us, frowning. She must know there's no way we'll let her fight her battles outside of our protection.

She takes the slice from Logan, then changes her mind. "I'll stick with Chinese. That's hot."

She gets up out of his lap, puts the slice of pizza on the table, and picks up a box of noodles with chopsticks. She then sits on the couch, crosses her legs, and starts eating. She says nothing more. Is she planning on doing her own thing? Rejecting our plan? I hope I'm wrong.

"Why don't I shower and change into something more like me, and then I'll take you out for a ride on my motorbike? Would you like that, Maisy?"

She nods, her mouth full. "Mm-hmm."

I turn to Orion and Logan. "We'll take your suits to the dry cleaner's, so bring them down before we go."

"Thanks, man." Orion nods, all the while watching Maisy. *He noticed too.*

I head upstairs to take my much-needed shower and throw this fucking suit away. It's been stuck on me for two days.

CHAPTER 7

KAI

I've changed into my usual gear, jeans, a shirt, and a black sweater, and of course, my leather biker overall on top. It's cold outside. And since I really wanted to give Maisy a ride, we improvised. I gave Maisy one of my winter leather jackets, as well as a balaclava for under the helmet. The flats she had on from Riyadh are sufficient for the ride but I'm glad Marina's bringing clothes for her. She needs proper winter shoes, and a coat.

Riding my black BMW K1600 with the girl I adore, is now my life. Her arms around my waist, glued to my back as I take corners, both of us leaning into the road. She's not afraid at all, moving like it's second nature to her. Us, the bike, and the road are all that exist.

The rest of the bullshit goes away, at least for the time we're riding.

The roads are empty as we zoom past houses, shops, and fields on our way to the dry cleaner's. I want to show her what it feels like to be free and judging by the laughter I've been hearing through her helmet, I think she gets it.

In a half hour, we reach the dry cleaner's. Through the window, I see a few people standing in line inside. I park out front and remove my gloves, hook my helmet onto the bike, and help Maisy with hers. She removes the balaclava and unzips the leather jacket, that now hangs from her frame, too big for her. I bet it's the adrenaline that's making her hot.

A smile is plastered on her face and she yelps in happiness. "That was crazy!"

"You liked it?" I grin at her with glee.

"Uh, *yeah* I did! It gave me such an adrenaline rush." She takes on a playfully scolding tone. "Even though Orion told you not to ride fast. How fast were we going?"

I shrug. "I don't look at the speedometer anymore. I used to, years ago, just so I could show off. But now, it's pointless. I just make sure I ride safely."

Riding a bike makes you aware of your own mortality. When I ride, I often find myself entering a place of peace and calm, a state of mind that allows me to access all of my senses, which in turn helps me with the smooth ride.

"Well, I loved it!"

"Yeah? You want me to teach you how to ride?" I feel excited, like a teenager. She does this to me, every time she opens her mouth.

"You think I'd be able to ride this bike? It's huge." Still sitting on the bike, her eyes linger on the machine underneath her. It looks so cool on her but she's right, it's a big one.

"A smaller one, you would."

"Sure." She chews on her lower lip. "But how about you teach me how to box instead?"

I raise my eyebrows in surprise. "You want to box? Since when?"

"Since I want to take care of myself. I want to be able to fight, at least. And I don't know how. All my life I've been using my brain, and that helped, but I've got my body too. And if I could throw a punch that would hurt... I'd love to be able to do that."

"Sure, sure. I'd love to teach you some self-defense techniques."

"Yeah, that, but also, how to throw a punch."

"Okay. Let's do that once we get back." I remind myself that all of us evaded death only three months ago and we're still healing. "Or maybe in a few days. I think you need to rest today."

"I'm fine, honestly! The women in Riyadh smeared something on my bullet wounds and you can barely see them now. Look." She lifts her jumper and bares her stomach to me, pointing to a few tiny ridges. I count four. Two under her left breast, one on the left side of the stomach, and one on the right.

She's right. Her wounds have healed much better than mine. I can barely see them. I reach out to stroke her stomach gently with my palm, when she recoils at my touch, as if I'm a stranger.

Worried, I withdraw my hand. "Are you okay?"

"Y-yeah. Sorry. I didn't expect you to–"

"Don't worry, baby girl, I won't touch you if you don't want me to."

"I... I do." She takes my hand and presses my palm flat against her stomach. Her eyes close. "It's hard. I know *you're* touching me but I still have to tell my mind it's you, and no one else."

I lean in and whisper in her ear, "That's all me, Maisy." I carefully move my hand north, reaching the mound of her breast. "This is all me. Remember me?" My cheek almost touching hers, I breathe across her skin as I get closer to her lips. "Hmm?" I roll her nipple tenderly between my fingers.

Her eyes open and she looks surprised to find me so close.

"Hey." I kiss her lips softly. "It's only me, baby girl." *Maybe Marina's visit isn't such a bad idea.*

I step back to give Maisy space, but she grabs my jacket and presses her lips to mine. *She wants me!*

My cock suddenly awakens, and I kiss her back, our lips crashing, and I weave my tongue inside her mouth ravenously. I've been longing for this kiss for months. I wrap my arms around her waist and pull her closer as her legs wrap around my hips. She's in my arms, but the power with which she's holding on to me is all-consuming. Her hands are holding my face, like she's extracting my soul that I'm willingly giving for free, because it's been hers all along.

Suddenly, she painfully wrenches her lips from mine but remains inches away, panting, breathing my air. After a moment she smiles, and her forehead touches mine. She grins. "I had to be sure."

"And?"

"Mm-hmm. It's you." She kisses me again. Her scent, her taste, *fuck.* I wonder if her cunt still tastes as good as I remember.

The dry cleaner's is behind me and her eyes dart to it. "You can go now. There's no one waiting in line."

"Do you want to come with me?"

"Naah." She laughs. "The floor is lava. Put me back on the bike."

I leave her on the bike and she watches me as I take the suit carrier into the dry cleaner's.

~

Our ride back took longer, but it gave me such a profound feeling of peace, love, the future, how I want it to be. We'd slow down at places that looked interesting, stop at a couple of lookout points, and if we saw any interesting-looking people, she'd wave.

She's back. Maisy's back. Is it possible to be even more stupidly in love with her than I was? I'm the head of my family, the Delgados, a gangster, a man who can crush a human skull with his hands, yet I'm jelly in hers.

After a good while on the road, we reach my house. On the approach, I see an unknown car parked in my drive. I slow down to take a look.

Recognizing my wariness, Maisy taps my shoulder. "Do you know whose car that is?"

"Nuh-uh. Marina's supposed to come, but I'm not sure if that's hers." I'm searching for any clue that could tell me who the owner of this vehicle is.

"Who's Marina?"

"One of mine, a Delgado. She's the one that told us who took you and where you might be. She found Logan and Orion for me. Oh, and she's a doctor." I park the bike at a distance and continue to observe.

Maisy persists with the questions. "Why is she here? Are you okay? Isn't Logan a doctor?"

"She's here for you. Wait. Let me see if that's her." I pull out my cell and that's when I see a message blinking.

I'm here. Waiting on you to get back.

"That's her. Let's go in." I restart the bike and make the short ride up my driveway.

"Me? Why me?" she asks when we pull up. She removes the helmet and gives it to me, her brows drawn together in a frown.

"Just to make sure you're okay, that's all, baby girl." I kiss her cheek as I help her off the bike. "Let's get inside. They must be waiting for us."

LOGAN

Marina's been staring at me inquisitively for the last half hour. I offered her water, coffee, something stronger. She didn't want anything. She just sits there on the couch opposite me, her eyes moving sporadically from me to Orion.

She almost got killed when she arrived. Orion was about to pull the trigger but lucky for her, I knew what she looked like.

Orion's currently behind her, towering over her with a watchful eye. No pleasantries with him. She's a Delgado and may be compromised. At least, that's what I imagine he thinks.

Finally, she breaks the ice. "How's your knee?"

I watch her carefully. There's nothing out of the ordinary in her question, nothing suspicious. Still, she irritates me. She managed to get to me at my penthouse, and I'm not particularly happy about it. "You do know I'm a doctor too, yes?"

"I know a lot about you. How d'you think I found you?" She leans back and crosses one leg over the other, looking like she feels in complete control of this situation.

"I don't know. How *did* you find me?"

"You see, as a doctor yourself, you should know this. But oh, wait, you're not a *practicing* doctor," she jeers.

Orion sucks in a loud breath. "Ouch, man."

I grit my teeth. I was willing to be nice to Marina but here she is, drawing out the knives. And Orion isn't helping by finding it entertaining. I'm not going to get pulled into this.

"No, I'm not a practicing doctor. I doubt anyone would want a mafia head as a doctor. People in New York still think of the mafia like we're living in the 1920s and I don't particularly want to be receiving cash in hand after each visit."

Marina stares at me for a beat before bursting into laughter. Orion joins her.

"That's funny!" she laughs.

"Honestly, you holding back your anger just makes you hilarious. Next time, don't," Orion chuckles.

I don't get the joke and I'm irritated beyond belief. But I know exactly why. It's her comment that I'm not a practicing doctor. That's what I studied for. That's what I want to be doing. Why the fuck must I kill people for a living? Why wasn't I born into an ordinary family? Just when I'm about to say something, the front door opens and Kai enters, Maisy following him.

I stand up. Orion takes a step. We only need to glance at each other to know what's going on. Kai just nods.

"Marina! Thanks for coming." He shakes her hand. "I suppose Logan, you know already?" She and I nod. "And I take it you met Orion?"

She looks at Orion. "Yes, I met him all right. He almost killed me."

"I wasn't gonna pull the trigger," Orion responds indifferently.

"But you aimed a gun at me."

"I'd aim it at anyone approaching this house."

"Fair. Let's move on," she retorts, cool as a cucumber.

"Agreed," Orion says.

"Good. Now that's all sorted, I want you to meet Maisy." Kai pulls Maisy in front of him.

She still has his jacket on, which makes her look even smaller than she is. She cautiously offers her hand and Marina shakes it.

"Nice to meet you, Maisy. For someone riddled with bullets, I see you recovered well."

"How'd you know I was shot?" Maisy asks softly, in stark contrast to Marina's voice, which is low and gravelly.

"I saw your medical chart. By the looks of it, you should've died. But even when you pulled through, they still got rid of you. I'm sorry, hon."

Maisy nods, seemingly not knowing what to say, and being nearest to her, I pull her under my arm. "Let's take this off." I help her with her jacket. "Did you have a nice ride with Kai?"

Her eyes sparkle. "Yes, I did."

"Marina, the reason I called you today was to check on Maisy," Kai says. "You were right. She was sold abroad. We just brought her back from Riyadh."

Marina's brow furrows and she turns to him. "Riyadh?"

"We need you to check if she's okay," he continues.

"Am I checking for anything specific?"

Orion cuts in. "Yes."

"No," I say at the exact same time.

With something clearly off, Maisy steps out of my space and throws probing looks at the three of us. "What's going on? Why's she checking me? I'm perfectly fine."

"Maisy, we want to see if you... if you were raped." Orion regards her authoritatively. "Marina's a woman, a doctor, and she can check that."

Maisy lets loose a melodramatic sigh. "I told you. I wasn't. Don't you think I'd know?"

"Yes, you told us, but–" Orion starts, but Maisy interrupts him.

"But what? You don't believe me?"

"It's not that, it's just that we want to be sure. We..." Orion exhales slowly. I'm not sure if he even knows what to say.

Lucky for him, Marina saves the day. "Look, Maisy, I'm not going to check you. I promise. Let's just go and talk. There's too much testosterone in this room, and if I know one thing that's not good for, it's heart-to-heart conversations."

I feel relieved that Marina's taking control because it would've been hard persuading Maisy to do anything.

"But..." Maisy looks at me, then Orion, and finally, Kai. The three of us can kill and skin a buffalo in less than an hour, but when it comes to dealing with sensitive matters, clearly, we're clueless.

"I promise, I just want to talk." Marina turns to Kai. "Now, do you boys have someplace to go?"

He nods. "Yeah, sure. We can go upstairs. If that's okay with Maisy?"

I hold my breath. None of us move and we're all watching her closely. She's going to decide. Here and now. If she decides she doesn't want to talk to Marina, fuck it. We won't make her, no matter what Orion says.

"It's okay. But she won't check me. We'll just talk. Only because I need to talk to a girl right now." Maisy crosses her arms over her chest and huffs angrily.

I exhale the breath I was holding. I nod at Orion and Kai, then head upstairs. They follow me.

We walk in silence up the staircase and Orion and I sit on the couch, underneath the dome-shaped skylight. Orion motions to Kai to sit down too.

"Let's talk about killing the Slavs. Every last one of them."

"Right." I've already thought about this. "The day after tomorrow I'll take Maisy to the penthouse, and I'll call a meeting informing my people that you're both alive, and we're joining forces to eliminate the Slavs. Milan must die."

Kai nods.

"I want to see if anyone has any objections, and who," I continue. "I'll squash each of them for sure, but it's good to do this strategically. Step by step. If I have

Maisy at the penthouse, I'm gonna make sure everyone around me is my ally."

"Makes sense," Orion agrees. "I'll do the same. I'll call them today, put a meeting in the diary for the day after tomorrow."

Kai nods again. "Works for me too."

MAISY

"Come, let's sit down." Marina beckons me to the couch, and I follow her. "Thank you for agreeing to talk to me. Men are made differently from women and they're just... *that*. Men."

"Sure." Having nothing to say to her, I simply check her out. She must be in her forties or fifties, and still looks youthful. Jeans, blond hair, buttoned-up red suit jacket and matching red lipstick. She definitely looks like someone who can take care of herself. Independent. Which is what I want to be at some point in my life.

"Maisy, have you ever seen a counselor before, or a therapist? I'm definitely not going to check you or anything, but I'd like to ask you a few questions and I'm wondering if you know the process."

"I've seen quite a few of those. I was a child prodigy. I guess I still am." I shrug. "They were asking me tons of questions back then, and again when my mother died."

"Your mother died when you were young?"

"Not really." I answer a little too fast. I don't want to talk about my mother. That's my memory to keep alive.

She smartly changes the subject. "So, child prodigy?"

"I have a photographic memory. Anything I lay my eyes on, it's stuck in my head indefinitely."

"That's why you're valuable to the Slavs," she mutters, almost to herself.

"Milan made me work for him, but then I ran away, and Kai, Logan, and Orion have been looking after me ever since."

She looks puzzled. "Why?"

"I know some stuff about Milan that could help them take him down."

"Like what?"

I shrug. "Dunno. There's too much information in my head and sifting through it's a long process."

"Sure. Okay, that's fine, Maisy." Marina shakes her head. "Sorry, I was supposed to ask you different questions. Tell me what happened. Why do they think you were raped?"

"I wasn't. When I was at Milan's place, he... I woke up a few times and he was in my bed."

"Touching you? Inappropriately?"

I nod, my eyes welling up.

"Was he touching you between your legs?"

"E-everywhere. Didn't stay in one place a long time. That's how I know he didn't rape me."

"Do you know why he was doing that?"

"Why? Because he felt like it. And nobody can stop him!" My voice wobbles and a sob comes out, and I can't stop the tears.

She moves closer and drapes her arm over my shoulders. "*I* will, Maisy. I promise you, he's a dead man walking as we speak." The tone of her voice is certain, deep, dark, darker than I could've imagined from her.

I raise my head and hold her gaze, tears rolling down my cheeks. Somehow, having her here gives me strength. "I know. He'll die from my hand. I swear to you!"

"Or mine. But let's not fight over that, okay?" I choke out a laugh and she chuckles too. "So you're good?"

I nod. "Mm-hmm." Apart from Lisa, I haven't come across one woman in my life who's so compassionate, and at the same time tough and inspiring. "H-he did rape me when I was twelve. I know that's a while back, but it's still painful. The history I have with that man is something I want to incinerate and burn to the ground."

"I'm so sorry, Maisy. If it's any consolation, that's exactly what keeps me going in my life. What I live for. Revenge."

"Did he rape you too?" As painful as it is to talk about, I have to ask.

She shakes her head. "He killed my husband. Who had nothing to do with the mafia. He was just saving lives. He was saving *their* lives. I told him not to get involved but he was a surgeon, he took the Hippocratic Oath." She gazes off into the distance. "So when they brought Kai's father to his operating table, he wasn't going to say no. I don't hold it against him. I wouldn't have said no, either. We're doctors first and foremost."

"Kai's father?" I'm stunned. My mind goes into overdrive to try to remember if there's anything I've read about it.

"Yes. He was the head of the Delgados, so someone wanted him dead. I mean, the mafia syndicate's full of snitches. They cut the brakes of his car. He had a horrific accident and they brought him to the hospital, straight to Richard." She stops talking and her eyes gloss over.

"You don't have to talk about it," I tell her. "I know how it feels to have to relive the worst moment of your life."

"I want to. *Please.*" She whispers the last word to me, her eyes engorged with tears. "I haven't said this to anyone. Not a living soul. Mickey Delgado was in a real bad state. He had a severed leg, but was conscious. He knew it was the end of his life, but all he wanted was to talk. I was there, you know. Not in the room with him, but... Maybe if I was–"

"If you were, you'd be dead now," I remind her softly.

She nods. "Richard." She blinks, and the tears roll down her face. I can tell she won't be able to continue with her story.

"What was your husband's full name?"

"Richard Connely," she says proudly, and sniffles.

"I... I think..." I'm trying to make sense of what's in my head for her sake. I want to give her anything at all that I have on him. "I remember a conversation Milan had about someone called Richard Connely. He was–" *Shit!* I remember, but it's too late now to go back.

"What?" There's so much hope in her voice, I hate to be the one to destroy it.

"He said he was, um... He said he was collateral damage."

Marina breaks down and starts to sob.

This time, I'm the one giving her a hug. "I'm so sorry. I shouldn't have said anything."

"No." She shakes her head. "Thank you for telling me."

"Mickey Delgado must've said something to your husband and Milan had to find out what that was."

"I know what. Just before he died, Mickey Delgado shared a date with Richard. My Richard got killed for a fucking number, even though he freely gave the information to Milan, without an issue. But Milan thought there was more. What more could he have? Or give...?" Her words die off as she sobs silently.

"Don't think about it. You'll get your revenge." I pat her shoulder, and as I do I spot Kai on the staircase, watching us from a distance. Logan and Orion are behind him too.

"Is everything okay? Marina?"

"Oh, yes." She wipes her nose with a scrunched-up tissue she pulls from her bag, looking uncomfortable and avoiding their eyes. "Ignore me. Please. I got emotional, that's all. I never get emotional, but I haven't cried since Richard died, and it was way overdue."

"Maisy, what did you tell her?" Kai asks as they all join us in the living room.

"I didn't tell her anything. We were just..."

Marina takes a deep breath, visibly pulling herself together. "I was telling her about my life, and how I ended up here."

It's okay that she cried. She's still the same strong, independent woman I wanted to be like a moment ago.

Kai looks uncomfortable. "I see."

"How *did* you end up here?" Orion asks.

She smiles. "That's a story for another time. I'm gonna head out now. Maisy's fine. We talked. Next time, if a woman tells you she wasn't raped, trust her."

Kai perks up. "So, all's good?"

"I don't know. Ask her."

I grin. "Yes. Kai, as I said before, all is good. You didn't have to get Marina to come here to tell you that. Besides, Logan's a doctor too."

Logan raises his eyebrows at us. "I said the same thing."

"Marina, I'll walk you to your car if you don't mind," Orion offers. "I'd like to ask you something."

"Sure. You can get the clothes I got for Maisy, too." Marina picks up her purse and coat, and turns to me, then gives me the biggest, warmest hug. It reminds me of my mother's embrace. I embrace her right back. "Thank you for allowing me to share my story," she whispers.

"Anytime."

"Don't forget, you and I are gonna kick some ass soon."

I nod, and laugh a little. She gives me hope that I too will be free one day.

"Kai, Logan. Good to see you again. I'll be in touch." She turns around and exits.

CHAPTER 8

MAISY

I'm a world away from where I was only a few days ago. Safe, warm, and protected by the men I love. Striking, fine-looking, ruthless boys who would kill anything that glances at me, and I'm experiencing them in a whole new light, like they're different people. When I stayed at Orion's, they didn't trust me. And why would they? I brought misery and downfall to their doorstep. I'm not sure if they trust me now, but then again, why would they make a twenty-eight-hour round trip to Riyadh just to get me back, and not trust me? Something's changed for sure.

We're upstairs, sitting on the couch under the glass dome, except Orion who's standing over us, admonishing Kai and Logan for not thinking straight. His demanding eyes probe mine from time to time. His hair's messier than ever, there's stubble on his defined jaw, and in that turtle neck sweater, and jeans, I'd say he's a different person than the one I know from months ago.

I roll my eyes, but make sure he doesn't catch me. Too much talking never helped anyone.

He points at me. "She's tired. Stop thinking with your cocks! Look at her!"

I'm sitting between Logan and Kai, my legs stretched across Kai's lap and my head nestling under Logan's arm.

I raise my forefinger. "Why are we discussing me?"

"Because these two want to fuck you."

I cock my eyebrow at him. "Only these two?"

Orion pinches the bridge of his nose and takes a deep breath. "Very well. The *three* of us want to fuck you." He looks at me and kneels down, placing his hot palms on my thighs. His touch, the heat from his hands, makes my insides melt. "But I do know you're tired. The flight took a lot out of you. You barely slept. On top of that—"

"I want you," I breathe softly in his face, interrupting him.

He doesn't respond, just stares at me in silence for a few moments. Then he comes closer, his eyes turning a shade darker. "Maisy, do not mess with me. I haven't jerked in months, and you don't wanna know what I'm like when my balls are full."

I lean forward and whisper against his lips, "What if I do?"

His lips curve upwards at one corner, and his eyes glint that black-as-night color, like an abyss out of which there's no coming back. He's waiting to see if I'll retreat, but I'm brave with all of them next to me. I don't look away.

"Fuck it!" he growls, and grabs me by the throat with both of his hands, his fingers curling around my neck as he pulls me up, like a marionette on strings, his hold tightening to an unbearable level. My fingers claw at his hands on my throat, and I'm gasping for air as he turns me around and bends me over the back of the couch. I cannot comprehend how fast all this is happening.

"Orion, wait! Wait! I was–"

"Hold her!" he orders, and Kai and Logan each grab one of my arms and push my head down on the couch. Orion reaches in front of me, hastily unbuttoning my jeans, and hooks his fingers into the waistband, pulling them down, revealing my bare ass. His fingers dip between my legs and he finds my arousal. "Fuck! You've been wet all this time?"

I hear him undoing his own jeans and I try to turn, but it's futile. "Orion–"

I feel the cold piercing of his glans, but he's not wasting time. He hisses as he slams his cock inside me, and the remaining air is expelled from my lungs with a groan. He's bigger, harder, rougher than any time before.

"Your only consolation should be that this'll be quick," he grunts, and grabs my throat with both hands, curling his fingers around my neck so tight I can feel my eyes bulge.

He pulls me upright, and Kai and Logan free my arms. My back is painfully arched and he uses my position as leverage, pounding into me, hard, fast, feral. Wordless, angry grunts tear from his throat as he slams into me. Hate-fucking me ruthlessly. *I'm flying*, I think. Without air, I fall in and out of my daze, and with my hands freed, I'm clawing at his for release, my mouth open as he pulls me to him, kisses me, then spits in my mouth.

"You like this, slut?"

Kai and Logan are gone from my peripheral vision as Orion operates me like a rag doll in his hands. His pace picks up speed, his grunts become shorter, and he's rougher as my insides split from the pleasure I experience. His groans tell me that this, his unraveling inside me, is my doing.

With a loud, guttural sound, he rolls his hips and stills, emptying his seed inside me, over and over and over, all the while still holding me by the neck, my back arched. *That feels like a huge load.*

Finally, he pulls me to him and kisses me deep, slow. Now that he has some sense of the time and space he's in, I tap his large hands on my neck and he slides them downward, wrapping his arms around me, pressing his large, muscular body to mine, my back flush against his front. "Don't be a brat next time," he whispers in my ear. He lifts me in his arms, his cock still inside me, and sits on the couch with me in his lap. The same couch I sat blissfully on with Kai and Logan a short while ago. Orion and I still have our tops on, except our jeans are down to our knees, and cum is dripping between my thighs.

Still panting, I glance around. Kai and Logan have their cocks in their hands, cum dripping down the side of the couch where they stand.

Orion laughs. "Good show?"

"The best!" Kai takes his sweater off, as well as his shirt and uses it to wipe the cum from the couch and floor.

"I didn't last that long. I was in pieces when I saw her wet cunt." Logan leans against the wall, slowly fisting his glistening cock. "But y'know, it's good that we had our first release now."

I raise my hand, still coming down from my own high. "I... I didn't." As exhilarating as it was, I couldn't focus on my orgasm while I had Orion breaking my body in half.

"Trust me, I know that. But it's good that we got it out of the way, that first, crazy call of lust you demand from us. Well, you sure did from Orion." Logan smirks as Orion burrows his head between my neck and shoulder and peppers me with kisses, before curling his fingers under my thighs and lifting me gently, pulling his cock free.

"We want to love you like you've never been loved before. Beautifully, softly, demanding, whatever way you want. Would you like that, sweetheart?" Logan's still regarding me with hooded eyes, and he hasn't stopped fisting his cock.

Lying serenely on Orion's chest, I grin and nod.

"Is that what our Maisy wants? To be worshiped?" Orion murmurs in my ear.

I giggle, too giddy to say anything. I love the love.

"Right, let's get you out of these clothes and into the biggest bed in here." He looks to Kai, who nods.

"The master bedroom, of course!" Kai exclaims, like he's just won at bingo.

Orion helps me take off my jeans and jumper. Francesca never gave me panties or a bra, but they'd be the wrong size anyway. He helps me stand up from his lap, all the while protecting his cock. *God forbid I fall back on it, sheesh.*

Kai holds out some pink lace panties from the bag Marina left for me. "Maisy, can I see how these look on you?"

I put them on. The lace is so soft, so intricate, I'm sure they're very expensive. Which reminds me, I'm still dependent on them because I don't have a cent to my name.

Oblivious to what's happening in my head, Kai just admires me in the panties, bless him. "They're looking so good on you. Keep them on." He takes me by the hand and leads me inside his bedroom. Logan and Orion follow us.

Kai's bedroom is large. It has a sturdy rectangular desk near the window with an office chair behind it, and enough space to fit another bed beside the one we're going to be sleeping on eventually, which looks like it can fit all of us.

I'm loving this minimalistic-style room. When I took a shower earlier, I took notice of the decor. The top-to-bottom windows facing the sea provide a stunning view. The days are shorter in November and it's getting dark soon, but from the leftover daylight we have today, the view is gorgeous. I don't think it would have the same effect once the night sets in.

"It's so beautiful in here," I mutter and walk up to the window, pressing my palm to it. Trying to see as far as possible. The sea is wild and boundless.

"I agree," Logan says, and when I turn around, I find him staring at my ass with a wicked grin. I roll my eyes at him and his lips quirk, his teeth flashing at me in a smile.

"Come here, gorgeous." He tugs me into his arms and presses his lips to mine, taking my breath away as he kisses me. I rake my fingers through his dark hair, responding to his kiss. His arms wrap tightly around my waist, his hands cupping my ass and pulling me into his perfectly buff body, clearly outlined by the sweater he's wearing.

I sense Kai coming up behind me. His hands go under my arms, around my body and over my breasts, kneading them softly. "We've missed you, baby girl." His hot breath caresses my neck.

This, here, is how I want to live my life. Between my men, held close, soothed. I try to hold Kai as I kiss Logan, ruffling Kai's blond hair with my fingers. I moan at the feel of it; it's longer than it was the last time I saw him. His bare, tattooed pecs and biceps, that any woman would die for, encase me, causing heat to pool between my legs.

"Come on, Maisy." Kai's nipping my neck. "We want to love you."

I glance at Orion sitting on the bed, granting them time with me. He got quite a fuckload of me for himself, so he can't complain.

"I'm sure she's gonna tell us what she wants." Orion chuckles. "Maisy?"

I'm lost between kissing Logan, grinding myself against his cock, his hands on my ass keeping me close, and Kai's torturous pinching of my nipples as he bites on my neck. Logan sets my lips free and I'm left breathless, but with a task at hand – to respond.

"I... I dunno. I want *you*." A burning flood is rushing over me, making me hot and needy. *What do they want me to say?*

"We want to love you the way you want to be loved," Logan mumbles against my lips.

What does that mean? Unexpected panic consumes me. Suddenly, the enclosed space they have me in is suffocating and I step out of it.

"Why?" I ask. I go over thousands of pieces of information in my mind. *What are they looking for? Will they find something about me that disappoints them?*

I sit down on the bed next to Orion. The distress must be visible on my face.

"Fuck, Maisy, stop overthinking!" he exclaims. "It's not good being this smart all the time. And you're safe with us. I want you to truly let go. That's all. But if it causes you this much agony, forget about it. We know how to love you, and we will."

"Nobody's asked me this before." My voice in this room sounds different.

Logan sits on the bed behind me, Kai on the opposite side. Orion's right, my mind is constantly on alert, checking if I'm safe. It's relentless.

"If you just want to be worshiped by us, we can do that too. Tonight, and every other night," Logan assures me.

"Baby girl?" Kai pinches my chin and pulls me to him. "We're here to love you. However you want." He presses his lips to mine.

"Sometimes, giving the control away is the only way to feel free," Orion adds.

I look at them, staring back at me in the most loving and beautiful way. I take a deep breath. *Why is it so hard for me to be frank? They love me.*

"Tonight, I want you all separately, and slowly. A-and maybe... maybe we all finish together." I watch them, warily surveying what kind of chaos my words have created.

The first thing I see is Kai's brow furrowing above his eyes. "You don't want us to play together?"

I shouldn't have said anything.

I turn behind me to look at Logan. His nostrils flare, subtly, but I notice it. *Is he mad? Angry? Shit!*

I glance at Orion, and his lips are quirked at one corner.

"No, it's not that," I say. "I... I want to love you. Look, it doesn't matter, okay? Orion? Kai? Logan?" I look at them all, panicked. "All of us will play together. Forget I said anything."

"It's okay, Maisy." Logan pulls me to him, calming me as I lay my head on his chest. "It's real scary having to speak your truth, but we got you. Okay?" He kisses my forehead.

"We got you, Maisy." Orion leans in and presses his lips against mine. "Honesty's always the best policy," he adds with a smirk.

"It is?" I breathe quietly, as if Kai and Logan cannot hear us.

He nods. "That's all we wanted to hear. I already had you, and you spent time with Kai earlier, so how about you let the doctor take care of you now?" Orion chuckles and looks at Logan's hard cock. "He needs you."

I nod, and smile.

"Good. Kai, let's give them some space." Orion winks at me and stands up. Kai follows him out.

The door closes behind them. I sit up on my heels and turn to Logan, grinning. "That was strange."

He raises himself to his knees and takes his sweater off. The perfect ridges of his abs staring back at me are delicious, and that small heart tattooed over his left pectoral muscle is cute. It tells me all I need to know about him. Fierce, but gentle. His jeans are unbuttoned, his cock out and swinging about. This man is ready to fuck, for sure. Seeing him without a suit is strange, but this wild look suits him well. The mischievous glimmer in his eyes cannot be mistaken.

"I guess you're all mine, sweetheart." He leans in and presses his lips to my jaw, nipping me gently, under my chin too, making my head tilt back. I pump his cock a few times, a drop of precum already formed at the top. He moans as he takes my hand and lifts it to his lips, kissing the back of it. "Let me show you what I have in mind, princess."

He pulls me up to my feet, smiling softly as he leads me to where the desk is. He's regarding me with hooded eyes, and suddenly that slow, dreamy manner he talks with is all I tune in to. *Princess?*

"Is it okay if I call you princess, Maisy?" His soft voice is magical.

He helps me sit up on the shorter side of the desk and softly presses on my shoulders. There's plenty of space for me to fully lie down on it.

"Y-yes," I say, barely audibly, as he lifts my feet onto the desk, and starts ever so softly stroking my inner thighs in slow, steady movements. My lower belly clenches. His green eyes are like an enchanted forest, pulling me inside, and I allow myself to be fully taken.

"You know the doctor's here to make you feel better?"

My mouth opens, and I nod. No words are coming out.

"Goooood." He fists his cock. "Now look how hard you made me, princess. You make me so hard."

I watch him, my eyes half-cast, probably floating because I've stopped breathing. The way he speaks slowly, elongating his words, soothing me, scorches my insides and, my juices gush.

"I could just look at my pretty girl forever." His eyes are on me as he rubs his cock against my panties, slowly. "And your pretty pink panties."

That slow movement of his cock over my lace panties, now soaked as he fists himself unhurriedly, creates a dip between my lips, and that's what gets me.

"You like watching me jerk my big cock over your pretty little panties, hmm?"

I nod and lick my lips. I'm keen, ready to do whatever he wants.

"You know you're such a good girl for me, don't you?" He pumps his cock slow and easy. It's his words that make me want to cum right this very moment. "Why don't you go ahead and say you're such a good girl for me, hmm?"

"I'm a good girl, d-doctor," I whisper, nervously.

"Mm-hmm, thaaat's right, princess." He keeps rubbing me over my slit. "Is it okay if I touch your pussy like this?"

"Yes. Yes," I moan, arching as I roll my hips. I want to get closer.

"Nuh-uh, I wanna tease you in your pink panties, sweetheart. Fuck, you're such a good girl. Right now, just watch me play with your pussy over your pretty pink panties."

I moan at his touch.

"My goodness, sweetheart. Maybe I love you so much I want to play inside of you. Hmm?" Another pass over my slit. His free arm is stroking my thighs. "Do you want the doctor's big cock inside of you?"

"Mm-hmm." I writhe under his caress.

"Oh, sweetheart, you're such a good girl for me, you deserve it."

I roll my hips closer to him, my mind lost somewhere between his soft, deliberate voice and his hooded eyes.

"You're so pretty, the doctor has the prettiest girl in the world. I got so lucky to have such a pretty girl, hmm?"

My panties are soaked, I'm totally ruined, and he hasn't done anything other than talk to me.

"Sweetheart, I can't wait any longer, I need to fill you up." He hooks his fingers in my panties and painstakingly slowly pulls them aside. "Oh my goodness, look at that pretty little pussy."

I've forgotten how to breathe, I'm totally under his spell. This leisurely pace is driving me crazy. He slides his cock between my silky folds, preparing me for something I've already had, but this time, this time is *so* different.

"The doctor's gonna put it in, okay, princess?"

It's mad, this teasing. I'm losing my mind. "Yes, please."

"Say, 'Yes, please, doctor, I want your cock inside me.' Can you say that, sweetheart? Hmm?"

I've been driven crazy by words. *Words!* I inhale desperately. "Please, doctor, I want your cock inside me."

And here it comes, my reparation. He groans as he slowly slides his hard cock inside. I don't know how he manages to keep himself under control.

"Mmm, such a tight little pussy. I'm gonna have to stretch it all right, but you're gonna take it like the good little girl that you are, okay?"

"Yes, yes," I pant. I'm out of my head, I need him pumping into me.

He takes it out and slides it in again. "Oh, thaaat's right, here it goes, sweetheart."

"Uh, Log– doctor, *please*," I beg.

"Oh my goodness, sweetheart, your pussy feels so good." He pumps inside me again. "That's it. Good girl, princess, you take my cock so good."

I moan in ecstasy. This leisurely fucking is bliss.

"That's it, you're doing so good, look at you taking my big cock." His hands glide over my thighs and rest on my pelvis. "Sweetheart, I'm so proud of you."

He's pressing down on my pubic bone, using it as leverage as he picks up speed. I don't know how he manages to last this long. I begin to climb toward my release.

"Feels so good, Maisy. The doctor loves you so much, you know that, right?" He's slamming into me faster now. "Fuck, you're doing such a good job, sweetheart. Just lay back and watch me pound your little pussy."

I moan and raise my head to watch him fucking me.

"You see my big cock stretching out your hole, princess?" he grunts. "Goooood girl."

Another grunt.

"Don't you worry, the doctor's gonna take good care of you. The doctor will always take good care of you, sweetheart." He growls and curls his arms around my thighs. "I promise you," he gasps, and increases his pace, slamming into me. "Yeah, take it like a good girl, I know you can do it. That's it, that's it, sweetheart."

The world is becoming distant. All I'm attuned to is his voice as he's pounding me hard.

"How about I play with your clit while I fuck your pussy?"

The moment he touches my swollen nub, I explode. Stars rain down on me as I writhe and start bucking into him, whimpering.

"Is your pussy getting all tight on my cock? Are you gonna cum on my cock, princess?"

I'm falling apart. "Yes, doctor, yes!"

"I want you to cum, but not just yet. The doctor needs to fuck you some more. But I love when you're messy, little girl."

"I... I can't hold it... It's started..." I whine.

"*Fuuuck.* Look at that creamy little pussy taking my cock. Come on, cum on the doctor's cock if it's started already."

Tossed around by my eruption and the waves that crash over my body, I come undone. It's overwhelming. Tears roll down my cheeks. His grunts become faster as he pumps into me for a while before he stills inside of me, emptying his hot seed into my cunt. He's fucked me so softly, so sensually, he gave me so much, none of the animalistic craziness I'm used to.

Spent, I'm still panting when I open my eyes to meet his. The desire inside is insatiable.

"You listen so good for the doctor, sweetheart." He pulls out and slides inside me again, slowly, over and over as he talks. "The doctor's so lucky to have such a good girl like you."

He finally takes his cock out and fixes my pink panties neatly over my cunt, soaking them properly with his cum.

"You remember the doctor's friends, sweetheart? Well, they're here now, and I thought that maybe I can let them all take turns fucking your tight little pussy. Is that okay, Maisy? Hmm?"

I'm watching him through wide eyes, my heart beating fast from the adrenaline. *Take turns?* I raise my head, trying to object, but he holds me still.

"Shh... You're gonna have to keep quiet for me, princess." He takes my panties off, scrunches them up in a ball, and gently stuffs them into my mouth. For some reason, I'm still aroused, like a nymph.

"She's ready for you," he calls out, his eyes not leaving mine.

The door opens, and I see Orion walking in with a glass of whiskey in his hand. His turtleneck sweater is gone and instead it's his six pack, tattooed arms and body are staring back at me. Kai has the bottle and a full glass of his own. They've been drinking.

"Well, it's about fucking time!" Orion snickers.

"I'm going in first." Kai leaves the bottle and glass on the bedside table and strides up to us, and between my legs, as Logan moves to stand next to my head.

"What do we have here, Logan?" Kai pumps his cock and smirks. "Good way to keep her mouth shut." He takes his cock and slides it between my folds, prepping me for his fucking as Orion walks up to me on the other side of the desk. He takes the panties from my mouth and throws them away.

"I know a better way to keep her mouth shut." Orion turns my head so I'm facing him and with his steely cock, slaps my face a few times. "Open." I show my tongue and he doesn't wait to insert himself throat-deep. "Theeere you go, darling."

Kai's not waiting either; he's thrusting inside me, my cunt, soaked with my juices and Logan's cum, providing the slippery passage needed. He places his hands under my thighs for leverage and pulls me faster toward him.

Logan's stroking my head. "Is my Maisy happy?"

I can't talk. Only the sound of me being face-fucked is heard, along with Kai's grunts as his speed increases and his cock gets firmer with each thrust.

"Oh my God, baby girl, aren't you a good little slut?" Kai groans.

"My princess is the best. Aren't you, sweetheart?" Logan keeps stroking my head. Orion pulls out of my mouth, his gaze meeting mine from upside down. I know what he needs. I nod and glance at Logan.

"Yes, doctor. For you. I want to make you happy."

"Theeeere you are." Orion pushes his cock inside my mouth again. "Take me all in."

"Fuck, she's such a slut, she's gonna make me cum so fast," Kai growls, and leans over my body, taking my nipple in his mouth, sucking on it. His feral pounding shows me he's close, and his focus is strictly on himself.

"Come on, princess, make him cum. For me." Logan's soft words do something to me because I start bucking into Kai's thrusts, milking him, doing everything he wants me to do to please him. Kai is there, on the cliff, when he explodes so powerfully, he almost crushes me on the table. Orion pulls his cock out and gives him the space to detonate. His hot cum spurts inside me, filling me, as he leans in and bites my shoulder so hard that I yelp. He looks pleased at what he's done. He falls on my body and kisses my breasts, then slaps them. "Good girl."

My body is on fire. Orion's cock is in my mouth again, and I moan and curl my fingers around its base and suck it, like a real slut.

"Look at you, taking cock after cock." Logan strokes my head as I'm choking on Orion's cock. "You're gonna be on your third cock now. You're such a little slut, sweetheart."

Kai stands up, strokes my inner thighs, and runs his fingers over my cunt. "Fuck, do you feel that cum inside you?" He takes the cum dripping out of my pussy and inserts it back again, a few fingers at a time, and I buck. I'm desperate for my orgasm. "Oh my God, you little cum slut, are you ready for the third load?"

"My turn." Orion pulls out of my mouth again and steps between my legs, his cock swinging around. He runs it up and down my slit, sloppy from Kai's cum. His piercing is evident as he reaches my clit. That's where I want him to be at. I move my hips, trying to get him to put it over my swollen nub, but no luck.

"Kai may have been nice, but I'm gonna destroy this little cunt!" he growls, and without preamble, he starts fucking me. Each time he slams into me I groan, almost being lifted from the desk.

I hold the sides of the desk as Logan turns my head his way and raises his hard cock, showing me his balls. "Princess, why don't you open your pretty little mouth, show me how you play with my balls as your tight pussy's being used?"

I do, without delay. I suck his balls and fist his cock with my hands as I'm banged.

"Thaaat's it, sweetheart." Logan's stroking my hair as his head tilts back, his eyes closed. "Suck the doctor's balls. Let Orion do to you whatever he wants. It's okay, your tight little pussy needs it."

I writhe madly. I'm close to my orgasm; they've made me fly already, but that one little push will make all the difference, and it's not coming. I whine in protest.

"What's wrong, you wanna come on this cock?" Orion gasps.

I moan a yes, and feel Kai's hands on my body, pinching my nipples. Giving me that extra push toward my heaven.

"Your slut is so pretty, Logan." Kai's kneading my breasts. "You must let us play with her again."

"Fuuuuuck! God, you fucking whore!" Just as I was close to my paradise, Orion pulls out. "All right, Logan, why don't you come back and finish your princess off. I'll make sure she's fed."

Orion hurries to where Logan is standing, seeks my mouth, and slams his cock inside it. Logan goes between my legs, his cock entering me so fucking sweetly, and continues with the feral pounding, taking over from Orion.

"Fuck, sweetheart, your pussy's full of cum. You like that, don't you?"

Logan picks up speed. He's close and Orion is too, suffocating me with his cock as he slams it deep in my throat one last time before stilling, spurting numerous ropes of cum directly into my mouth. "Drink it. All of it." He holds my head in his hands, watching me from above. I swallow all too eagerly, all the while being banged by Logan, my whole body lurching upward with each thrust.

Kai must feel sorry for me because he spits on my cunt, making me shiver, and when I feel his fingers over my clit, I know he's just about to bring me to my death. He rubs me so hard, so fast, that the moment Orion pulls his cock out of my mouth I whimper loud and long, then explode into a bucking bronco, taking Logan with me. He growls as he cums, his hot spunk filling me for the second time, trying to hold me as I'm soaring somewhere in the sky.

"Whooooah. Whoa, Maisy."

I sense all of them holding me, concerned I may fall from the desk. If I did, I wouldn't care. But I know they've got me. They always have.

ORION

I don't remember ever sleeping this soundly. Quiet, peaceful. But someone rolls over me, wakes me. I smell her, Maisy, and I don't let her go. My arm hooks around her waist and I pull her close.

"O-Ryon!" she whispers. "I need the toilet."

"Make sure you come back right here, in my arms," I grumble sleepily, and release her. She kisses my cheek and jumps from the bed. I always sleep closest to the door, at the end of the bed. Nobody's running away from me anymore. Control freak? Fuck yeah!

I open my eyes to check the time. My cell's on the floor. I reach down to touch the screen and the time flashes up. It's late. Almost noon. We've slept eighteen hours, probably getting that jet lag out of our systems. I lift my head and look across the bed. Without Maisy, the three of us naked just look odd, our arms and legs crossing each other's, but our cocks, rock-hard at this time of morning – or afternoon – kept to ourselves.

I lie back, my eyes closing, and smirk. What a fucking sight we are without her between our sheets.

Maisy flushes the toilet in the bathroom, and then I hear her running the shower. We've crowded her ever since we got her back. I'm sure she wants time to herself.

Logan's searching for her in the bed. I sense him sitting up, listening for where Maisy is.

"Leave her be," I croak, my voice deeper than usual. I'm still not properly awake. "She needs some privacy."

He sounds annoyed. "Fuck you, Orion. Do you wanna blow me instead?"

I chuckle. "Only if you do it first."

Kai's still asleep as Logan and I eagerly wait for Maisy to come back to bed. Fuck, she's like the north star to my cock.

"There she is, my sweetheart."

I open my eyes and see Maisy leaning against the doorframe, her hair wrapped in a towel, her body too. Her arms are crossed over her chest and her teeth flash with a grin as she watches us. I didn't hear her stop the shower. Perhaps it's good, this, me sleeping so deeply with her around.

"Come here, darling." I grasp my cock and wave it up and down, my piercing flopping about.

"Someone's weeping for you here." Logan takes a drop of his precum with his index finger and shows it to her. "One drop of this'll make you fly, Maisy," he smirks.

She drops both towels, revealing her majestic body and all its curves. Her damp hair falls over her shoulders and she runs back to jump on the bed, directly straddling Kai's legs. He's in the middle, and still asleep.

"You all look so delicious," she giggles, and runs her fingers down his stomach, heading for his morning wood. Her tongue glides up and down his shaft, taking it in fully, and I start pumping my cock. Kai moans and opens his eyes. *What a fucking way to wake up.*

She gives him another swirl of her tongue, then raises her head and looks at us. "Now that you're all awake–"

"Oh, no, no, not a chance, baby girl, you're gonna finish what you started," Kai complains, pulling her by her hands to get her to go down on him again.

"But Kai, look at your bite from last night." She points to her shoulder, distracting him. *Clever girl.*

"Oh *shit!* Does it hurt?" Instantly awake and obviously feeling guilty, he sits up. "Let me see."

She laughs excitedly. "It's fine. I love it. I love it so much, I'm gonna tattoo it on my skin."

Kai's eyebrows shoot up. "You are?"

Tattooing is a personal choice, and you either love it or hate it. Although for Logan, the jury's still out. He doesn't have any tattoos, but he never voiced anything against them, either. And I'm not counting that one small heart on his pec. That's another matter.

Maisy beams. "Yes! Won't that be cool?"

"Sure will. I love it!" Kai says.

"It'll be a really cool tattoo, Maisy," I agree.

"Logan? What d'you think?"

He smirks and kisses her cheek. "If it's on you, I'm gonna love it."

"Great! Now that's out of the way, wait here." Still stark naked, she runs out of the room then back in, carrying the bag of clothes Marina brought for her. "Help me choose what to wear." She tips everything out onto the bed.

"Where are we going?" I ask.

"To get a tattoo!"

"Today?"

"Yes." She pulls underwear from the pile –
another pair of pink panties and a matching bra – and
puts them on. She finds a loose black top, one that shows
off her shoulders, and a black skirt. A miniskirt. *Does she
really need a miniskirt in this weather? It's cold.*

As if she heard me, she puts on a brown furry
jacket and some short matching boots. Fuck, she looks
fuckable, but for *us*. I'd hate for other men to ogle her.

"I thought we were helping you choose," I object,
but Logan interrupts.

"It's okay, we'll work with this. The three of us'll
be chaperoning so I doubt there'll be any issues. Right,
O-Ryon?"

I nod sullenly.

"We can pick up your suits and go out for
breakfast too. Kill two, or three birds with one stone,"
Kai agrees.

~

Last time we attempted to take Maisy out, all
hell broke loose. Now, I'm wary of any outing. Kai's
insisting it's safe. On Long Island, we're far enough away
to not be recognized, but still, it's dangerous, especially
in our case, when none of our families know where we
are.

Maisy's insisting on going to a tattoo parlor she spotted yesterday, and is certain she wants a tattoo of Kai's bite mark. The fucker just had to do it. Like I didn't want to make her ass red with welts. If I can reign myself in, he should be able to too.

But he's like a teenager around her. He even brought out his black Ford Mustang, which the four of us are riding in right now. He wants to show her what life with us would look like, I know. But he doesn't need to. Our lives will always be different. She just needs to accept it.

I glance over at Kai. He looks at home again in his boots, jeans, shirt, and leather jacket. Logan and I are not like him. As much as this jeans and turtleneck suit me, in addition to my long overcoat, I personally need my orderly suit and vest. Logan looks good in jeans and sweater but again, he's methodical like I am, and we love stability. I can't wait to pick up my clean suit.

The car slows and we pull up to the tattoo parlor. Kai parks just in front. "Come on!" he shouts impatiently, and exits the Mustang.

Maisy grins and shoots out of the car, too. They run toward the shop, holding hands.

Logan and I follow them closely to the parlor, which looks like any other tattoo shop, with photographs of different tattoos displayed on the window, back-to-back, so we can't see what's going on inside. In places, the glass is tinted.

We enter and a tattooed man with a goatee greets us from his seat at the counter. There isn't a spot on his skin that's not tattooed. I look behind him and see a reclining chair in the back room, plus loads of ink and tattoo guns.

"I'd like a tattoo, please," Maisy grins, while Kai, totally smitten, takes out his wallet, counts out five one-hundred-dollar bills, and leaves them on the counter.

The young man hesitates for a minute, then looks past Kai and Maisy to us. In our long overcoats, I guess we look too menacing to just be asking for a tattoo.

"Is that all you need?" he asks.

"Should we ask for something else?" Logan steps up, towering over him.

"Um, no, man." The man stands up, looking alarmed. He tries to match Logan's height but fails miserably. He's shorter, by a lot. "That's what we do here. Tattoos. Nothing else."

"Great, then." Maisy laughs softly. "Where do I sit?"

"Over here." He points at the reclining chair. "What d'you want done?"

Maisy jumps into the chair, takes off her coat, and lifts her top halfway up, damn, near giving the three of us a heart attack. *She shouldn't be revealing so much of herself.*

Kai's closest to her but Logan and I rush in too. Fortunately for the goateed man, he manages to stop her in time.

Looking confused, she lets go of her top, dropping it back down to her waist. "What?"

Kai saves the day. "He doesn't need to see you naked. It's your shoulder only. Just the bite mark. Do this." He pulls the top down over her left shoulder and addresses the tattooist. "We need you to trace the bite mark on her shoulder. Her top's gonna stay like this."

"Y-yeah, yeah, man. All good."

"Logan, let's wait for them outside." I turn, not waiting on him to respond. It was more of a statement.

"Here." Kai throws his keys to me. "You can wait in the car."

I grab the keys and with Logan, exit the tattoo parlor.

~

In a half hour, Maisy and Kai are back in the car. Logan and I are sat in the front so Maisy and Kai take the backseat. Maisy's grinning from ear to ear as Kai kisses her neck. They look like new lovers who only have eyes for each other. I won't take this away from Kai; she's not going to stay with him, and this is his chance to enjoy her fully. For finding us and Maisy, and keeping up morale –

because we were pretty much dead, even though we were breathing – I'm cutting him some slack, for sure.

"Let me see, Maisy." Logan sounds excited as he turns to check out her tattoo.

She shimmies down her coat and top, showing her bare shoulder. "Here. It's cool, right?" Her eyes sparkle as she looks at Logan and me. *That fucking tattoo looks sexy as hell.*

Logan tries to touch her skin, but she recoils. "Careful, it's quite sore."

"Sorry, sweetheart, I was just checking the skin." He kisses her head as she admires her tattoo some more.

Kai leans back, evidently content that this went well. "Right. Now that's done, I'm starving! Orion, take us to the Black Llama Bar to eat."

"Sure." I drive off, realizing that this Mustang needs to be taken for a proper ride. Alone.

Within five minutes we arrive at the Black Llama Bar, thanks to Kai's directions. It looks like it's still open from last night.

Once I park, we leave the car and enter the bar in twos. Kai and Maisy go in first, as a couple, and Logan and I follow closely behind, like their bodyguards.

It's dark inside. The music's still on and the dancefloor's nearly empty, but on seeing it, Maisy's eyes light up. She turns to us. "I've never danced on a dancefloor before."

I guess the adrenaline's still coursing through her blood from getting the tattoo, so this must feel like a day when she can try everything she's missed out on in life.

"You could dance if you want," Logan suggests.

We find an empty booth and make ourselves comfortable in it. The waitress, who's been watching us ever since we came in, immediately approaches, looking like she can't decide who to flirt with first. We shouldn't really be drawing attention to ourselves at all, but being big, tall, and tattooed makes it inevitable.

Maisy's oblivious to her surroundings, just staring at the dancefloor, not paying attention to anyone.

I nod at Logan, who's at the edge of the booth, and he takes over. He's our smooth talker, the diplomat. His broad shoulders block any view of us as he talks to the waitress.

I overhear the food order, and it's the full shebang: an American breakfast of pancakes with maple syrup, eggs, bacon, and the rest.

Finally at ease with the place and its security, I lean back, just as Maisy stands up. She throws her coat onto the seat and heads off to the dancefloor.

Alarmed, Kai looks at us. "What do we do?"

I laugh. "D'you want to dance to Taylor Swift, Kai?"

"Fuck you, Orion."

"Logan?"

"I'll pass, thank you."

"Then we sit and watch her shake her booty."

The three of us sit back and enjoy the view. I may even tap my foot on the floor along with the music. I'm calm, content, and fuck am I sated.

Maisy's on the dancefloor by herself. Her hips are hugged by the tight miniskirt she's wearing, and the loose top reveals her pink bra straps. On her feet are the short furry boots. She waves at us, deliberately showing off her tattoo, her top falling low on her bare shoulder. She twirls and moves her body in what looks like a very awkward way. I'm not sure she's taken any dancing lessons exactly, but fuck, what is dancing if not being happy and free inside?

A girl approaches her and they dance face-to-face. Then the music changes and a guy appears behind her, turning her and starting to dance with her. I'm not worried. Considering the clothes he's wearing, he's clearly gay. He grins at Maisy, who doesn't seem to have any normal dance moves; she's all over the place, yet utterly charming. Everyone else is watching and loving it.

The girl she was dancing with is still around, and now she steps behind her, swaying her body with Maisy's rhythm.

Logan leans forward to get a better look. "What the fuck?"

I snicker. "Relax. They're dancing. What, you gonna go and fight them?"

"Wait. Did you see that?" Kai sounds put out too.

"What?"

"She's getting groped by that woman."

"You're imagining things, Kai. They're dancing, Calm your testosterone, both of you. It's dark here, anyway. How can you tell?"

I take a better look. The woman has Maisy's back pressed to her front and as she sways to the music, she runs her hands down to her hips and then up to her breasts. *WTF?*

Maisy takes the woman's hands and puts them back on her hips. I turn to Logan, whose eye is twitching, and then Kai – his fingers are already curled into a fist. But I know we can't start killing in here. Especially not women.

As Maisy dances, she gets turned around by the woman, and now they're face-to-face again. The moment she pulls Maisy in for a kiss, the three of us jump to our feet.

Everyone sitting in our vicinity looks shocked, and stares at us before following our eyes to Maisy.

"I'll go. Let's not make a scene." I gesture with my hand at Kai and Logan. "Sit down."

I stride over to the dancefloor and reach Maisy just as she gives the woman a shove.

"What the fuck are you doing?" she yells over the music.

I stand behind her as the woman looks at me, then Maisy. "Oh, I'm sorry. I thought you were friendly. I got a different vibe from you."

"Well, you should've asked!" Maisy sees me behind her and grabs my arm. "I'm here with my man."

"That's your man?" She raises her eyebrows. "Wow. Hot. Can we share?" She winks at me, and I smirk.

Maisy straightens up, standing as tall as she can, and lifts her chin. If I've ever seen her angry, and dead serious, it's right at this moment.

"I don't share," she says and walks away, dragging me with her. I laugh to myself as I follow her.

We return to the booth and sit down, Kai and Logan's eyes following us closely. Maisy's chin is still raised.

Logan seems to be wondering what the fuck's going on. "Sweetheart, you okay?"

"Mm-hmm," she says, turning to him, and then looks back at the woman who's still on the dancefloor, searching for someone else to grope. "That bitch wanted me to share my men. Like hell I will."

Kai's eyebrow quirks. There's a grin in his eyes.

"So you don't want to share us, is that what you're saying?" Logan teases.

Maisy's eyes go wide, in shock and maybe fear, and she looks between us, like she's searching for some reassurance, but as we're failing to stifle our laughter, she gets it. She relaxes and smacks Logan on the arm. "Logan, stop being such an asshole. And no. If you must know, I *don't* want to share you."

Kai and I burst out laughing. Just then, our food gets wheeled out on a trolley.

"Ah, it's Tania with our food," Logan announces.

Tania grins at Logan. He must've got her thinking she'll get some later. She leans over and starts setting the food on the table, her boobs almost spilling out of her uniform.

"We have pizza, ribs, water, coffee, eggs, pancakes, and..." She smiles flirtatiously, adding the last item to the table. "Toast!"

"Thank you, sweetheart." Logan kisses the back of her hand, gentleman-like, and she giggles and waves goodbye.

When she's left the table, Maisy turns to him. "Logan, um, 'sweetheart' is mine. I don't want you to use it on other women."

Now my brows fly up in surprise, and Kai makes a whiplash sound. We watch Logan, whose head tilts at Maisy. Clearly amused, he's considering his response. The right response.

He narrows his eyes at her. "Are you telling me I'm not allowed to say 'sweetheart' to any woman apart from you?"

Maisy takes a bite of a pancake and there's a sassy smile in her big, dark eyes. She nods. "Mm-hmm." She swallows and reaches for a slice of pizza. "I'm starving!" She lifts it to her mouth, her tongue darting out before she takes a big bite of it. "Finally, a pizza I can eat!" she mumbles through a mouthful.

There's something so fucking sexy about a woman who eats without shame, and it makes my cock hard again.

She looks at us, realizing we're watching her, and gestures to the table. "Don't look at *me* – eat!"

"You're too delicious, Maisy. I'm not sure if I should eat you or the food," I say, and raise my coffee cup to take a sip.

Kai dives into the food and starts stuffing his face while Logan continues to watch her, apparently entertained.

"Very well," Logan finally says. "It's gonna be hard for me, but as of today, you're gonna be the only sweetheart in my life. However..."

"Here it comes," Kai snorts, then continues plowing through the BBQ ribs on his plate.

"Because you'll be my only sweetheart, you're gonna have to satisfy my desires, however, whenever, and wherever I want." Logan shrugs. "Because I have many desires. Not all sexual, mind you. I'm not sure you'll be able to satisfy them all."

"I can!" Our sweet, sweet Maisy; she's so gullible sometimes, it's endearing.

"Well, now you're gonna have to." Logan takes a slice of pizza and bites into it.

~

The drive back is smooth, no issues. I hate to say it but I'm beginning to love this place, and being anonymous. I glance at Kai in the rear-view mirror. Judging by the look of him, this could be the best day of his life. By far, better than any he's had. As mafia heads, we shouldn't be having days like this one, but I'm feeling it too. It's almost too good to be real. Maisy completes us in so many ways.

I look at her staring through the window in silence, the bag of dry cleaning in her lap. From time to time, she checks her tattoo and smiles to herself. She's happy. We've *made* her happy. And she's given us hope, hope that this life has something good to offer.

"Hey." Kai calls out to her and she turns her head. She's the epitome of gorgeous. At peace. Like she belongs here, with us, at this very moment and beyond.

"Were you serious about learning how to box?" he asks her.

She nods. "Can you teach me today?"

Kai's always ready to oblige her. "Sure, I can show you a few moves."

"I want to know the best ones." She leans over and kisses him.

Kai catches me looking at him in the rear-view mirror and I nod in approval.

Logan turns to her. "You want to learn how to box?"

"Yes," she replies sweetly.

"Don't you want to learn how to throw blades?"

"Sure I do!"

"Great. Once Kai's given you a lesson, you'll come to me."

She grins and looks at Kai. "I'm gonna become a badass bitch."

I smirk, and all of them laugh.

She looks at me. "What?"

I grin at her. "You're gonna be the *best* badass bitch, Maisy."

CHAPTER 9

KAI

"No, not like that. Hook your left hand."

I've been teaching Maisy how to box for the past thirty minutes, but it's not easy. Nothing gets through to her. I groan in frustration.

Logan's driving me nuts too. "Come on, Kai, did you think it was gonna be easy? Man up, grow some patience, and start again. Maisy wants to learn, that's the important part."

"Yes, I do!" she agrees, and bangs the gloves I gave her against each other before throwing a punch at me, the way an ant would. All it does is reveal her shoulder more. Her top slides so easy off her, it makes my cock twitch.

"Yeah, but not like that, baby girl. You're not gonna hurt anyone with that move."

I hear sly snickering behind me. I turn to see Orion leaning back on the couch, his feet on the coffee table, glass of whiskey in hand.

"You okay there, O-Ryon?"

He smirks. "I sure am. I'm not used to not doing anything. And this really does me good. Watching a live comedy show."

Logan's in the chair next to him, also with a glass of whiskey, but he's been acting like a live commentator of my struggle.

Maisy hits me two, three times while I'm taking to Orion, but I barely feel it. I dismiss all her efforts; how else will she learn?

"What if I hit you here?" Her voice sounds frustrated and I'm too late to react before she kicks me straight in the balls. Pain sears through me, one I never thought I'd experience in my life. Should I feel lucky that she's still wearing her miniskirt and couldn't really swing her leg any higher? It's better for sure that she's wearing those cute socks rather than the boots she had on earlier.

I yelp and crouch down, dropping to the ground, holding my balls with both hands and looking at her in disbelief. I can feel how red my face is. "What the *fuck*, Maisy?!" I gasp.

Logan's on his feet and laughing out loud. "Oh, fuck! Haha! That's my girl!"

"Shit! I'm so sorry, Kai, I didn't mean to hurt you." Maisy removes her gloves and kneels next to me, but it's pointless. The pain is zinging through my balls and I feel like someone's cutting my body with a saw.

"Sorry, sorry, sorry, sorry..." She peppers kisses all over my shoulder and back as I roll on the floor in agony.

"You okay, man?"

I hear Orion, but I can't talk. My suffering is all-encompassing. It will go away soon, that I know.

"*No*," I mouth, unable to breathe.

"I think I've had enough. I don't want to learn to box anymore. I'm so sorry, Kai. I really am. You got me so frustrated, and I was hopeless at learning," Maisy admits.

"You... *think?*" I manage to retort after a sharp intake of breath.

"Hey, that doesn't give you the right to insult me." She frowns and punches my arm.

What is she *frowning about?* I'm on the floor, injured, weak, and in agony. If it was anyone else, I'd kill them on the spot.

"Come on, Kai, don't be such a baby," Logan says, but if I hit him in the nutsack, we'd soon see who's the bigger baby. "Okay, Maisy, let me teach you how to throw blades."

I manage to sit up and lean against the wall, taking small breaths, still in agony.

"Here, go on, touch them." Logan offers a blade to Maisy and she reaches for it.

"Those are sharp, Logan," Orion warns. "Are you sure you want to give her sharp blades from the get-go? She could hurt herself." His lips form a straight, disapproving line. I don't approve either.

"She'll be fine, won't you, sweetheart?" Logan asks.

"Sure. What do I do now? Do I throw them somewhere? Maybe over there, at that wooden pillar?"

"Sure, if you want to. Let's see what your aim's like."

She raises the blade and I turn to see where the pillar is – literally right behind me. Fuck this, she may actually kill me today, but even then, I can't be mad with her.

"Wait…" I raise my hand, still unable to shout. "*Wait*." I drag myself away from the wall and onto the couch. "Now you can do whatever you want."

Orion grins and Maisy giggles. "I wasn't gonna hurt you again, silly!" She takes aim and throws the blade, hitting the exact spot where I was sitting. Her top slides down her shoulder again, revealing the tattoo.

She makes an O shape with her mouth and then covers it with her hand, looks at all of us, and bursts into laughter, so sweetly that we all join in.

Despite my literal ball-ache, I don't remember that I ever had a night with Logan and Orion that was as relaxing as this, or as enjoyable. I'm sure Orion's thinking the same thing because he has a calmness in his eyes as he sips from his glass and watches us. Well, watches Maisy, mostly.

"Okay, let's start again. This is how you hold the blade." Logan demonstrates. "Notice the weight. You hold it just a little higher than where the middle is."

"Okay, I am. Now what?"

"Now, swing your arm like this." He swings in slow motion, and Maisy copies him.

She's obviously eager to learn. "Okay, okay, I think I got it."

"Here, Kai." Orion passes me a glass of whiskey. "I'm sure you need one."

"Cheers." I clink glasses with him and drink mine in one go. Fuck, did I need that. The pain dissipates slowly, though more of this whiskey would help.

"Okay, now swing," Logan tells Maisy. "Like this." He swings and hits the pillar dead-on.

Maisy swings and misses.

"Here's another." Logan hands her another blade. She swings and misses again. "Here, one more."

She grins, and this time, she hits the pillar low. The blade stays, which means it was a good strike. "Woohoo! Yes!" She leaps into Logan's arms. "I can do it!" She turns to us. "Did you see me? Did you?"

"Yes, we saw you. Really good, Maisy," Orion praises her, a clear hint of pride in his voice.

"Great job, Maisy. Keep training," I add.

Logan nods at the pillar. "Right. Go pick them up and we'll try again."

"Yes!" She runs to the pillar and reaches for the blade.

I see it happening before it actually does. I stand up quickly. "Logan, does she know how to–"

Maisy screams.

Orion jumps up and runs to her. She's holding one palm in the other, blood dripping down her arm.

She looks like she's having a panic attack. "Oh no, nononono... I can't do this, no..."

"Fuck! Maisy, you don't grab the blade like that!" Logan scolds her.

"It's okay. It's fine. Maisy, look at me. Maisy!" Orion raises his voice. "It's only a small cut. Logan will close it now and you'll be fine."

Her eyes are big and teary, her chin trembling, and she's biting her bottom lip. I can tell she's trying not to cry like a little girl.

I fetch a towel to soak up the blood and press it against the cut. It looks deep, going through the side of her left palm. "It's okay, baby girl, it's all good. No big deal."

"It hurts a lot," she sniffles.

"It will, but only for a short time, sweetheart." Logan strokes her face and wipes her tears away with his thumb. "Kai, bring me a sewing kit, any sewing kit you have here."

"Right." I run upstairs. I know exactly where the sewing kit is, the kind he needs. I bring it down quickly.

Orion sits down with her and takes her in his lap. "Come here, darling. Let's get you nice and cozy on the couch."

"Here it is," I say. "You got everything in there, Logan."

LOGAN

I shouldn't have let her play with my toys. *What was I thinking?* I should be looking after her, not exposing her to my blades. I can see it's just a little cut, though, and I'm not worried at all. I've dealt with worse. But the pain of seeing her suffer, I feel it. It feels as if I'm stitching my own skin.

The thing is, had she been whining, or cursing, it would've been better. But she's not doing that. This is where it's fucked up for me. She's silent, chewing her bottom lip, her eyes tightly closed, but that can't stop the tears from rolling down her cheeks. The ridge between her brows keeps appearing and disappearing. She's controlling herself, and the pain she's in. Being brave. Was it like this when she was raped? Holding it in? Hoping it would be over soon? Was it like that for her, and every woman who went through my father's club, my club? Rosa, too? *They don't fucking matter*, I heard my father say too many times. *We're Vitalis*. Well, fuck that! I'm a doctor!

"No more of your blades around Maisy. Clear?" Orion's being overprotective, though there's no need to tell me twice. Of course it's clear.

I glare up at him. "D'you think I'm stupid?"

"I mean it. I don't want you to teach her to throw knives. And I know she's not gonna listen to me if I tell her. So this one's on you."

"Don't worry," Maisy cuts in, her wobbly voice betraying her. "I won't be asking anyone to teach me anything. I hurt Kai, and now I've cut myself. I don't want to cause you any more trouble."

"This is no trouble, sweetheart," I respond softly. "We're just worried. We don't want you to get hurt."

"Yeah, well, I won't."

"Good," Orion says, with finality. He watches me threading the needle through her skin, and her stifling her whimpers.

"One more, aaand it's done." I cut the thread with the scissors, tie a small knot, and wipe her hand with iodine. Five stitches are nothing.

"Let me see." Orion takes her hand and examines it as I prepare the dressing.

Kai's also watching us. "Logan, your needlework's getting better," he jokes.

"Ignore him, Maisy. He's still angry that I practiced on him when I first started to learn stitching. Check out the scar on his forearm."

"Can I see it?" she asks sweetly.

"Here." Kai presents his tattooed forearm. "But you can barely see it."

Maisy's tracing her fingers over his forearm when his cell beeps. With his free hand, he pulls it out of his back pocket. I can't see who the message is from, but I see his expression harden and his brows draw together. "I gotta take this."

"Everything okay?" Orion asks.

"Trouble at the club," Kai responds, and heads to the kitchen to talk in private.

Orion's cell beeps too, and we look at each other. He checks it, but gives no indication of who it might be. "Let me take this. Sorry, Maisy, let me put you down here." He lifts her from his lap and settles her on the couch next to me, then walks out onto the porch.

"Give me your hand, Maisy. And hold still." I prepare a large Band-Aid and fix it over her wound. "There. You're good as new." I smile and wipe her tears.

She leans into me and closes her eyes. "That hurt. A lot."

"I'm sorry, sweetheart. I should've told you to look out for it, but I've been working with blades for so long I'd forgotten how dangerous they are."

She checks her Band-Aid and the movement of her fingers, and I take the opportunity to look outside at Orion. He's not talking to anyone, just pacing up and down the porch. At one point he stops, looks at his cell, and swings wide. Just as I think he's going to throw it away, he changes his mind.

Maisy gets my attention again. "How long will this hurt?"

"Four or five days. Don't worry, it's only five stitches. But I hate that you'll have a scar on that pretty hand of yours forever."

She shrugs, not looking at me. "I don't care."

"I do. Every time I see you it'll be there, a reminder of my recklessness. It could've been much worse."

She lifts her eyes to me. "I don't see it like that. This stitching, this scar, is made by you. It hurts, but you gave it to me. So I got *you*. Right here, in my palm. Forever." She closes her palm.

I felt that. I lean in and press my lips to hers, salty from her tears. "I'm so sorry. I promise to be more careful with you. You're... You're so fragile."

"Don't be." She laughs softly. "I wanted to learn. I still do."

"You heard Orion. They'll lynch me if anything happens to you."

"We don't have to tell them..." She bats her eyelashes at me, but Kai coming back interrupts her flirting. Orion walks in from outside at the same time.

"We'll talk once you're at mine, okay?" I whisper, and kiss her cheek. She nods.

I raise my eyebrows at Kai. "Everything okay?"

"Fucking Slavs. They started a turf war an hour ago. We lost a few people already." He curses under his breath.

We all look at Orion.

His brows are drawn together, his lips set in a straight line. He rubs his jaw as his eyes roam around the room, though his mind's clearly elsewhere.

Maisy's sweet voice breaks the strained silence. "Orion?"

He looks at her and his forehead flattens and his lips quirk up, but if I know Orion, that's not normal behavior. That's a mask.

"Um, yeah. The Slavs are causing us headaches too. Uncle Leo can't handle anything without me. The fucker!" He shoots Kai and me a grave glance. "I think I'm gonna have to head home today."

I nod. "Maybe all of us should."

"I agree. I wanna be fighting my wars too," Kai says.

"When am I gonna see you again?" Maisy asks. Her naïve voice is so pure.

Kai drops down next to her on the couch and kisses her forehead. "Sooner than you think, baby girl."

"Definitely soon," Orion confirms automatically. "I'll head upstairs to change, and call a cab."

Kai and I exchange a glance. *Something's off.* "Now?" I ask.

"Yes, now," he states as he walks toward the staircase, lost in thought.

"Wait up!" Maisy jumps up and heads after him, leaving us on the couch.

As soon as Maisy's out of earshot, Kai looks pointedly at me. "That was fucking odd."

"I agree."

"Why d'you think he has to leave so soon?"

"I'm sure he'll tell us." I check my cell for any messages in case the Slavs are attacking us too, but I got nothing.

In my head, I'm trying to figure out what really happened, and I'm sure Kai is too because we sit in silence until Orion shows up again.

His voice is grave. "I don't have much time and I don't want Maisy to know this. I got a message from Milan." He's regarding us steadily as he passes his cell to me. Kai leans in to read it too.

I'm coming back for what's mine. And this time I'll make sure you're all dead, except for Maisy Roy. She has a special place in my heart. Didn't she tell you? She belongs to me. The rat's blood should have given you a clue. She's a rat. And that rat is MINE.

"Fuck! Fuck! Fuck!" Kai curses. "How? How the fuck did he find us?"

"The better question is how the *fuck* he has my number. No one knows this number apart from you two and Lisa. *Lisa!*" Orion takes his cell back and dials his sister's number.

"You called the Cartes from that phone earlier, remember?" I remind him, and he nods at me as he waits for her to answer the call.

"Lisa. All good?" he asks. "Where's Mya? Good. Stay there. Do not come to my house. I'll let you know when it's safe."

He cuts the line. "She's safe, thank fuck." He stares at his cell. "He could track my cell to this place, if he hasn't already."

Kai stands up and looks out through the window. Apparently not seeing anything, he draws the drapes.

Orion looks at us. "We need to find out what else she knows. I hate to say it, but clearly there's still something she's not telling us."

I shake my head doubtfully. "Is it possible? Really? We were ready to die for her, and still you think there's something else she's hiding?"

"One way to find out." He turns and charges back to the stairs.

"Orion!" Kai calls out, but Orion only raises his hand.

"You two get ready to leave!"

"Kai, he won't do anything to her, I promise you," I reassure him, although I'm not so sure myself.

He smirks nervously. "Yeah. I wouldn't wanna have to fight him later, that's all."

CHAPTER 10

ORION

Un-fucking-believable! This again. Why am I even wondering? We never asked her about her history with Milan. Smart girl. She only fed us what was needed. I stride up the stairs and storm into my room, making her jump. She's sitting on the bed, on top of the covers. All of us slept in Kai's bedroom last night and the bed here's still made.

She's leaning on the pillows, her knees bent. That damn skirt's too short, and her panties are staring me in the face. Goddamn, this girl's gonna be the death of me. She's skillfully elusive, and we're all like teenagers, me included. Infatuated.

She chews on her lower lip. "What's wrong?"

I start pacing around the room and rake my fingers through my hair a few times, thinking. The *fuck*. Milan's gonna get what he deserves.

I stop and point my index finger at her. "You tell me."

"Wh-what? What do you mean?" She swallows hard, staring at me as I search her eyes, trying to find something, anything that she's trying to cover up.

A *lie*. That's what I'm looking for. But I can't see shit.

"Maisy…" I sit next to her. "It's been three months since all of us nearly died in the setup you planned with the Slavs. I don't want you to get me wrong, but for some reason, I think there's still something you're not telling us."

"Y-you don't trust me?" Her eyes narrow, like she's reading my face, but I got nothing more to give her. She's burned me too many times. She's played with our lives as if we're toys in her crib. Getting nothing from me, she scoffs sarcastically. "You *don't* trust me."

"No, I don't trust you," I confirm. No lies coming from me.

"How can you say that? I didn't ask you to save me from Riyadh!" She raises her voice. "You came. Remember, you *came*!"

"We came because you belong to us. You're mine, and no one's gonna sell you on my watch," I snarl back.

"I don't fucking belong to you! I belong to me!" She pushes me and stands up, yelling in my face. "To *me*! You think because you saved me, now you own me?"

I stand up slowly, taking my time as I tower over her. She wasn't this feisty before. *Where did this come from? We gave her safety, security – and now she's yelling? Nuh-uh. No.*

"Don't make me remind you. The deal was we protect you, and you give us all you know on Milan. The fact that you got fucked was a bonus." *No one screams at me and gets away with it.* "You haven't kept your part of the deal yet."

"Oh, and you have? What kind of protection did you give me? Milan came to your *house!* The one place where I should've been safe!"

I felt that. A jab right below the belt. My jaw tightens, and I can tell I'm about to spew out something neither of us is going to like. I close my eyes, take a deep breath, and exhale. When I open them, she's still standing in front of me, craning her neck to stare up at me.

"Which begs the question, why are you still alive?" I demand. "What does he want from you?"

"I don't know." Her voice is different, and I see it. I–see–it. *She's lying.*

"Start at the beginning," I say calmly, although a full-fledged storm is thundering inside me.

"I don't know what you're talking about. There's nothing to tell you!"

"And now I *know* you're lying!" Only with a diversion will she crack and start talking. Questioning techniques are my forte, but I keep getting tangled in her net and I still don't know if she's the prey or the predator. "What about Rebecca Trellis? Remember, in the cab, you asked me if I know her."

"Yeah, I know where I was when I asked you!" she snaps.

All of a sudden, *she's* angry? "What are you not telling me about her?"

"You didn't figure it out?" she mocks.

"For fuck's sake! Your side of the deal was to tell us, not for us to figure anything out! This is not a game, Maisy!"

"She's named on your birth certificate. You must've seen it by now. Your mother's name!"

"So why did you ask all of us if we knew her? Why not me only?"

"You were all in the car, and I... I was feeling guilty. I wanted to distract myself from what was about to happen."

"What else?"

She shrugs.

"I'll remind you. You mentioned some article."

She looks away, frowning, then looks back at me. "Yes, there was an article about her in one of Milan's offices. I didn't read anything else apart from her name. Not even the headline."

"Headline?"

"It was a cutout from a newspaper."

Fuck. I've had it with her short, cryptic answers. "Lies by omission in a court of law are actual lies. You know stuff you're not telling me." I take a step closer to her and roar in her face. "*What-else?*"

She stands her ground, still glaring up at me as she crosses her arms over her chest. Before speaking she licks her lips, and my already hard cock reminds me just how bad I crave to feel them wrapped around it. "No. You're gonna start treating me with respe–"

That's it. I grab her throat and push her backward, taking her with me for a few steps until I slam her against the wall. She gasps under my hold. "You don't get to say that. I own you. Remember that."

She desperately claws her nails at my hand, needing air, and I let her breathe just a little.

"I–own–me." She strains to get each word out. Even with that little air that I let her have, she fights back.

"You do?" I brush my lips against her cheek, squeezing the column of her throat tighter, making her eyes roll back. "You do, huh?" In haste, I unbutton my jeans and free my cock. I've become hard from frustration, anger, and the sight of her sweet ass parading around the house in that miniskirt. I reach down under the skirt and in one move, I tear her panties from her. "Let's see what you're gonna do about this."

She pushes me off, tries to kick me, but I'm bigger, stronger. I insert my knee between her thighs and slide it up the wall, spreading her legs with it. With my free hand I hold her leg up, leaving her open and ready for my cock. Without warning, I slam inside her sweet, juicy cunt. *Fuck* – on top of it all, she's wet.

"I own you. I own your cunt. I own the air you breathe."

I ram her against the wall, hard, furious, and in my anger, I bite her earlobe. She yelps in pain. "Go on, aren't you gonna scream?" I wedge her leg over my knee and with my freed-up hand, I slap her face a few times as I pound her. "No? I wanna hear you scream!" I plunge into her, using all the frustration I have against her. She's holding me like a prisoner and I hate it. I hate loving her. My animalistic, angry grunts drown out her cries as she fights back with all her tiny might.

"Tell me I don't own you again. I wanna hear you!" I'm hate-fucking her and I know I'll hate myself after this. But she's looking at me with those stubborn eyes, begging me to teach her a lesson. My orgasm comes way too soon, and with a long growl and all the control I can muster, I pull out and jerk off on the carpet, ropes of semen falling one by one.

"You don't deserve my cum, you whore. Out! Get *out* of here!" I yell.

That didn't do me any good. I was angry at Milan, and I fucked Maisy. The door opens and closes and I hear Kai outside, and Maisy crying, no doubt in his arms. We cannot keep falling for her fucking sweet body, and mouth, and cunt, and ass, and *fuck*, I'm giving myself another hard-on.

I head to the bathroom to clean up, Maisy still in my head. We saved her from Riyadh, so she's ours. I wanna dare someone to say otherwise. *She's ours.* I groan loudly. Milan's giving me too many headaches.

I take off my clothes and step into the shower. I cannot wait to put my suit on and head to the club. I'm moving the meeting to tonight. I won't sleep until Milan's caught and every living Slav in New York is dead. *Why the fuck does he want Maisy?* He could've killed her, but he didn't. He took her from the shooting, near-dead, brought her back to life, and sold her in Riyadh. Why? To make money? No. Something else is at play.

She's out of the picture until Milan is caught. At least for me. I can't allow another near-death experience coming upon us.

MAISY

My fingers hurt from clawing at his hands. I wish he'd killed me; that's the only way I'd really be free. Exquisite torture, that's what Orion's intense fucking felt like. I knew he needed a release, and I was willing to do anything for him to get it. It's the reason why I ran after him in the first place. I offered my body freely. I just didn't tell him. But I got more than I bargained for. The reason why I fought back. Hurt. Betrayal. *Men.* They're all the same. They keep showing up in my world as invaders, ready to hurt me when I least expect it.

I don't know what brought his hatred on. But it's clear he never trusted me, and never will. Family? That moment we had as a family, it's gone. Shattered. He did this. Singlehandedly. Although, I know Logan and Kai would join him. They'd follow his footsteps to the grave. It's like we're back to square one, right where we started. I don't lie. I... I just don't say everything. If I did, people would be on my case all the time, demanding more. But sometimes they need to figure things out for themselves. Like I'm doing. We all have stuff to deal with.

Coming back from Riyadh was an eye-opener. Had I stayed there, had they not shown up, I'd have been happy to die, away from the horror I was forced to live in. I'd given up on life anyway. As luck would have it, them saving me from certain death opened a new avenue for me. I was so stuck in my way of thinking that I couldn't see a way out. But now I do.

After the day I've had, I realize that there could be a happy ending in life. Today, I felt at home. With them, I'm at home. There's no denying that. But clearly, I should stop fooling myself – my happy ending is not with them. Orion will never fully trust me. He sees through me, I'll give him that. His eyes penetrate my very being. They're like a night sky without a single star, no guides, just dark, lulling me into false safety, a place I can hide, and then he touches me and, like neon signs, my sins light up. One by one.

And when he sees through me, I'm back to square one.

They don't own me. Orion doesn't own me. He. Does. Not. Own. Me.

I was fucked but never owned. Milan's been trying to own me all of my life, but he never did and he never will. And he raped me to prove it. Fucking my body means nothing. Orion's too stubborn to see some things. But throwing me out of his room, that was different. He was disgusted. *That hurt like hell. As if he* really *saw through me.*

I'm just glad Kai was outside his bedroom, a shoulder to cry on after being discarded like a piece of trash. He heard the way Orion treated me. Still, every protest against him falls on deaf ears. He insists Orion will eventually come round, that we need to give him some time.

Now, Kai seems rushed. He has my bag of clothes with him and is eager to take me downstairs. He hands me a pair of panties when he realizes mine are torn and I put them on in silence. He watches me go through the motions, but doesn't say anything. Any other time, he would.

Logan's downstairs, dressed in his suit. His smooth, carefree southern smile turns into a troubled frown when he sees me, his brows drawing together.

Kai nods at him and passes him my bag. "We don't have much time."

"Time for what?" I ask. I don't understand what's happened. I wish they'd talk to me, but nobody ever explains anything.

"You and me are heading to my penthouse, sweetheart."

"Do we have to? Let's stay here one more night," I beg.

Logan takes my coat and helps me into it. "Change of plans."

I comply, and proceed to step into my boots.

Orion comes downstairs, his hair damp and sleek. He's wearing his suit, looking like... Orion. An ever-consuming being that draws you in with his own gravity.

He ignores me. I ignore him too, except to steal a few glances in his direction, careful not to be caught. He's different. It's like there was a switch, something got triggered inside him, and I was his punching bag. Am I strong enough to say no? To part ways with him? Them? I never counted on finding life in the epicenter of death. But again, they're the reason I'm still alive at all.

"Did you call the cabs?" Orion asks.

"Yeah, all three cars are outside," Kai says as he turns to me. "Baby girl, I'm gonna miss you." He smiles and wraps his arms around me, kissing me on the head. "Please stay safe, okay?"

I nod in his embrace. My arms wrap around his waist and I press my cheek hard into his chest. A tear rolls down my face. Why am I crying? This feels like goodbye. I inhale deeply. I want to etch his scent onto my brain.

He pinches my chin and makes me lift my head to look at him. He rubs my cheek with his thumb, looking into my eyes. I see uncertainty. Hesitation. And love. "No more crying, okay? You got a tattoo now. You're hardcore, just like us."

I smile and blink, more tears brimming in my eyes. "When am I going to see you again?"

"Don't know. Until all this is over, I don't know anything." He hugs me again, deep but brief, and moves away. I get no kiss. I take a deep breath and wipe the fresh tears from my eyes.

Logan pulls me to him, his arm draped across my shoulders. I'm with him now. Orion's standing at the door, his back to us. I wasn't going to say goodbye to him anyway. But it hurts. I should be the one who's upset, not the other way round.

~

It's dark and rainy during the cab ride. I'm looking through the window as the droplets roll down the glass in front of my eyes, but everything outside is blurry.

Logan's next to me. Wearing his long overcoat, looking too serious, he's been quiet for some time now. I look over at him, and as if he was waiting, he opens his arms to me. I scoot closer and fall into his embrace.

"What's going on, Logan? It's Milan, isn't it?"

"Don't worry about it. Please." He strokes my hair, like he's trying to lull me into a false sense of security. But I feel it, it's in the space. Unsaid words, undelivered communication that permeates deep. We all feel it.

"I want to know. Is it?" I sit up straighter and look at him.

He nods. "He found you."

I gasp, my hand flying to my mouth. I knew it was Milan, I just didn't know he'd found me. *Me?* I thought they had problems with him elsewhere. This, this is too close. My heart, pounding in my chest, is picking up speed. I think I'm having a panic attack.

"Please don't worry. You'll be safe at my penthouse, and this time we're planning on killing him," he assures me.

Little does he know that what Milan wants, Milan gets. He has a way with people. He kills too easy. "H-he knows where we were?" I whisper.

Logan isn't listening to me. His attention is drawn to the Toyota truck driving alongside us. I can't see who's driving because of the rain, but we see their intentions when they suddenly sideswipe us.

"Asshole!" the cab driver yells as we teeter.

Logan pulls out his gun but the moment our driver sees him through the rear-view mirror, he slows down. "What the fuck?"

"*Drive!* Do not slow down. Try to get rid of them." He turns to me. "Quick, put your seatbelt on."

I buckle up, my hands shaking in fear. "Who's that, Logan?" My PTSD is as real as this car.

"I'm hoping it's Milan." His voice is barbed; his eye is twitching.

The truck speeds up and slams into our bumper. We swerve wide into the road but our driver manages to maneuver around the cars coming from the opposite direction, which respond with angry, long blares of their horns.

"Shit!" Logan opens the window and shoots at the truck.

"Give me a gun!" I shout at him. My heart is racing, and I'm sweating.

"Stay low, Maisy!" he barks as he looks behind us. I ignore him and peek over the back of the seat. I want to see what's going on, but he shoves me down. "Maisy – stay the *fuck* low!"

"I won't go to Milan's house again! Do you hear me, Logan? Don't let him take me!"

"Yes, I hear you. You won't." He's assuaging me and shooting at the same time.

Being in a car chase is petrifying. The cab driver maneuvers for his life. His knuckles are white from gripping the steering wheel, and he peers back through the rear-view mirror much too often, his eyes wide.

The fear that I'll end up at Milan's again paralyzes me and restricts my air flow. Terror mounts in my body with each gunshot and screech of tires that I hear.

The truck chasing us slams into our bumper again, then tries to overtake us. An oncoming car toots its horn, but it's no use; it's nicked sideways and flipped over somewhere on the road.

We speed down the road with the truck continuing to sideswipe us and trying to tip us over. Skillfully managing to avoid a few collisions, our driver is doing good until we reach a sharp, almost ninety-degree corner. That's when the car starts skidding, and even before it happens, I see it. We're open and vulnerable on the road, and the truck plows us over, the sound of crunching metal turning my world upside down.

We drive directly into something on the road, and this is it. Time slows down as I see my life flashing in front of my eyes, inside the car that's now flipping over. I see my hair hanging down, following gravity as we roll, and notice pain in my ears from the noise of the windows shattering. The airbags at the front activate and everything becomes covered in a fine powder that smells like burnt rubber.

At the first direct hit, the driver is thrown through the windshield and the car rolls down into a ditch. I'm getting soaked in something. I can guess what it is by the strong smell: gasoline. It's all happening so fast but I know Logan's still here, being thrown about in the car with me.

The density of trees helps us stop, finally. Somewhere halfway down a ditch. The eerie moment of silence is disorienting. Nothing and no one can be heard, just the final creaking sounds of life the car can muster.

"L-Logan? Logan... *Logan!*" I scream, my voice like that of a stranger as I hang upside down.

"Y-you're okay?" he croaks from somewhere.

"I... I can't see you. Where are you? Logan?" Everything is black. I don't know if my eyes are open or not. I can't see a thing.

"Try to unbuckle yourself," he tells me, his voice weak.

My hands search for the buckle fastening but when I find it, I stop. "I... I'll fall if I do."

"You gotta be quick now, Maisy. They're coming. Unbuckle your seatbelt." His voice is faltering.

I follow his order, pressing on the button and dropping like a dead weight onto the roof of the car, head-first. I groan in pain. Everything hurts. Only now do I grasp the gravity of my situation. Still, in my head I'm focused on three words only – *They are coming*.

I swallow nervously. "Logan? Who's coming?"

"Milan's men."

I immediately hear a noise outside. Someone's approaching.

"Logan, I can't see you," I start feeling my way about the car and find a way out through the broken window. It's still raining; the weather doesn't care about my troubles and soaks me thoroughly. On top of it, it's freezing. Having adjusted to the darkness, I still struggle to find Logan. "Where are you?"

I barely hear him. "Go. Just run, sweetheart."

"Take my hand," I say, finally seeing him sprawled across the driver's seat. "I'm not going anywhere without you." Without looking, he feels for my hand and once I grab hold of him, I start trying to pull him out.

"Listen to me now. Just go." He's struggling to talk. "Leave me. I'll be fine."

I start to sob, the feeling of helplessness crippling me. "No! I will not let you die here. I won't..." I'm bawling.

"They don't know you're with me. Go. Save yourself. And... tell Orion and Kai, I tried."

I kneel in the mud, in the path of the rushing water flowing down the ditch and under the car, holding his hand and sobbing. "I won't go anywhere without you. You hear me, you asshole?" My voice is unsteady. "So if you wanna stay here, I'm fine with that!"

I can make out the shadow of him in the car, and his head turns to me. He's not talking, but I know he's watching me. It feels like an eternity as I wait, hoping he'll come to his senses, when the whiff of gasoline reaches me. That, and two distinct voices, becoming clearer as they get closer. He must hear them too.

"You're very stubborn, Maisy."

I manage to laugh through a sob and pull on his hand. This time it's much easier; he's doing his part. Just when I get a small win, the sound of a shot pierces the stillness of the trees and rushes past my ear, missing me by an inch. I yelp, and Logan scrambles fully out of the wrecked car. They're here.

Dread sinks in as my stomach begins to burn. This is it. I look at Logan in the darkness, and see the blood on his face. He strokes my cheek and smiles. Undefeated forever.

I press my hand over his on my face. I know the men have their guns on us, and running would be certain death. "For what it's worth, you made me believe in life again. I love you for that," I tell Logan.

"We're still alive, sweetheart." With his last ounce of strength, he pulls out his blades and throws them toward the men. I hear a thud, an angry bellow, and immediately after, three shots are fired at us, one after another. I flatten myself on the ground, but I hear Logan collapsing next to me.

"Logan! You're hit!"

I have no time to run as thundering steps reach us. In my final seconds of freedom, I check on Logan. It's his shoulder.

"Got ya, little birdie! You keep running away, but I got ya!"

My hair is grabbed, and they pull me up by force. I shriek, fighting to set myself free, but their grip's too strong.

"Let me go, you asshole!"

"Maisy..." Logan attempts to stand, but a kick to the face knocks him straight out.

CHAPTER 11

MAISY

Logan lies unconscious in the large cell opposite mine. The bleeding from his head has now stopped, and only dried blood can be seen. It's cold in here. I lost my coat in the car crash, and I'm freezing. My legs are covered in scratches and cuts, as well as my arms and face. My miniskirt and top did nothing to protect me; they're way too flimsy. Luckily I still have my boots, which keep my feet warm somewhat.

It's dark; only a few slivers of light come through the heavy wooden door and land directly on the table at the far end of the room. The place reeks of blood, death, and metal. It smells like a basement, and it's paved with stones. My eyes have adjusted enough to be able to make out my surroundings. There's a filthy blanket in the corner of my cell, one that I know at some point I'll have to use. My cell is smaller, and another, same size cell is adjacent to mine, separated with metal bars. On the other side of the room there is a chair next to the table, with what looks like a vise, ice picks, blowtorch and other torture devices on top of it. There are no windows.

Logan, wake up! We gotta get out of here, they're gonna kill us.

Something moves in the cell next to mine, and my heart jumps. The hairs on my arms stand up as panic surges through me. *We're not alone.*

"Logan, I... I need you!" I croak, dread twisting in my gut. I'm afraid, and I'm lonely. I'm back to where I started from.

"M-Maisy?" someone whispers, but I don't recognize the voice. It sounds distorted.

"Wh-Who's there?"

"Maisy, it *is* you!" They shuffle closer across the floor, the clanking of metal accompanying them, until I hear them hitting the bars separating our cells. Thank God for the bars. "It's me, Marina!"

"...Marina?" I try to make her out in the darkness. Her clothes are torn, her face is swollen and bloody, and she has metal cuffs on her arms, legs, and neck. "Oh my God, Marina! What've they done to you?" I run to her and slide my arms through the bars to hold her and as if she was waiting for it, she breaks.

"Please – please tell Kai I didn't give him up. They tortured me, but I didn't give him up."

"You'll tell him yourself, I promise. We'll get out of here."

"They found my cell and checked every number in it. I stupidly added Orion's number without a codename. H-he gave it to me when he walked me to my car yesterday." She coughs and spits blood, turning her head to the side. Only now do I see what they did to her. She has teeth missing, and there's dried blood around her mouth.

"Oh, God!"

"Don't worry about me, I managed to take Milan's eye out." She tries to laugh, but it comes out as a cough. "They'd have to kill me before I stop fighting."

The sound of a lock turning makes me jump. The heavy door is unlocked and opens slowly.

It's *him*.

A dark shadow moves through the doorway – Milan. I'd recognize his walk anywhere. Two goons follow him and close the door behind them. A switch is flipped and a weak yellow bulb lights up on the ceiling. Milan's dressed in black slacks, a robe, and slippers, as if he just woke up. He has a bandage over his eye, wrapped around his head. He checks on Logan and then walks to my cell, making my blood freeze in my veins.

There's no way out of here. Only enough chains

to tie up ten men.

"Well, well, well. Look who the cat dragged in." Milan laughs sarcastically.

"You leave her alone, you sociopath!" Marina yells. She manages to get to her feet, the clattering of her metal cuffs echoing around the basement as they meet the bars. "You fucking psycho!"

"Oh. You're still here," Milan says matter-of-factly. He turns to his goons. "Why didn't you kill her already?"

"Um, boss, I-I don't know. Um..." they stutter.

"Kill her," he orders calmly.

"No!" I shout, and run to the front of my cell. I realize this is the first time ever I've raised my voice at him. It's how easy he ends lives that always gets me. Dispensable. To him, everyone is dispensable.

"Tell me, and let me die in peace!" Marina yells. "Why did you have to kill Richard?! He gave you what you wanted. He told you what Mickey Delgado said to him." The goons take their guns out but she continues, clearly running on adrenaline. "He told you, Easter, Good Friday! I was there, I heard him! He was killed for something that happened thirty-three fucking years ago! Why? It had nothing to do with him, with us!"

"Shut that bitch up, for fuck's sake!" Milan snaps.

"No, Milan, please, don't!" I beg, my panic

flaring. Only begging works with him.

Marina turns to me. "Maisy, promise me you'll kill him."

And there it is. I hear the shots fired, so loud in the basement.

"No! No! Marina!" I try to reach her, but she's fallen further away from the bars.

Her eyes are still open. She's looking at me. "*Promise me...*" she mouths.

"I promise!" I say, my vision blurring from the sudden invasion of tears as her eyes close. I see her final exhale. She's... dead.

"Haha, I'd like to see that happening!" Milan's vile laughter makes me sick. He turns to his goons and points to Logan. "Throw a bucket of water on him."

One of them walks to the corner, takes an empty bucket floating in a barrel of water, and dunks it. He swings and the cascade of water falls on Logan. He groans.

"Shall we get him out of the cell, boss? Put him in the chair?" the other goon asks Milan.

He waves him off. "Get Marina's body out of here. Make sure it's burned."

Milan turns to Logan as his men enter Marina's cell and pull her out by the legs. What little hope for humanity there is when I see something like this. She deserves revenge. I'm going to get it for her. *I swear.*

"The great Logan Vitali," Milan taunts. "I don't particularly like when I sell a piece of meat to a friend and then someone steals it from him. Then on top of that, you kill that friend. Now *that's* vulgar." Milan pulls a gun from his robe and plays with it. He aims it at me, then at Logan, and then at one of the goons. The man cringes, but doesn't move. He doesn't dare.

One of Logan's eyes opens, and it lands on the goons first, then Milan. Finally, he sees me across the room, sitting on the floor in my cell with tears rolling down my cheeks.

"Maisy! Are you okay?"

I nod, sobbing, and point to Marina's empty cell. "She's dead. They killed her! They killed Marina."

Logan's gaze coldly travels back to Milan. He stands up, with some difficulty, and straightens his bloody suit. He must have lost his overcoat somewhere. His lip's cut and one of his eyes is closed and bruised, but he acts as if nothing's wrong.

"Milan the Dog," he jeers, and points to the bandage over his eye. "Don't worry, I'll finish the job when I get to you. Clean cut – whoosh! Just like I was trained at school. You know which one, right? You've already read my medical certificate."

"Tell me something," Milan says. "The night you killed Zed, was it because you found out he was my son, or was it because he was his usual obnoxious, insufferable, asshole self?"

Logan's brows draw inward slightly; this is a surprise to him. And to me. "Why do you think it was me who killed Zed?" he asks.

Milan places his gun in the pocket of his robe. He locks his fingers behind his back and starts walking up and down, thinking, it seems. Logan uses the moment to motion to me to ask if I'm okay. I nod.

"He was under Vitali protection. Although, that meant something when your father was alive. With you, I guess, you just kill as you please." Milan stops to look at Logan and catches him staring at me.

I can feel Logan's pain. I did this. He's here because of me. And yet, he feels guilty.

"Wait. Wait a second, I may have all of this wrong. You killed Zed because of *her?* This dumb, attention-seeking whore?" He points to me, but his eye's still on Logan. As much as Logan is fighting to remain impassive, his jaw tightens, his nostrils flare, and his whole face darkens, like clouds before rain. "Yes. That's right. Zed took her, she was gonna make him money. She needed to be put in her place. Now I see it... It wasn't personal, it was protection? She made you believe you're protecting her? Hahahaha!" He laughs, and the goons nervously laugh with him.

"You don't know anything!" I shout.

Within a split second, Milan turns to me and

grabs my throat through the bars, pulling me forward and slamming me against them. His breath reeks, a combination of ashtrays and vomit.

"I should've broken your neck a long time ago." He's choking me and I fight for air, my nails clawing at his hand. Only a gurgle comes out of me. "Give me one reason I shouldn't crush your windpipe this very moment."

"Let her go! Milan! LET HER GO!"

I hear Logan's voice, but the room starts spinning and I feel heavy. The grip on my throat is released and I slump down onto the cold stone, gasping for air.

"You're lucky I still need you."

ORION

"Fucking sociopath! Stupid douche! Are you gonna threaten me in my own goddamn house, you fucking asshole? I'm gonna throw you out in a bag of laundry so I never have to fucking see you again!"

I've had it with everyone. We got no more time left. It's been ten fucking days without word of Logan or Maisy. We're monitoring all of the Slavs' hideouts, but no one's saying a thing. Sitting at the head of the table in my three-piece suit – because what other clothing screams authority – I slam my fist down in rage. I'm losing this game with the Slavs and I'm close to killing everything that stands in my way to get to them.

Uncle Colletti's brought a new face into the Cartes, Adam. Apparently he's part of the family, his son-in-law, and reliable. From the look of him, he's barely out of diapers. He's never been part of mafia life before and has no idea how you address the boss.

And clearly he's an idiot, because he's not backing down after my outburst. He just puffs his chest out even more, like a peacock. Lucky for me he's sitting close, and I could easily just reach out and pull his esophagus out through his throat.

"All I'm saying is that *if* you talk about working with–" Adam's on his last words as my hand itches to draw my Colt, but Uncle Colletti catches me reacting and hurries to warn him.

"Adam." He raises his palm at him, but fuck that.

Everyone knows I'm not happy. I shoot to my feet and pull my gun on him, pressing it to Adam's temple. He freezes.

The boardroom is full, and everyone has been listening to me, paying attention. Ever since I got back, there's this fear in their eyes. Plus respect, and dignity. Because I survived, they survived. I feel it. But I'm not choosing my words carefully anymore. I'm strung up, and all it will take is something small for me to explode. This, I don't need. I know I don't. But I also do.

"Hey, hey, calm down, Orion, please...What are you doing?" Adam's petrified, and he doesn't even know how close to dying he is.

"You see that door, Adam? You're gonna go through it and close it behind you. And you're gonna stay on that side of it, because I need just one little grain of sand to tip the scale. If I see you in here, ever, you're dead. Not even Angelina can save you. *Run.*"

"Y-yes. Yes, Orion." He jumps to his feet and runs out of the room. I caution Uncle Colletti with my glare, and he just shrugs his shoulders.

"He's family. He gotta learn the business one way or another."

"If you want him dead, just say the word," I warn. *I'm not gonna be a babysitter.*

"Um, no. No, Orion."

"Good. Now, back to business. Where was I?"

"You were talking about your meeting with Kai Delgado and Logan Vitali. They want to get rid of Milan too," Celina reminds me. She's been listening attentively ever since I walked in the room. I need more like her — on the outside, just a delicate woman, but upset her and the jujitsu master inside her makes an appearance. You don't want to mess with Celina. She's been crucial to some of our racketeering for some time now.

"Yes. Except–"

"Except no one's seen or heard from Logan Vitali for more than a week," someone at the back interrupts.

I raise my eyes, searching for where the voice came from, and I spot Emilio. He's mid-twenties; his father was my father's bodyguard, and he and I grew up in the same circles. When his father died, he stayed. He's a good muscle to have, and a good driver too. He doesn't get involved much, doesn't talk much either. He just needs company.

"How d'you know that, Emilio?"

"I... I..." he stutters.

Clay pipes up beside him. "He has a Vitali girlfriend." He turns to Emilio. "Sorry, man, they have to know. You can't just fuck a Vitali and not tell anyone."

"You're an asshole, Clay," Emilio mutters, but we all hear him.

"Fuck!" I growl.

"Orion, I'm so sorry, I-I'll break it off immediately. Please..." Emilio's begging for his life. Smart, given my current state.

"This is what I'm talking about, idiots!" I exclaim. "You can fuck whoever you want if we all work together!"

Silence ensues. Nobody's sure what's going on. Everyone's afraid to speak. This idea of working together has been great, but I never expressed it out loud before.

"A-and after we kill Milan?" someone asks.

"I don't fucking know! I just know we need *everyone* to defeat the Slavs. And I mean every fucking person in New York should be on our side! Because we tried, and we failed. We fucking *failed*. I'd rather be dead than go through the same fiasco as three months ago."

Emilio smiles. "Okay. I'm in."

"As long as your cock gets some action, sure!" someone jeers, and everyone laughs.

"Me too!" Clay says. "I got kids. I wanna see them grow up. How we've started, there ain't gonna be enough of us left if we keep fighting everyone in our vicinity. What's happening with this world these days, you can't even make an honest racket anymore."

Everyone agrees; heads are nodding. I glance at Uncle Leo and Uncle Colletti. Their heads each make an infinitesimal movement, their way of showing agreement.

"Right. I have to ask something now: is anyone against this move?"

They all look at each other.

"A real Carte speaks up. I don't want cowards walking among us."

"There's no cowards here, Orion!" someone yells.

"I hope it stays like that. Because from now on, I rely on you."

"Cartes!" someone else shouts, and the rest follow. "Cartes! Cartes!"

I raise my hand; there's still conversations to be had. "I'm gonna reach out to the other mafia families today. As of this very moment, if you see a Delgado or a Vitali, you do not engage. Do not shoot or fight. Because they'll have the same order from above."

"The Vitalis too?" Emilio asks. He doesn't know I've already had a word with Jon, Logan's uncle.

"Vitalis too. I'm gonna speak with them today. We believe Logan Vitali's been kidnapped by Milan."

"Why? Why not just kill him?"

"He was with Maisy Roy. The girl who got Milan by the balls. Now he finally has her."

"Didn't she die in the shooting?" Emilio asks.

"It's... It's a long story. But no. We just fucking failed her." I clear my throat before continuing. "In any case, I'm glad I stand here among brothers who, just like me, want a better life."

"Ey-ey!" the Cartes exclaim.

"As soon as I make a plan, you'll be informed." I nod and leave the boardroom.

The plan is in fact already made; I just had to make sure everyone's on board. In the last week, I've met with my people four times. Each time something new would come up, and I'd clear it. This time I learned about Emilio's little girlfriend, but I let it be, because who cares.

I think we're finally ready. Because that surge of guilt that pulses in my chest is not going away.

Kai's losing it, and so am I to be honest, but for his sake, I'm more reserved than before. I'm going to do this right, and no pussy is going to make me lose my mind.

Maisy.

I had to tell her to get the fuck out of my room the last time I saw her. All the fuck she does is lie. But fuck me if I'm gonna let her die by his hand. I'll slaughter every living Slav if she does. She's in too deep. I feel her in my blood, like a contagious disease. I hate it so much but it's too late now; she has a grip on every part of my life. Kai's and Logan's, too.

The thought of Logan being there burns in my chest. A searing pain that cannot be controlled. It hurts, and in a way, I allow it. Because of me, they took them. Had we stayed together, none of this would've happened. But I know he has it in him to survive. If Maisy's there, he's gonna survive.

Kai chose to follow my plan because he knows he's too impulsive, and his reasoning is utterly gone when he's angry. Also, not having Logan with us is a first.

When we didn't hear from Logan, Kai and I went back and found the car wreck. That day, I went to the Vitalis' club to see Uncle Jon. I explained everything and told him our plan. At that point they suspected Logan may be dead, but me telling them he's alive and at Milan's gave them a reason to celebrate.

They do love him – after all, he got rid of all the snitches. They sharpened their knives and got the guns out, ready to attack the Slavs.

I explained the plan, and they're ready, waiting on me to say the word.

The Delgados are already surveying Milan's house 24/7. We needed to know every single person coming in and going out to find our way in. As luck would have it, we found it. There are many girls coming and going from the house, but only one was free to move about – only one had a key.

One of us had to approach her and question her, or fuck her, whichever worked, and make a copy of the key. That was it. I couldn't let Kai do that. Us taking different routes was my suggestion, my fault.

I approached her, and I completed the task at hand. Got the copy of the key. That's all. It was easier than I thought. I didn't enjoy it, though.

What's bothering me is this feeling I have after fucking her. Empty. Hollow. Like I cheated on Maisy.

CHAPTER 12

LOGAN

I don't know how many days we've been here. I
lost count. I'm naked bar my boxer shorts, which are
torn. I'm bloodied, beaten, swollen, aching in every
possible place on my body, and on the inside, I'm
furious. *Where the fuck are they?*

My name rings in my ears over the pounding
pain. I hear the same questions Milan and his goons
have been torturing me with for days. Each time I try to
answer, my swollen tongue stops me from clearly
enunciating what I'm gonna do to him. I bit the fuck out
of it when I got a fist to the mouth. Right now, pain
shoots up my arm like fire as they pull my nails. It tears
up the nerves and explodes in my head with a blinding
flash. Like millions of needles dipped in salt are jammed
into the skin of my fingers, the sensations are wired
directly to my spine. But the moment my mind comes

back to this forsaken cell, I think of Maisy. Is she okay? What has she been doing except watching me helplessly from afar, her face pressed against the bars, screaming at them to let me go, crying? There's dried blood from the accident all over her; her bare legs are shivering every time I look at her. At night, when she covers herself with the measly blanket she has, I hear her sobbing. It breaks my heart that I can't reach her to console her. But maybe that's good. Thinking about her keeps me going for sure.

When I get my hands on Milan, he's gonna find out what real torture is. I'm only worried my body will give up on me before I can. My eye is constantly twitching. If only I could get my hands on a blade, I'd know what to do with it. I'm fed once a day, and he lets us use the bathroom – the only place I've seen a razor – but his goons don't let me out of their sight. I just know that's my only way out.

"Logan, I know more about the Vitalis and your operations than you do," Milan declares. "I know where you're stashing the money you take from the club each month. I know how much it is. I got eyes and ears everywhere. And I don't ask for much. Just give me the name of your Uncle Jon's wife and kids. I want to send them a nice pretty package for strengthening the roots of the Vitali family. You see, without you, and them, there's not gonna be a Vitali family within the syndicate. And what does a leftover pack of wolves need? An alpha to lead them."

I laugh sarcastically. "And that's you?" I doubt they can understand me though.

Milan's words linger in my head. I finally see through his intentions. Kill every Vitali. Stupidly, I helped him by killing Vince and his two brothers for running the porn studio, but I'm not sorry. They were distant cousins anyway and they'd have been killed sooner or later with that behavior. But what's apparent right now, at last, is the reason my father was insistent on secrecy around our family. That secrecy is why, I thought, I never found out about my mother. There are only two Vitalis left in the family, myself and Uncle Jon, who, together with my aunt Dina, has been an absolute lifesaver while I was recuperating. Their son Gino died young. Nobody knew about him, and it stayed that way. My father started a rumor that my Uncle Jon had three sons, and now I'm being tortured to give the names of children that don't exist. So very fitting for my father, torturing me even from beyond the grave. He also said that I have an older brother. But when I got made the Vitali head, it was clear that this older brother didn't exist. Still, in an extremely gruesome way, he's saved my life. For the moment.

Milan's two faithful dogs grab me from behind, yanking me to my feet. I don't fight. I clench my teeth so I don't make a sound at the pain that shoots like lasers from my fingers, now bare of nails. Still, this is better than being strung up like yesterday. I'd rather not have Maisy watch them doing this, though. I can't stand her screams.

"Eventually, you'll break," Milan continues. "D'you know how I know that? Because I knew your mother. If she could see you today, the kind of son you grew up to be, she'd vomit. A *doctor!* Ha! Her intentions for you were the best. Become a murdering machine. Kill everyone that's in your way. But look at you now, getting tortured for a whore you don't know shit about."

I'm tossed inside my cell. The grimy floor is hard as I fall. I groan. Everything hurts.

"Logan!" There's so much pain in Maisy's voice. I can only raise my hand. I have no strength to talk.

I hear the heavy wooden door being unlocked and opened. I don't see Milan. I just hope he's left, as my mind is elsewhere. Repeating his words in my head. *He knew my mother? He's messing with me. He has to be.*

"And you."

I hear Milan and lift my head. He's now turned to Maisy.

"Don't expect Orion Carte to come and save you anytime soon. He scored the cunt of my main girl. They had sex all night long, I'm told, and she stayed over at his place. She couldn't shut up about him, how good they fucked, what he did to her, the whole nine yards."

Maisy's chin wobbles. She's trying to stifle her emotions but it's of no use. Her face shines with fresh tears rolling down her cheeks.

I somehow manage to stand up, and hold myself against the bars. "Maisy, you know Orion better than anyone," I say, sucking in a breath. She needs to focus on me. My pain is irrelevant.

Milan leers deviously at me, then at Maisy, and continues. "He told her he'll keep her safe, just like he told you, Maisy."

"Stop it! Stop it! I don't believe you! I would never believe you!" She's sobbing, and banging on the bars. "Why are you doing this? Why?"

Milan reaches for her neck, yet again. *Goddamn, Maisy!* She's so naïve. She should be at the back of the cell, not the front.

"Go on, kill me! What are you waiting for?" she sobs as he grips her throat.

He looks at her with the scowling grimace of a psychopath. "Not yet, Maisy Roy," he taunts.

"Why? You sent me to Riyadh to die! What could you still want from me?"

"Riyadh? You were on loan there. On *loan*, whore. Which now I have to pay!"

He throws her to the floor, and she crawls back to the corner where he can't reach her. *I hope she stays there.*

MAISY

Where's Orion? Did he really...?

I pull my knees to my chin and hold my legs as I sob. He's not going to take away the only thing I have in life. *He's not!*

Milan leaves the basement, turning the light off and leaving us in darkness. When I hear the lock turning I let go, my sobs quickly filling the air. Why aren't Kai and Orion here already? Why are they letting Logan go through so much agony?

Logan manages to talk through his strained breathing. "He's trying to play with your mind. You must be strong."

"Where's Orion? Or Kai? Where?" I choke through a sob. It breaks me that they're not here. Not for me, or for him.

"They'll come."

"You really believe that?"

"Yes."

"Milan wants to kill you." I let out a shuddering breath. "I can't lose you, Logan," I whisper. "I just can't."

"Naah. You won't lose me, Maisy. You'll never lose me."

Logan's on the floor, leaning against the wall, just like I am, his eyes closed. They're feeding him once a day but he needs so much more than that. *Why am I fed more than him? Wasn't Milan supposed to kill me?* I tried to hide food for Logan but I was caught. So now, I'm under constant surveillance. I try to reject the food, but I'm weak, and I sometimes reach for the piece of bread on my tray. And then, Milan's goons don't move from my cell until I finish it.

"Logan, do you think he lied? About Orion?" I shouldn't be thinking about Orion now, but I got nothing else to think about. Imagining any of them with another woman breaks me. My heart constricts at the thought and dread twists in my gut, and all the while, I'm afraid it's a real possibility. No matter how scary it feels, I'll eventually lose them, just like everything else in my life.

"In our world, you'd do anything for a piece of information. Orion, well, I can't say for sure. But I know Milan plays fucked-up games. He also said he knew my mother. Ha, can you believe that?"

I can, actually.

"Maisy... you're gonna have to tell me eventually why Milan needs you."

Logan's eyes shine from across the basement; the few slivers of light coming through the heavy door are enough. I know he needs more – Milan's getting inside his head too – but I got nothing.

"I don't know. I really don't know."

He closes his eyes, and I want to think that he believes me. I want to believe myself. I know Milan wants to own me and never really succeeded, but why is he so persistent?

Before long, the sound of his breathing evens out. He's fallen asleep. Maybe for just a few moments he'll be able to get away from this place. I'm watching over him, and in a selfish way it makes me feel good. As if I'm actually doing something, even if it's me imagining it. Because I can't sleep. I don't think I will ever be able to sleep again.

~

I'm dozing off, my head resting against the wall, when a sound from outside the door wakes me up. It must be very early; at this time, we don't usually see anyone around. I lift my head, listening carefully. There's definitely someone outside the door.

The lock releases and the door's pushed open slowly. Four or five flashlight beams illuminate the basement, searching, going from corner to corner, but I... I can't move. I find solace in the beams of light.

"The cameras. Up there," someone whispers. Another person aims and shoots at them. It makes a suppressed sound.

"Found him!" A familiar voice. "Over here! We need a crowbar." All the beams point to Logan and I see him clearly, at last. There's so much blood on him. His body is black, blue, and red from bruises and cuts. My tears start again. It feels like all I've been doing here is cry, helpless to do anything about what's going on.

"I'll get it!" another person says, and runs back outside.

"Logan! Logan! Wake up!" It's Kai. I blink as my eyes become blurred from the tears. I want them out of my eyes – I want to see him. "We're gonna get you out of here, buddy."

"What they've done ..." Another familiar voice reaches me, Orion's, as he moves the flashlight beam up and down Logan's body. "Milan's gonna pay for every second you were in here," he mutters through his teeth.

"Took you long enough to get here... assholes," Logan finally croaks, raising his arm to shield his eyes from the light.

"Where's that crowbar?!" Kai shouts impatiently.

"Fuck you, both of you," Logan continues.

None of them are looking for me. It figures; if Orion was making the plan, they'd go for Logan first. My heart tightens, but I'm happy for Logan.

A single flashlight keeps moving about until, finally, it lands on me.

"Maisy!" Orion hisses.

I haven't moved. I'm still sitting in the corner, but I hide my face between my knees and my chest and a strained sob comes out. I sense more flashlights on me;

it's getting much brighter.

"Maisy!" Kai's louder. "Where the *fuck* is that crowbar?" he growls.

"Maisy, darling, look at me!" It's Orion.

He's been with someone else. He's been having fun, and all the while Logan was dying in here. Now he wants me to look at him?

"Maisy!" he keeps yelling, but I just can't make myself lift my head.

"I got the crowbar, Kai! I'll get on opening Logan's cell!" someone shouts.

"Do that, then we need this cell opened, too."

"Sure."

"Maisy! Hey! Look! At! Me!" Orion orders as I sob harder.

"Orion, go to Logan," Kai mumbles. "You're more helpful there."

I hear the metal bars being banged, a frustrated sound, but then Kai's soft voice. "Hey. Hey. Maisy. Baby girl, you can stop crying. We're here. We'll get you out and we'll go home."

I finally look up. The three flashlight beams shining on me are blinding. I raise my hand, trying to shield my face to be able to see him. "Home?" My voice shakes. "What home will I go to? I have no home." A fresh flood of desperation hits me and I burst into another loud sob.

"Yes, you do. You got us. *We're* your home."

"You'll save me, and then what? Milan will never stop hunting me. He'll succeed, too." My voice is trembling. "Look where I am. Maybe you shouldn't bother with me anymore."

"Baby girl, don't talk like that." Kai's trying real hard.

Across the basement, I see Logan's cell is finally open. Orion helps him get to his feet.

Two other men help Logan. "Take it easy now," one of them says.

"Maisy... Get Maisy." Logan points to me. Sweet Logan. Always thinking of me, even when I don't deserve it. Not one bit.

"Don't worry, we got her too." Orion turns, his eyes landing on me. The determination in them stirs my soul.

"Shhh! Someone's coming, close the door!" one of their men shouts, and two others jump to close it. Everyone lines up along the wall behind the door, except Orion, who gets the crowbar and tries frantically to break the lock on my cell.

A hushed shout comes from one of the men. *"Orion!"*

He doesn't stop. The noise could easily give them away.

Kai runs to him. "Orion! Stop it." He tries to take

the crowbar from his hands but Orion holds onto it firmly. "We'll get her out. Let's see who's coming first."

Orion finally yields, giving the crowbar to Kai, but doesn't make much effort to hide. He moves to first in line just behind the door. Logan's standing with the help of two men, his cell door now wide open.

"Where is everyone?!" It's Milan. That's his voice.

My heart stops pumping; my adrenal glands are working overtime, shooting adrenaline throughout my body that's now vibrating a new shade of scared. I'm creating all these deadly scenarios where everyone loses their lives, until I'm left alone in this forsaken place. Everyone dies, because of me.

Milan opens the door and turns the light on. He's in his robe, half-asleep. From the moment the yellow bulb lights up, he doesn't have time to blink before everyone descends upon him. A big scuffle and plenty of thuds are heard. I can't make out a thing as there's too many people involved.

Finally, Kai's voice signals the end. "Okay, okay, we got him. Stop hitting, we need him alive."

"You fucking assholes, do you know where you are?" Milan shrieks. "I'm gonna fucking mince your bodies and feed you to your families! Let go of me!"

I see Orion swing wide and knock Milan's face so hard, his nose gushes with blood. It's all over him and running down his robe. But Orion doesn't give him any more attention. He takes the crowbar back from Kai and resumes jacking the door of my cell.

"Hold him," Kai orders, and he too takes a swing. The boxer inside him must have wanted to do this for a long time.

"Kai, don't—" Orion turns at the last moment but it's too late. Kai's hit Milan so hard that he's knocked him out straight.

"What?" Kai asks, baffled.

"I was gonna say don't knock him out yet. But never mind now."

"It's fine, we're gonna wake him anyway. I'm cutting his dick off here and now." *The Vitali calling card.* "Logan, you don't mind, right?" Kai glances at Logan, who's still being held up by one of their men.

"Naah. I'll take something better. The skin off his face, maybe," Logan mutters.

"Great. Tie him up. Then we're taking him with us."

The metal bars finally give way and Orion manages to pull the door of my cell ajar. He throws the crowbar aside and runs to me, crouching and wrapping his arms tight around me where I sit. His scent is overpowering, instantly taking me to my safe place, which I hate right now because it's his house.

"You okay? Tell me you're okay. Have they done

anything to you?" He checks my body, my arms, my face.

No. Orion doesn't get to save me again. Being next to him is comforting, but how can I forget his hurtful words?

"If I tell you they haven't touched me, you'll be asking me why they haven't," I sniffle, my voice betraying me as I speak. "You'll be asking me what I'm not telling you. You'll say I'm lying, yet again. Spare me your concern, Orion."

I see Kai entering my cell and I manage somehow to get to my feet. Orion gets up too.

I run into Kai's embrace with a choked wail. He holds me tight. "It's okay, it's fine. We're getting you out of here."

"I got movements again! Someone's coming!" the man on lookout shouts. They kill the light, and all of us stand behind the door, waiting.

We hear light footsteps that stop outside. Someone knocks on the door. "Milan? Is... Is it okay if I come in?"

We look at each other. Kai partially opens the door in invitation. It gets pushed fully open.

"Milan?"

There's that voice again.

My heart starts thumping in my chest. I recognize that voice. She turns the light on and as she does, they all pounce on her.

Rosey.

I remember seeing her with Milan. I remember her laughing. *Or was I dreaming?*

"D-don't hurt her," I manage to croak.

She's not thrashing the way I would if five men pounced on me in a basement. She's meek. Passive. Like she's given up on life. They overpower her easily and hold her still. Almost instantly, everyone's eyes turn to me, then back to her.

I'm frozen in place. I'm looking at my sister, after so many years of searching. I know I can talk to her and ask her everything, but I'm too afraid because I may say something I'll regret. I could be wrong about her.

Orion and Kai step back and leave a clear space between her and me. She's wearing a robe, too. Looks like she's naked underneath. Just like Milan. *They're sleeping together.*

The bags under her eyes make her look hollow, empty. Ghostly almost. She squints as she looks at me. She's much skinnier than I remember, making her breasts look bigger. This here is my sister. My family. My blood. She is mine. I'm hers. That's what my mother used to tell us. No matter what, we stick together. I've given my life to find her. Has she forgotten?

"M-Maisy?! You're here?" She's taken aback, and her words trail off. "I... I didn't know..."

"Spare me the lies, Rosey," I rasp.

"Maisy…" She tries to take a step forward but she's held firmly in place. She looks at the men holding her. From here, I can see the tears glistening in her eyes. If I know one thing about her, it's how easily she can start crying. Something that saved us a few times when we were growing up. The sight of her tears reminds me not to trust her.

I don't move, only blink while cold tears fall down my cheeks. This is my family. My family who changed sides. She sent me to Riyadh. I remember her laughter.

"I did everything to find you. To save you. And here you are, in the wolf's lair." My raspy voice turns wobbly, ending on a whisper. "Why would you do that?"

"You don't understand, Maisy. Please," she pleads.

Milan's groans get our attention. He's coming round.

Rosey shrieks. "Milan! What have they done to you?!" She tries to run to him but Orion's men hold her firm. "Let me go! Can't you see he's hurt?"

I use the distraction to turn my back to everyone and regain my composure. I'm openly crying and I'm trying to still my wobbly chin. It's obvious. Even so, I wipe my tears away and clear my throat.

"He's awake? Great! Pass me that chair!" I hear Kai ordering and pointing to the chair at the far end of the basement. "I'm cutting his dick off right now."

"No! You can't do that! He can't die!" Rosey yells, and again attempts to pull herself free.

I turn and look at her in disgust. "The man who raped you as a child, and God knows how many times more, the man who sold your body to everyone and anyone, *that* man" –I point to Milan– "you now want to *save*?"

"Rosey, honey, please, tell them not to do it, they'll listen to you," Milan begs, panic-stricken. "That's your sister over there. Tell her she's gotta save me. She has to."

We all watch Kai taking the chair that's been brought to him and placing it in front of Milan.

"Hold him tight." Kai looks at his men, then grins wickedly at Milan. "This might hurt a little. A preview of what's to come."

Milan starts crying as he's held tight. He begs for his life, no, for the life of his dick, as Kai pulls the robe's belt and allows it to open up. Milan's big, fat stomach and his limp, shriveled cock hanging underneath it make me want to vomit.

From the inside pocket of his leather jacket, Kai pulls out what looks like a chef's knife. It's pretty big, possibly too big for cutting off something so small. He lifts Milan's cock with it and flops it over the chair's backrest. "There. This should be a clean cut."

Milan's writhing and thrashing about, but with more than five men holding his hips firmly against the backrest, he stands no chance. "You can't! No! Please! I'll give you anything! Please…"

"Don't move or I'll cut your legs too. I don't want you to bleed to death." Kai winks at him. "At least not yet."

Rosey's screaming, Milan's pleading like it means anything to the men in here, and Kai's grinning. I don't think I've ever seen him this crazy.

"Um, boss?"

Kai rolls his eyes at the interruption and turns toward the voice.

"Look what I found. A baby."

"A baby?" Kai chuckles as one of his men pushes a stroller into the room. It does indeed have a baby inside.

I gasp in shock. "*What?*"

"What the fuck?" Orion frowns at the extra variable thrown into this scenario. He must have organized everything to the last detail in here, but this…

As if he wasn't crying just a moment ago, even with fucking tears still in his eyes, Milan's demeanor changes the moment he sees the stroller. "You fucking whore! Are you fucking crazy, bringing the kid in here?!" he barks at Rosey.

"I… I didn't want to leave him by himself."

Rosey's voice cracks as she looks at me. "Please let me go to my baby. He'll be hungry."

I'm frozen, but for so many more reasons than I was before. Stunned into silence, I nod to the guy holding her to let her go and she runs to the baby.

"I'm here, Damien, Mommy's here."

We're all silent as she picks him up in her arms. *Mommy?*

"Who's the father?" I ask. If this is Rosey's child, I'm... I'm related to it. I have a right to know.

Rosey shrugs, a clear signal that says *I don't know*. Is she lying to me? I could always tell when she was lying to me. But now? She's too unreadable to figure out.

"Right. I'm sorry, but we gotta leave this place before everyone figures out we're here." Kai's waiting for no one, and instead uses the moment to swing with his knife and in one quick move, Milan's dick is cut off, just like Kai promised.

As shocking as it is to witness, I watch his junk plop down on the chair, then on the floor. This is basically what I've dreamed of all this time. Rosey screams, Milan's screaming. Lucky for us, this basement was made to contain the sounds of screaming.

"No! No! What've you done?" Rosey's terrified as she holds her baby close to her body, her hand on the back of his head, hugging it to her chest. *She should be happy Milan won't be able to rape her ever again, or anyone else for that matter.*

Milan's screaming fades as he blacks out, and Kai's men use the opportunity to duct-tape his mouth and zip-tie his arms and legs. They're clearly taking him with us.

"Is this baby his? How *could* you, Rosey? He raped us when we were twelve! *Twelve!*" I yell at her, no longer able to ignore what's plainly in front of me.

"You're so stupid, Maisy!" she shrieks back. "So clever, and yet so stupid! We were always gonna end up here. We were promised to him before we were even born!"

I take a step toward her. "How many years have they been brainwashing you?"

I know she's holding a baby, and I haven't been this close to her in years, but all I want to do is hit her. Orion must realize my intention, and quickly holds me back.

"My rightful place is here, with the Slavs," she goes on. "You know why? Because–"

"How could you be so stupid? *How?*" I turn to Orion, who's got me by the arms. "Let me go! Let me slap some sense into her!"

"Maisy, stop shouting," he replies. "We're leaving. And I need you to be quiet. We'll deal with everything once we get home."

Home. There that word is again, taunting me. I glower at him, ready to spew fire as my anger is now aimed in his direction, and *he knows.* Before I can speak, he places his large hand over my mouth, quieting me by force.

"Yes. I'm taking you home. Whether you like it or not. Now, should I duct-tape your mouth too, or will you be quiet?"

I groan and shake him off, pulling back. I don't want him to touch me. Every time he does, I'm reminded of my reckless need for him and that's what I want to forget.

"Walk in front of me," he orders.

"What are we doing with her, boss?" one of Kai's men asks.

Kai and Orion both look at me.

"Leave her here to rot," I say. "She's made her bed, now she can lie in it."

"Stay here, Maisy, with me. You're supposed to be by my side, not over there, with *them.*" Rosey scowls at Kai and Orion as if they're her worst enemies. "Mom told us—"

I take a step forward, and she stops talking. I'm so close to her that I'm practically breathing in her face. "You're dead to me. I have no family anymore."

I leave the basement first, with Orion and Kai following me. I don't know the layout of the house but I walk up the stairs, through the corridors, towards the cold air.

Once I'm out of the building, I see Logan being taken care of as he's led inside a van, with Milan being already inside, lying unconscious on the floor. Orion overtakes me and leads us towards the van, with me next and Kai behind me. Everyone else has disappeared. It's dark, quiet, too quiet, and only the rustling under our feet can be heard.

"Give me one good reason why I shouldn't raise the alarm right now and hand you over to Milan!" Natasha's voice slices though the silence. "Hands where I can see them!"

CHAPTER 13

MAISY

I freeze. Orion and Kai stop too as I turn to see Natasha. She's facing Kai and has a gun aimed at his head.

"What the fuck? You're working for Milan now?" Kai hisses through his teeth. "I should've killed you when I had the chance, Natasha!"

If she shoots, all hell will break loose. She doesn't know we have Milan, but still, there may be many of Milan's men in that house. Then again, this is only an assumption. Right now, I just want out of here. I'm filthy, hungry, and disconnected. I have no family left. I lived my life for Rosey, and now... now I've got nothing and no one. In a way it's freeing, as I don't have to be afraid anymore. Milan had me in his tight grip because he knew I'd do anything to save Rosey. She should've never been hurt. But Rosey... No matter. This is it.

There is a standoff between Natasha and us, and trigger-happy fingers are all around.

"Oh, Kai, you know you don't have it in you to kill an innocent woman," she mocks, rolling her eyes. "Oh, okay, a *woman*. Don't know about the 'innocent' part."

Kai's back is to me and his gun, tucked in the back of his jeans, is staring at me.

"Maisy, don't," Orion whispers.

How? How does he know what I'm about to do?

"You broke my heart, Kai. I loved you," Natasha declares.

I have no time for a sob story, nor for Orion figuring out my every move. Seeing Natasha's act, I really have had enough of it all. I reach out with my right hand and pull Kai's gun, my movement shielded by his big, strong body. He tenses and steps back.

I get the message, Kai. I shouldn't be doing this, especially when she has her gun pointed at you.

"Maisy," Orion warns me quietly.

Kai's unperturbed. "Either shoot or let me go, Natasha."

"Let you go?" She breaks into a bitter laugh. "I'll never let you go!"

I use the moment when she throws her head back in laughter, and drops her aim on Kai's head. That's when I raise the gun in my hand and shoot her, hitting her forehead and killing her on the spot.

With the gun in my hand, I look at Kai and Orion in panic. They're staring at me, speechless.

"I... I just wanna get out of here. M-maybe I shouldn't have..."

We hear a few dogs barking in the background and Kai immediately bends and grabs my legs, draping me over his shoulder. I drop the gun on the ground and brace myself for a bumpy ride.

"Run!" Kai shouts at Orion and everyone outside the van.

By the time the lights go on in the house, we're driving down the street at a crazy speed.

Logan's staring at us in confusion. "What happened? Why did you fire?"

We're still panting and getting seated on the benches in the back of the van. Orion and Kai eye each other and then look at me.

"Maisy killed Natasha."

Logan raises his eyebrows at me. "*Killed?*"

"I-I made a mistake. It's not as easy as they say. I-I took an innocent life." I'm conflicted.

"She was everything but innocent, Maisy. Don't beat yourself about it." Kai puts his hand on my shoulder.

"She wasn't gonna let us go. You could've been hurt." *Yes. That's it.*

Orion cocks his head. "He wouldn't."

"You deserve a bullet, too." I cross my arms over my chest and look away. *How I see it, I saved us.*

ORION

"As the top dog of an organized crime syndicate, and as the head of the Slavs, Milan has overseen racketeering, illegal waste dumping, money laundering, and drug trafficking for the past twenty years.

"He's protected by a very dense network of complicities, deeply-rooted and extremely powerful throughout New York and beyond. Over the years, a sort of smokescreen formed around him, made up of a network of people loyal to him. And for years, our fathers have tried to enter this circuit, but separately. They each craved the power Milan had, which shouldn't have been his in the first place. He's not from the Slav bloodline. He's not a Slavinovich. The last head of the Slavs, Goran Slavinovich, got killed in a drive-by shooting twenty or so years ago. That's when all this started. Milan proclaimed himself head of the Slavs and everyone supported him. Which is totally unheard of, and enraged our fathers even more. At their persistence in trying to kill Milan, gradually, the Cartes, Delgados, and Vitalis got weakened. Eventually, those wars made us all more vulnerable. But this is where things change. Now, we got a joint front. Milan's smokescreen has started to clear, and we got him."

I stop and look at Kai and Logan, checking if they're paying attention. We're in my kitchen, takeout on the table, a few pizza boxes and my laptop in front of me. It's been a week since we got Logan and Maisy back. Logan's been recuperating speedily, while Maisy was fine when we got her. A little dehydrated, but well fed and otherwise healthy. She'd been in a cold place in filthy conditions but once she took a bath, she was fine, if I can say that. The thing is, she's been spending most of her time in her room with Kai and Logan. She doesn't want to see me. Or talk to me. Which is good. Agonizingly painful, but this way's for the best. I need my cock clear of her cunt in order to think. Just a thought of her crossing my mind makes me hard. I'm not going to allow myself to be weak in these times. Not until Milan and the Slavs are fully decommissioned. I also remember that she shot Natasha. See, that's another red flag I'm going to explore. Not yet, though. I trust her enough to not turn on us when we're sleeping, but handling a gun so easy, when only three months ago it looked like she had no idea how to shoot, does look suspicious. She tried shooting at Milan so many times at Gianini's, but didn't get him. And now, suddenly, she shoots and kills

Natasha without flinching?

I glance at Logan. He's back to wearing his usual gear, a three-piece suit, which gives him an air of authority. We thought he was shot in the shoulder but luckily, he was only grazed. And now only his face still wears the cuts and bruises, those that we can see. The torture he went through at Milan's comes to my mind when I see the haunted look in his eyes. He's strong, too strong to say anything. He didn't even tell us what Milan wanted. Of course, he'd never give them anything they wanted, I'd bet my life on that, but he avoided the question altogether when I asked him. Alas, that's not important right now. At this very moment, all I know is that with Milan in my basement and getting his dues for the past seven days, we will reciprocate the hospitability. Logan has an extra motivation over us, of course.

"Any questions so far?" I ask.

"Goran Slavinovich. I haven't heard that name in years." Kai props his black boot on the chair next to him. His black shirt has seen better days, but he likes to be dressed like that, scruffy. Even his shoulder-length blond hair is messy. I'm like Logan when it comes to dressing – a three-piece suit all the time. My suit jacket is off right now and my shirt sleeves are rolled up, since we just ate takeout, but everything else remains, including my gun in its holster.

"We're going after Milan with all our might. But

we need to hit the rest of the Slavs at the same time. When we shake the foundation of their leader, they'll want to leave him."

"They'll never abandon him," Logan says darkly. "After twenty years, their foundation's solid. They wouldn't be this strong otherwise."

"Of course they will, when they find out. I know the story in detail, my father—"

"Your father knew nothing!" Logan snaps.

I'm confused, and enraged. "What the fuck, Logan?"

"What d'you think Milan wanted from me?!" Logan shoots up to his feet, irritated.

I'm the one that's usually angry, not him. *The fuck?* "I don't know. You didn't tell us." I take a step forward, daring him to disclose whatever it is. "But now that you mention it, what *did* Milan want from you?"

"Never mind." He turns his back on me, his shoulders slouched, and starts walking away.

"Hey, fucker! You come here and tell us what he was after!" I growl.

Logan rakes his hands through his hair and sighs. "I can't tell you. This is ultimate Vitali shit."

"You don't trust us, Logan?"

"It's not that." Logan still has his back to us, and I wonder if it's because we let him down, we came so late to get him. I allowed that maniac to torture him for days, and it kills me to think that I was the one who made that decision.

Kai pushes back the bench he was sitting on and stands up, walking up to him. "I love you, man." His puts his hand on Logan's shoulder. "Whatever it is, I'll still love you. Even if you snitched on us."

Logan punches Kai jokingly. "You're stupid. You know me better than that."

"Thank God! Cause I'd have punched you so hard, just to get it out of my system."

"Asshole!"

I make it clear I won't let them forget what we're talking about. "What did Milan wanna know?"

Logan turns back to me. "If I tell you, I don't want any more questions on the subject."

I nod. "I'll give you that."

"Milan wanted to know the name of my Uncle Jon's wife and kids. That's all."

Kai's eyebrows shoot up. "What the fuck?"

Logan takes the bottle of whiskey, pours himself a glass, and drinks it in one go. He pours another and sits back down on the bench. Kai follows.

I'm trying to think of what the implications are for Milan having this piece of information, but can't think of any. *His uncle? Why?*

He knows I'm about to say something and raises his finger at me. "That's all I'm sharing. That's what

Milan wanted to know."

Kai looks as stunned as I am. "He tortured you for that? Surely that information's available to anyone."

"It's not."

"Come on." I open the laptop in front of me and do a quick search online. "Uncle Jon... Jon, J-O-N?" I ask, my eyes flicking from the screen to him.

Logan nods. "You won't find anything."

I continue searching for one Jon Vitali. I find him. Single. No wife or kids. "He doesn't have a wife or children," I state. I look up and we regard each other for a beat. Then I look at Kai. Then back at Logan. "*Does* he?"

Logan drinks his whiskey. And pours himself another.

"What the fuck, Logan? Why is this important?" I demand.

His eyes flick to something behind me and I know we're not alone anymore, but I couldn't care less. I've been ignoring Maisy all this time for a reason. I refuse to swoon over her so I can finish my job successfully. Any job that I'm doing without thinking of Maisy is usually done successfully.

"I don't understand how your uncle's wife and kids are connected to Milan," I press.

Logan shakes his head. "This is something that none of your fathers mentioned to you, or mine to me. I found out by accident and was sworn to silence."

I said I wouldn't question him but also, fuck me, I want to know what this is all about. I will not ignore it.

"Logan?" Kai prompts.

I raise my eyebrows at Logan. "We're waiting."

"Fuck off, Orion. I told you. This has nothing to do with you." He glances at Maisy, who's behind me, patiently waiting to enter. "Maisy, sweetheart, come here. I need some loving right now."

Maisy's in her jeans, sneakers, and sweatshirt. She's been wearing proper clothes lately, but I can tell she's not wearing a bra and I bet there are no panties either. *Fuck.* I can tell everything about her. As she walks past me, I grab her wrist.

"No. You don't get Maisy 'til you tell us."

Logan gives me a malicious smile, one I've never seen before on him. "D'you think I took this torture lightly? D'you think I enjoyed it? Feel free to skin me alive if you want. I've given my word to someone and I'll be goddamned if I break it."

"And... if they find out from a different source? Would that be okay?" Maisy asks him, so sweetly that you'd think butter wouldn't melt in her mouth. I pull her toward me and even though her body's facing me, her eyes are on Logan, waiting for his response.

"You *know?*" Kai's clearly shocked, just like I am. Although I'm more annoyed than shocked. *How come she knows fucking everything?*

"I doubt you know, Maisy. But if you think you know, please, share," Logan says.

Maisy forcefully pulls her arm from my grasp and I let her go. If I wanted her next to me, she wouldn't have been able to free herself.

She sits down between Kai and Logan and stares at her hands, her fingers fidgeting.

"Why is this all too familiar?" I mutter as I sit down opposite them.

She's silent as she looks up at Logan, searching for some agreement from him, or approval, fuck knows what.

"Talk, Maisy!"

My command startles her and she jumps. Her dark eyes meet mine, and whereas before she'd instantly succumb, now she shoots daggers at me from under her lashes. I hold her stare, and she soon yields. Again her eyes drop to her fumbling fingers. It's how she tells stories to us. Or lies. Who knows, maybe one of these will be the truth.

"When I worked at Milan's, I came across a lot of information. Most didn't make sense until I met you. What you're talking about, only now I understand. Or at least I think I do. I couldn't get why they were torturing you over something so trivial." She looks at Logan, then back at me. "But I think I figured it out. It was in an old notebook, with something scribbled on it. I saw it close to five years ago. Some doodles... but I remember. I remember seeing the names Delgado, Vitali, and Carte. It looked like a family tree. I've no idea why this was important, but now I think I do." She glances at Logan again. Waiting for him to stop her.

But Logan's not looking at anyone. He's miles away in his head, the fingers of one hand on top of the other, where his nails used to be, and he's gently touching the bare skin. It breaks my heart how much they fucked him up. There are not enough hours in the day to torture Milan in the basement as much as we should. But we'll try.

"Milan had written down the names of the members of your families. For you, Orion, it was Willer Carte, you, your sister, and an X next to her. I think that's Mya. Underneath was Uncle Colletti, and then, um, someone called Angelina. I'm presuming his daughter. Underneath, Uncle Leo and Uncle James. You have a big family. I think he feared you most because of it." She turns to Kai. "Kai, for you it was your father, Micky Delgado, and then you. And Logan, for you," she looks at him, but he's not interested in her story. "It was Lorenzo Vitali, then you. Underneath that line was Uncle Jon, with two Xs next to his name. I'm presuming those are his children."

Logan catches my eye as Maisy continues. "You

each had a number next to your name. 1 Vitali, 2 Delgado, and 3 Carte."

Kai's confused. "I don't get it. Why did he have this information?"

"He's going after us first," Logan says. "Once he killed my uncle's kids, who, by the way, don't exist, it was gonna be easy. Killing me and Uncle Jon in a shootout would render the Vitali family terminated, and my people would be in search of a new leader. If that happened, guess who'd come to save the day. He'd find a way for everyone to join him."

I'm trying to make sense of this. "What do you mean, the kids don't exist?"

"Those are the lies my father spread. For this exact reason."

"He already had you. Why didn't he kill you when he had the chance, and then go after the kids and uncle?" Kai asks.

"Because then the dynamics of the game would be different. Then it would be about revenge," Maisy replies. "Logan has you, he has people in the family that he trusts. Milan knows that. Milan knows a lot of things."

"Huh."

Maisy continues. "Once he's broken down the Vitalis, he'll go after the Delgados. They're not his priority. He'll just use them to tip the scales in his favor."

"The fuck he will," Kai snaps.

"Well, if he does succeed and get the Vitalis on his side, he'll be after you next, Kai. And take over your patch, and people," she says.

"You're dreaming, Maisy. You're talking nonsense now." Kai's riled, but she continues, for my sake. I'm the only one listening to her with a cool head. As much as I can.

"And lastly, having two syndicate families from New York joining the Slavs, it would be easy killing you and everyone else in your family, Orion. The order wouldn't be relevant."

"So the hit on Lisa's husband..."

"I wouldn't be surprised if it was planned for Uncle James to kill Mya too, if he'd had it in him."

"There's something missing here." I rub my chin. "He's not a Slavinovich. If we shake the Slavs, he has nothing to lean on. Every Slav will change sides. My father said when Goran Slavinovich got killed, with him died the name, the family. And when that happens, we know, it's the end."

Kai looks like he's trying to recall anything relevant. "How come all of this is unknown to me?"

"Kai, you never wanted to be the head of your family," I remind him. "When you were old enough to get involved, you hated it. And created the bike club to run away from it."

"That was true in the past, but not now. Now my

life's purpose is to slaughter every single Slav out there. Dammit, I have some catching up to do on the theory, too."

"You sure do. The way your upbringing went, you're lucky you can read and write." I snort. "Remind me, how many nannies did you have looking after your spoilt ass?"

"Can't remember." Kai shrugs. "Too many. Too many 'moms.'" He turns to Maisy. "That's what I called the nannies that looked after me. 'Mom.' My father insisted on it. I was never really bothered about my real mother. I got to see that anyone could've been my mom, they just had to care for me. And they all did."

"Huh." Maisy tilts her head. "In a way, that makes sense. So you never met your mother?"

"Nuh-uh. I got enough love when I was young and I lacked nothing. It's when my father introduced me to the mobster's way of life, as a teen, that I started to hate my life."

"And you don't know who your mother is?"

"I don't."

"What does your birth certificate say?"

He shrugs again. "I never had reason to look at it. I know my legal name, I know I'm a Delgado, and the rest I owe to my two fists." He kisses the knuckles on his left hand, then his right.

Logan's still lost in thought, withdrawn. So

much has happened in such a short time, and he's suffered most. His hands are now curled into fists and his jawline's flexing.

"Logan, what are you thinking?" I ask.

"That I wanna find out how come that bitch downstairs knew my mother. And then kill him."

"Your mother?" Kai and I ask at the same time. We know how hard Logan's been searching for his mother, with none of his investigation amounting to anything. *And Milan knew her?*

I nod and stand up. "Then it's time."

Maisy shoots to her feet too, but she's mistaken if she thinks she's coming with us. I glare at her for a moment, making her slowly shrink back into her seat.

Kai kisses her cheek. "Don't wait up, baby girl."

"I want to come." She's pleading with her eyes, a skill she has that's worked on us too many times. "I want to find out what happened to Rosey. It's my right–"

"Like hell it is," I snap. "Go to your room. Or do whatever."

Logan is already out of the kitchen.

"No." Maisy crosses her arms and stares up at me through her long lashes. I'm towering above her and *fuck*, her mouth is level with my cock and what I wouldn't give to just shut her up with it.

I don't look away from Maisy. "Kai, go with Logan. I'll be there in a minute."

"Is that how long it takes you now?" Kai chuckles, and I shoot him a warning look. *I will not fuck her. I will not fuck her.*

"Since when do you answer back, Maisy?" I demand after Kai leaves.

"Since you're being a real asshole to me."

"Did you shoot Natasha to show me you can use a gun?"

"What? No."

"Did you pretend you couldn't throw Logan's blades, too?"

"No! No, I don't know how to throw a blade. And why would I cut myself?"

I sit opposite her and sigh, then pinch my nose and close my eyes, deliberating over what to do with her. She's driving me mad, and the fact that I haven't had her in a while is literally making me weaker. She's the poison and the antidote at the same time.

"Right." I open my eyes again, but she's not there. She's not far, though, as I suddenly get a hit of her cherry-blossom scent like a shot to the veins. She's sitting next to me, on the bench. Too close. It's pure and heaven, and... *Wake up, Orion!*

"Orion." Her palm's on my thigh; her lips brush my ear. I don't move. I don't want her to see how much she affects me. But fuck me if my cock didn't just go full-on hard. It makes me groan under my breath, and now my pants are too tight to withhold the animal trying to set itself free.

She bites my earlobe. "*Please.*"

Fuck! She knows. She knows I'm barely staying sane. *Sly fucking slut.*

As if this tornado raging inside me can be stopped once it's let out. My nostrils flare. I know what happens when the inevitable comes forth. She has the audacity to stroke my thigh, and with the other hand, rub my rigid cock over my pants. In a split second, my fingers curl around her neck, reddening her skin, tightening, hoping she'll beg me to stop. But she doesn't. Her eyes bulge, her mouth opens to gasp for air, but her deft fingers pull at my belt, then buttons.

"Stop what you're doing," I order, grazing her lips with mine as I talk. If she doesn't, I may hurt her right here, on the table.

She's trying to say something and I release her throat enough for her to speak.

"You hurt me. This is how I take my power back."

"By trying to get fucked again?"

"By jerking you off. While you do nothing."

I touch my forehead to hers. "Not possible, Maisy. Don't do it."

"Let me." She surges toward my lips but I don't let her reach me. She whines, enveloping me in her eyes, the black fire singeing me, not giving me space to think. I didn't know I was this far gone.

"You must let me do this. Please. I need it."

My eyes slam shut. I know I'm frowning because I don't want this, and yet, my grip on her throat eases off. I don't understand myself – have I become a total wimp around her? I just know that last time I hate-fucked her and spat her out. Didn't have a chance to do anything after, and then she got kidnapped.

"*Yeees...*" She kisses my neck and manages to free my cock from my pants. This is so fucked up for me, and new, and I don't know how to deal with it. I want her to get her power back, but I also want to spank her ass so hard it bears red welts for weeks.

"Don't think, just let me take care of you." She curls her fingers around my cock and pumps me slowly as I groan and open my eyes, fixing them on hers.

I keep hold of her neck and my other hand roams under her sweatshirt, grabbing her breasts, one after another, like a hungry child being given two breasts and not knowing which one to take first. "Maisy..."

"Shh..." She sucks on my neck, then bites me, hard. Fuck, I needed that. I'm still holding her by the throat, but I let her. I let her do whatever she wants to me. She's my door to heaven and hell, like an orgasmic prayer taking me to another dimension. She sees through me, she knows what I need. She pumps me faster, and moans as if I'm fucking her, and yet, *she's* jerking *me*. I'm so close to orgasm it's embarrassing.

Her bites come one after another, aggressive, forceful, as she nips my jaw to the rhythm of her pumping. She's taken me to another planet in such a small space of time and I'm... *Fuck*, I'm powerless.

It's coming, like a volcano. I feel my whole being shaking and thundering. I groan and shoot to my feet, taking her with me, and thick cum spurts out of me as she massages my balls and pumps me dry over the table. It's all over the food. *Lucky we finished eating.*

I'm growling under my breath. *What the fuck just happened?* I can't get my head around it. My hand's still around her neck, although not squeezing hard. I'm just holding it because had I let her go, I may have done something I'd regret later. She was my anchor.

I gotta say something. "Look at the mess you just made." *I'm ridiculous.*

"Nothing needs to be wasted." She smiles mischievously and picks up a slice of pizza covered in my spunk. I let go of her neck as she takes a bite. My cock twitches again.

"On the table. Now," I order.

"Nuh-uh." She shakes her head, her mouth full. "That wasn't the deal." She straightens up but I shove my hand under the waistband of her jeans. I was right. She's not wearing panties, but when I reach her cunt, my hand slides through her arousal, seemingly still surging.

"Fuck! Maisy!" I bring my fingers to my lips and taste her. If her body makes me weak, her cunt debilitates me.

She bats her eyelashes. "I want to see Milan."

I close my eyes and smile to myself. *Did I really fall for her conniving ways again?* My cock needed her so much, I'd believe any story she tells me.

I tuck my cock in and button up my pants. "Nothing's changed. You're not allowed downstairs." *Little slut.* She thinks she can jerk me off and I'll fall at her feet? "Go to your room, or stay here. I don't care. I just don't wanna see you in the basement."

She pouts, but since she's still chewing her pizza, she doesn't look particularly upset. She's endearing more than anything else. Especially when she's trying to alleviate the spicy taste. She always wants pizza, but changes her mind when she remembers how hot Logan has it.

I leave her standing there as I turn and head to the basement door, then descend the stairs into the darkness.

CHAPTER 14

MAISY

What if life gives you more than you expected?

What if it opens a door that was never there before, and now you have a choice? A choice you never wanted to make in the first place because you knew in your heart of hearts what you wanted.

I lived my life for Rosey. She was the reason I woke up in the morning.

Little did I know that she'd turn against me. Which still baffles me. Me and her, we used to be tight. So tight. What happened?

Milan happened.

He knows how to get between people. Divide and conquer. That's his motto, the sign hanging above the desk in his office. That's what he's doing, constantly.

I want to find out everything. Every gory detail that Rosey went through. It will be easier on me to get over her. I have no sister anymore, but I'd be lying if I said I'm not hurt. And, fuck, I don't even want to think of the baby. That baby, Damien. It's hers. And I'm an aunt. If Milan raped her and she had to keep the baby... What is she to do? I wouldn't know. I've read of some women who were raped and kept their babies, because it's not their fault. And some gave them up for adoption. I'd do the latter. In those circumstances, I couldn't look at a baby every single day and be reminded of what happened.

For the first time, without Rosey in the picture, I see my life. Who I am. Should I take everything life offers, or should I keep living on the periphery – in fear, and for others, fulfilling *their* life's purpose? A place that is way too familiar and comfortable.

The door I feared to even glance at, Marina opened. She gave me courage. That was all I needed. She reminded me of the anger and resentment I'd held onto for too long. And she made me promise to kill Milan. And I will. This is the second time I've promised something to someone before they died. *What's wrong with me?*

How will I kill him? I know how to shoot. I taught myself that right after I was raped by Milan. But he was smarter. He knew. The moment he got me in his clutches, he threatened me with Rosey's death, should he ever see me with a gun again. I got so scared that I couldn't hold a gun, even if I knew Milan was miles away. I knew he had snitches everywhere. I couldn't lose Rosey just for holding a gun.

When I shot at Milan at Gianini's, I could still feel that threat looming over me. And I stupidly missed.

But knowing Milan was in the van with his dick cut off, that gave me power. And Kai's gun was in front of me. It was either Natasha or us. I feel guilty, somewhat. I think. It comes to me from time to time. The blood on my hands.

I decided. I'm not going to be a burden anymore. To anyone. I love when my boys take care of me; I've needed it. I got shot at, sold in Riyadh, and they got me back. I got kidnapped, they saved me again. And now, here, I think it's enough. Enough running. I was running because of Rosey. I'd have done anything for her. I'd live my life out of a box just to see her happy. But I was too late.

God knows what her life's been like.

When we were born, I got to see the world first. I always felt guilty, because I was luckier. I suppose that's normal for twins. If I remove the emotions and the guilt, we got physically separated when we were born, but I feel the emotional separation now.

And if that's the case, can I live my own life? Or should I finish what I started? I know it's over now. Milan's downstairs and he'll die, one way or another. But my boys? Don't they deserve to know?

Not fearing for other people, not being threatened or blackmailed, is giving me access to more air. And courage. Maybe boldness, too. What would happen if I went downstairs? Quietly?

I finish the pizza slice – Logan's fucking hot pizza, but I'm slowly getting used to it – and wipe my hands clean.

I go to the door of the basement, and slowly and carefully, soundlessly, I open it.

I remember doing the laundry downstairs and I can guess where they've taken Milan. I take a few steps down and wait for my eyes to adjust to the dark. While I do, I question my courage. Am I brave enough to go against Orion's orders? Kai and Logan follow them, and I also want to, but he never asks for anyone's opinion. Like he knows best. Whatever he decides, goes. Well, I don't agree with his decision. Because Milan can't die before I find out about Rosey. And Milan knowing Logan's mother, well, that's another matter. As long as I'm not asked about it.

It's dark as I take the last steps down, but I can make everything out thanks to the few slivers of light coming out of the room where they keep Milan in. The wooden boards of the door are not properly stuck together.

I pass the metal bars of the gym that shine in the dim light and raise my chin. Two of Orion's men who I haven't spoken to before are sitting on tall barstools, having a rest while guarding Milan's door. They've been here since he arrived, making sure his stay is well remembered. Beating him, torturing him, doing God knows what to him. All well-deserved.

They know me, I know them, I've seen them around the house, mostly in the kitchen. But we haven't spoken to each other. Probably on Orion's orders.

Logan says that the Slavs think Milan's dead, and that they won't attack Orion's place. There's a truce between the families at the moment and Kai and Logan have been coming and going from the house as they wish, which is good for everyone.

I must pretend I'm meant to be here. If it appears that I'm out of place, they'll send me away. At the very least. They'd probably immediately tell Orion. I don't want that.

I move quietly toward the room, and hear what sounds like someone grunting and hitting a punching bag. Which is probably Milan. Reaching it, I peek though the crack in the door.

Milan's body is spread-eagle against the red brick wall, chains holding his wrists and ankles wide apart. He has a metal collar around his neck, secured to the wall and keeping him upright. He's stark naked, with a red blotch where his cock used to be. It's a bloodcurdling image. I grimace as I watch him but deep down, I know he deserves more.

It's Kai's voice I can hear, and his fists I see raining down on Milan one after the other. "Answer him!" he shouts.

Milan's unrecognizable, and barely alive. He's been kept here and beaten ever since we got back, nearly seven days straight without a break. He's about to say something when Kai interrupts him.

"Wait, don't answer yet." Another shower of blows lands on him. It's obvious Kai's enjoying this.

Eventually he steps aside and Logan takes over, like they're a tag team.

"Aren't you going in?" one of the guards asks me.

"It could be too much for you," the other one pipes up.

I'm here, and I'm going through with it. So I knock, swing open the door, and quickly close it behind me. I catch everyone so off-guard that they say nothing for a moment. Logan stops mid-punch.

Orion's the first to confront me. "What did I tell you?" He moves to stand in front of me, blocking my view with his body. The sleeves of his rumpled, bloodied shirt are rolled up to his elbows. The splatter of blood all over his face makes him look scarier than ever.

Logan and Kai are both staring at me in silence. Milan's groans tell me he's still alive, but he sounds like he's hanging by a thread.

I look down. I don't want to challenge him. But I want to be here. "I have a right to be here," I say to the floor. Orion can be mad as hell, but he knows I won't let it affect me. If I even glance in his direction I'll know his anger, and he'll know I know, and of course, that would mean it's either him or me, and the battle would be lost. So patiently, and may I add, smartly, I stand in place and continue, trying to remain emotionless. "He raped me. He sold me. He almost killed me. He raped my sister. He ruined her life. He ruined my life. He kidnapped me. He did so much to me, and you're now trying to save me from seeing him suffer. No. I'm staying."

I know they're looking at each other because Orion takes a step back and turns to where Logan is, then Kai. They haven't seen me like this before. It's because even I don't know what it is that gets me this way. Courage? Hatred? Revenge? Whatever it is, it's working.

"Maybe you're right," Orion agrees. I look up at him in surprise, then at Kai and Logan.

Logan turns to Milan and resumes throwing punch after punch. "Eventually, you'll talk," he says.

At the back of the room is a large metal sink and a hose. Orion walks over to it, turns the water on, and picks up the hose.

"Step back," he warns Logan, and as the water rushes out he sticks the hose into Milan's mouth. He's gurgling and choking while Orion watches in silence. Just before he fully drowns, the hose is removed from his mouth. Orion takes it back to the sink and turns the water off. Milan is left vomiting, coughing up water and blood.

"I won't ask again," Logan says, an eerie calmness in his voice.

Milan mumbles something and nods in my direction, if you can call it nodding. Logan continues pummeling him.

I remain standing awkwardly by the door, looking at Milan. It's a sight I never want to forget. For every life he's taken, for every woman he's raped, he deserves this.

"Can I hit him?" I ask quietly.

Orion answers without hesitation. "No."

I look at him and frown.

He eyeballs me, chuckling. "I think we all know about your boxing skills."

"Just once. I just want to hit him once."

"Okay. Go ahead," Logan says, and steps back.

I approach Milan. He squirms like a worm on a hook. I swing with my foot and kick him right where his dick used to be. I can hear Kai, Orion, and Logan groaning under their breath, but Milan, he squeals, loud, like a pig being killed. Fresh blood starts gushing onto the floor, adding to the bloody puddle of water. I ruined my sneakers, but I don't care. It was worth it.

"You like this, you cocksucking asshole?" I kick him again and he's crying, begging, fuck knows what he's doing. "I'll keep doing this 'til you tell me everything you've done to Rosey! Why didn't she want you dead? I know how much she hated you. *Why?*" I swing again and he opens his palms to signal me to stop, even though his hands are still chained to the wall.

His words come out with difficulty. "I'm... I'm the only one... who knows where her children are..."

"You've taken her *kids?*" I swing and kick him yet again, the puddle of blood deepening below him.

I'm crazed and I half-expect someone to hold me back, but no one does anything. I turn and they all nod at me.

"I told you... Please..."

I spin back to Milan. "Where are they? *WHERE?*"

"With Ma. Ma Molly... in DC," he croaks.

"Ma Molly?" Orion ponders behind me. "I thought she died."

"Naah, she's still alive," Logan states.

"Someone fill me in, please?" Kai's confused; so am I.

"The head of the Irish mafia," Orion explains. "She became the first-ever billionaire criminal, making eighty million a month from the proceeds of smuggling cocaine from Colombia to the US. She's based in Washington DC. But she should be old now. I remember my father mentioning her, he was mad at her because she invented modified women's underwear for her smugglers to wear. Molly took over the Blanco Clan after her husband died and his brothers were arrested. She's also one of the founders of the strategic alliance between the families. Where I got the idea of us working together. Except this fucker wanted it all. Last I heard of her, she introduced the sex trade into the gang's criminal profile. And that was a while back."

I've heard enough. "How many children does Rosey have?" I yell at Milan, landing another kick.

"Four... Damien's the youngest!" he squeals.

"And the father?"

Milan has barely enough strength to talk, but Logan motivates him with a few more blows. He finally raises his eyes to me.

"She.... She was bred by all of us."

This is the moment I have to stop listening. I shriek in frustration and double over with the excruciating pain that I feel for my sister. Kai, Logan, and Orion all come to me, to support me, to calm me down.

But the moment I spy Orion's gun in its holster, the anger gets the better of me. I reach out and take it. He could stop me, I know, but he doesn't. Probably afraid we might struggle and the gun will go off.

I point it at Milan. "You don't deserve to live, you piece of shit." I cock the gun but don't shoot. I want my boys to know I'm not a loose cannon. I turn to them, not sure what to do because with this gun, I'm all-powerful. I remember what it was like holding a gun for the first time.

Logan's watching me carefully. "Shoot, but don't kill him."

Orion nods.

As I turn back to Milan, it all feels like it's in slow motion. I look at him down the barrel of my gun, the one thing I've wanted to do since the day life changed for me.

I aim at his head, then down at his knees.

"This is for you, Marina," I whisper.

I shoot one silenced round at his right knee. Then another at his left. Milan squeals again like the pig that he is. He buckles as his legs are no longer supporting him and, held up only by the collar around his neck, he starts to choke.

I let the gun dangle loosely from my index finger before passing it to Orion. "Let's go," I say, and walk over to the door. They don't say a word. Kai opens it for me and I leave, the three of them following.

The two guards outside jump the moment they see us coming out. "Pour some salt on his wounds. And make sure he doesn't choke to death," Orion orders them.

I'm first in line as we walk out, but the silence behind me is loud and clear. They're wondering, just like I've been doing lately, who I am.

I know there'll be tons of questions, but right now, I'm taking my power back. The man who raped me is almost dead. I will kill him, that's for sure. One promise, fulfilled.

I reach the top of the staircase and head through the hallway, leading them into the kitchen. The sexual tension that's strung taut like a wire is tightening with each step we take. It seems to vibrate as I feel them watching me walk.

One of my sneakers is totally ruined, and I have blood splatter all over my jeans and some on my top. I know for sure my face is bloodied too. I have so much adrenaline in me I could run a marathon. But instead, I want them. I haven't wanted them this much, ever. It's always been about their needs, their love, but right now,

I'm the one calling the shots. And I say, fuck me. Right now.

In the kitchen, I turn and see the three of them lined up next to each other, towering over me, oozing power that invades me on so many levels. They all have the same gleam in their eyes, just as I know I do. We feel it; like animals, we sense when we're about to mate. Orion's anguish comes and goes, he's fighting it desperately, but when I glance at his cock, I can tell he's failing miserably.

"Maisy, we need to talk," he says, his nostrils flared.

I take off my top, my nasty sneakers, and as for my jeans, I unbutton the top button and let them drop to my ankles. I kick them away. I wear no bra or panties. Stark naked, I reach out to stroke their crotches, one by one. I get to Orion last.

"Okay." I nod and unbutton Orion's pants. His cock's steel-hard, and springs out of his pants by itself. His eyes close as he sucks in a breath. I move to Logan's pants and do the same, and finally, Kai's.

"Fuck. Maisy, baby girl…" Kai looks lost in the idea of what's to come and pumps his cock energetically. They all have blood splatter everywhere. Kai's knuckles from the day's previous activities are red and raw. I choose to ignore it.

Logan pushes his hips forward and smirks mischievously; he's waiting, waiting for my lips to wrap around him. In one hand I stroke Kai's cock and in the other, Orion's, who I can see is still fighting his inner demons. I pump them both and feel their veins pop up. The muscles clench deep in my belly as Logan locks eyes with me and I slowly get down on my knees.

I crane my neck to look up at the three of them staring down at me. I open my mouth, and with my tongue fully out, I lick the precum from Logan's cock.

He hums. "That's it, sweetheart."

Just like that, I make his cock disappear into my mouth.

Orion appears to give in, and change sides. He's one of us now, and his demons won. He tangles his fingers in my hair and pulls me off Logan.

"Nuh-uh, darling. You're starting here." He pushes his cock deep into my mouth. "Mmm, yes!" he groans, totally oblivious to the fact that my air intake is obstructed as he pushes my head down. "They had you for a week. And I know how hungry you are, slut. Now, take me like a big girl who can shoot."

He releases me long enough for me to take a big gulp of air just before he begins to fuck my mouth, the piercing on his glans hitting my throat. Each time it does, he growls. It hurts; I can manage it, but not for long. Eventually, the lack of air and burning throat make me try to push myself off his thighs. I gag, and choke, drool running down my chin, but he's got my head in both hands.

"Juuust a little bit longer. Yes, yes, yes, yes..." He fucks my throat as I choke, dribbling, desperate for air, literally suffocating while he slaps my face, not allowing me to pass out.

Finally, I'm let go and allowed to fall to the floor, gasping out loud. Orion looks down at me and strokes his cock with his bloodied hand. "You're a big girl now, you should be able to take us longer than that."

"Sweetheart, don't waste time." Logan's impatient. I look up to see both Kai and Logan have taken their clothes off, fast.

Logan does the same, fucking my mouth as I jerk Kai and Orion. The heavenly sound of their moans reaches me and I know I'm doing a good job, but just as I start to drown in them and get comfortable, I'm gasping for air again. In panic, I slap Logan's thighs. I feel my eyes bulge, and I'm drooling and coughing yet again.

But I'm crazed with need, and Logan is not as cruel as Orion. He takes me up to where I can manage before it becomes painful, and the pulse between my legs and the surge of my juices signal my body's approval.

He releases me and guides my lips directly onto Kai's cock. I expect Kai to do more of the same, but he just looks down at me and grins. "Yes! Come on, baby girl, you do the work, go on." I grab him with both hands, wrapping my palms around his sturdy cock, and give him a few long, wet licks, from his balls up to the head. He groans, tilting his head back. I take him entirely in my mouth, throat-deep, and as I pull out, I swirl my tongue around the tip. Again, I bob my head, sucking him a few more times before I feel someone's fingers tangling in my hair. I open my eyes to see Orion's taken off his clothes, and, gripping me tightly, he starts controlling my head on Kai's cock. He loves to use me, I know.

Logan's pumping his cock as he reaches over, slapping my breasts. His knuckles are still bloody and red, but I don't care. I'm going to celebrate Milan's death with his blood on me. That's a promise I'm making to myself.

Orion's pushing my head harder and faster as he makes me suck Kai's cock. "You're a little whore, aren't you, Maisy?" he whispers in my ear. Kai grunts in pleasure each time I'm thrust against his groin.

His groans are a warning of what's coming, and we can all hear it. Orion pulls me back, his fingers still tangled in my hair, which he uses to hoist me to my feet.

"Let's see what we're gonna do with this little slut." He pinches my breast, then slaps me hard over one nipple, then the other. My legs buckle, the sharp, shooting pain almost sending me back to my knees.

"Logan, clear the table," Orion orders, and Logan sweeps the table clean in one move of his arm, sending everything to the floor. I'm put on the table, made to lie on my back with my head hanging over the edge.

"Perfect!" Logan exclaims. I watch him from upside down as he positions himself. "Show me your tongue." I do, and without preamble, he grabs hold of my neck and his cock re-enters my mouth. He leans over me and starts pumping. Each time my throat is filled, he groans in pleasure.

Orion opens my legs wide, bending my knees and pushing them up toward my chest, exposing my cunt. He slaps me there.

Sharp pain zings through my body, making me jolt, and I stifle a moan. Logan's oblivious to anything else happening to me, totally committed to ruining my throat.

Orion slides two fingers inside me, then hooks them upward and takes them out, sticky strands of my juice stretched between my cunt and his fingers.

Kai's losing it as he jerks himself. "Fuck, Orion, stop playing! I need her, *now!*" I love him like this, all impatient.

"Agreed," Orion growls. I'm grabbed by my hips and they're lifted up. Orion lies on the table under me, at a right angle, and places his cock between my buttocks.

With my new position, my head drops lower off the edge of the table, allowing Logan to enter a few centimeters deeper. Which is beginning to cut my air intake, again.

Orion slaps my pussy with his cock a few times from below, coating himself with my arousal as he holds my ass cheeks.

"This might hurt, but I don't care." He tries to enter me and I try to protest by thrashing about, but he's not going slow. After a few tries he manages to force himself in, and I cry out. I know it will be godly in a moment, but right now, I feel a burn that hurts. I try to push Logan off, to get some control of my body, but he doesn't ease off, and Orion holds my hips firmly in place as he begins to pound my ass. Kai just pushes my knees up to my chin, climbs onto the table, and enters me so hard and so deep that my whole being transports to another dimension. A place where I have no body, only nerve endings, and they're all working for me, feeding me pleasure.

This, right here, is heaven, I think, as they start their game of undulating, driving in and out.

"Fuck, Maisy, how's it possible that your tight cunt is so... *Fuck!*" Kai growls and pistons harder as Orion pinches my swollen clit and slams his cock into my ass. Without available air, I'm asphyxiated already, my body jerking uncontrollably. I shoot to the moon, flying in frenzy as I orgasm between their bodies.

Logans pulls out and I gasp for air, gaining some semblance of consciousness. One long strand of drool connects me to him. Seeing where I am, I don't want to land from the heights I just reached.

"My turn." He slaps my cheek and goes around the table to where Kai is. "Let me get a hit of that drug."

Kai gets off the table and makes space for Logan, who leans down between my legs and gives me a wet lick across my clit before climbing onto the table and entering me.

They start again, Orion with the everlasting thrumming of my every nerve as he pounds my ass and takes me flying with each thrust, and Logan, chasing his own stars.

"You look so pretty like this, baby girl." Kai's looking down at me, but all I see above me is his balls. "Say aaaah." I open my mouth wide, stretching out my tongue, and take his balls. I suck them, lick them, pumping his cock as I do, while my body is used by Orion and Logan.

Kai's velvety skin tenses. His veins stand up; he's close. I play with his balls in my mouth, swirling my tongue over them, and suck them until they pop out of my mouth, fighting to keep my focus as the pounding I'm taking is making me lose all cognition.

"Fuck, I'm gonna cum," I hear Kai exclaiming, and I know he's had enough of playtime. He pushes his cock into my mouth, throat-deep, and starts to face-fuck me. I'm choking again, tapping his thighs for a reprieve as I search for air, but he's not pulling back.

Orion and Logan somehow take harder, more vicious turns with me. I'm tossed about, pushed, flung from side to side as each take a different part of me. And they use it, take it, absorb it into them as I begin to fly, asphyxiated again with no air to breathe.

Just when I think I'll black out, Kai stills inside me, his hot cum spurting deep in my throat, his balls squeezing out every last drop. He finally pulls out, granting me air. I inhale loudly, breathing raggedly as I feel my whole body dislodged.

My position is not the best as my ass is speared on Orion's cock. He's lying perpendicular to me while Logan, above me on the table, holds my knees to my chest and rams into me. All the while my upper body is pressed to the table, my head still hanging over the edge.

"I want to cum without thinking of my knee killing me," Logan announces, and pulls out of me. I hear Kai chuckling, and I do, too. Not Orion, though; he's like a soldier. He pulls out, lifts me up, and sets me softly back on the table, then he gets off too.

"Lie on the table, Logan. Maisy, on top of him," Orion orders. Logan climbs onto the table and lies on his back, and I straddle him. His hard cock is not at all concerned if his knee is hurt or not. He slides inside me fast, as if we never stopped fucking, and he quickly regains his tempo, pounding into me.

Orion climbs up behind me; it's lucky this table's large and sturdy. Logan takes one of my nipples in his mouth; he sucks it and plays with it, and bites me softly. He then takes my other nipple and does the same as I moan and arch my back, pushing my breast into him, needing more. His groans tell me he's loving this new position much better.

Orion presses on my lower back and slides inside me as easily as Logan did.

"Ohhh, *fuck!*" I gasp. They start moving, rising and falling, all of us chasing our own summit. In my frenzy, their groans and grunts take me that much higher but when Orion pinches my clit, I'm there. I cum violently, thrashing between them and crying out with the loudest howl I've ever made. I know it's loud because they slow down for a split second, but continue pounding me, allowing me to ride the waves of my ecstasy.

"You fucking queen!" Logan moans, his spunk shooting inside me. Orion's fingers are still digging into my ass cheeks as he rams his cock into my body. The waves come over me, leaving me soaking wet, and I whimper and then moan, again, loud. Really loud.

"Let me see you cumming, Maisy," Orion commands.

I look back at him and our eyes meet. Those eyes are my true home, and at the same time, they take me flying to all the planets in the universe. He presses his forehead against mine, all sweaty, and curls his fingers around my throat for leverage as he pulls me to him. The way he growls as he rams into me, I know he's close. His cock is a solid rod and with one more thrust, he stills inside me, my ass tilted up as his cum spurts, rope after rope.

I have no voice. We're entangled, sweaty, sated, and breathless.

"Sweetheart, you're enjoying yourself, right?" Logan asks. He always makes sure.

I grin, still panting. "Was I too loud?"

Orion chuckles. "That took me by surprise, too."

All of a sudden, we hear heavy footsteps. Someone's at the kitchen door. Kai runs over and holds it slightly ajar, placing his foot strategically so it can't open fully. Naked, he peeks through the gap.

Someone speaks. "Is something wrong? We heard screams."

Kai ignores the question. "You shouldn't move from downstairs. No matter what," he says, reminding the guy exactly where he should be right now. It's one of the men in charge of Milan's torment.

"Oh, okay. Is the boss there?" He sounds suspicions of Kai. Of course, they're enemies – a Delgado and a Carte. Eventually, they'll have to learn not to question each other.

"You-shouldn't-move-from-down-stairs. No-matter-what," Orion calls out, repeating Kai's reprimand word for word.

"Sorry, boss," the guy responds, and I hear his footsteps move away and down into the basement.

Kai closes the door and bursts into laughter. "Really? You had to scream that much?"

Sandwiched between Logan and Orion, I giggle, and the others crease up laughing.

KAI

She's becoming a woman. I don't know how or why I know that, but it feels as if she's growing up in front of our eyes. Do I want that? Yes. Yes, I do.

And if we succeed in joining up as a syndicate, then New York will be ours, and Maisy will be in our bed. *Fuck. Who wouldn't want that?*

I lift my head and search for her. She's lying on top of Orion, whose arms are wrapped tightly around her. Everyone's asleep. Logan's next to them and I'm next to Logan.

Maisy's bed is bigger now. After seeing my bed in Long Island, Orion upgraded. He made sure everyone could fit in Maisy's bed. Which we finally tried out last night.

There was something new and crazy inside her last night. It turned me on so fucking much, seeing her torturing Milan, and using the gun so skillfully.

Like a phoenix rising from the ashes, she came through to the other side as new, but meaner. Louder. Braver.

She told me what happened to Marina. It was how Milan found us. God rest her soul. Marina lost everything for me, for the Delgados. That woman deserved so much more than what she got. *Fucking Milan. Why didn't we see through him before? Why didn't our fathers?*

Orion's right. We've been working separately for too long, like our fathers, and failed to see his plan. But his obsession with Maisy is what we're all baffled about. Why? He could've killed her so many times. A mystery we've all fallen in love with, and we still can't get enough of.

I lift my head. "Hey, are we up?"

Logan grumbles something, and Maisy moans sweetly. Orion just tightens the hold he has on her. *I know, buddy. I've held her like that for the past week. It's your turn now.* He's been dying on the inside but was too stubborn to admit it. She got to him, finally.

She was mad about what happened in Long Island, but also because of the woman he had to sleep with to get the key to Milan's place. Logan and I had to really get the point across that it was all business. We would've done the same. She's not happy when we talk about it, though. We all saw her jealous streak in Long Island when she forbade Logan from using 'sweetheart' on other women. That's still funny. Logan can't help himself, so let's see when he makes his first mistake in front of her.

Maisy moves and rolls off Orion's chest. He turns to her, scoops her up in a spoon hold, and pulls her back to him.

"I'll get the coffee." I sit up, my cock hard as always in the morning, jutting up.

"I need extra large," Logan mutters.

"I'll give you extra large right now if you want," I snicker as I put my boxers on.

"Don't remind me, my extra large is painful in the morning," he replies.

Orion pulls Maisy even closer in the spoon he has her in. I hear him groaning in her ear.

I know if I go for coffee I'll miss the fun, but fuck me, Orion needs her. And Logan, well, after what he's been through, he can have her before me any time he wants.

Maisy rolls over Orion and ends up snug between the two of them. I wonder if I should actually leave after all. I rub my cock a few times. This will only get spicy from here. She rolls onto her back, her head pillowed on Logan's bicep. Everyone's naked, but Maisy's body is just exquisite to look at. Her white, soft skin, her ample breasts, pink nipples, her trimmed pussy. I'd have her for lunch, breakfast, and dinner, every day of the week.

Logan's hand slides across her thigh and moves up until it reaches between her legs. She gives a little moan and turns her head toward him. Orion, clearly awake now, props himself up on an elbow and leans over her until he's only an inch from her face. He grips her chin and turns her face to him instead. Her sleepy eyelids flutter open.

"Hey, gorgeous," he rasps, and kisses her. His hand moves from her chin to her throat, wrapping around it, and for a moment he devours her mouth. His hand then wanders slowly down over her breasts while his face turns to the side, burrowing into her hair. He wraps an arm around her and slots her into the curve of his body.

She moans, seemingly frustrated now that Logan's hand is no longer between her legs.

Her head moves from Logan's to Orion's bicep. I know this move. Orion bends his arm and fists her hair, using her body as leverage as he pushes his hips against her ass. *Fuck. I want that.* He bites her shoulders, her throat, her jaw while rocking his body against hers.

Fuck this. I'm going to get the coffee. Otherwise I'd have to join them. And it's not fair. Maisy can take it, but I don't want Orion or Logan pulling back on my behalf.

LOGAN

She's wet all the time, constantly, for us. Her pussy's so hot and sweet, my hands could live there forever. As Orion pulls her out of my reach, I open my eyes and meet hers.

"Logan," she whispers, her voice thick with desire.

She's held by Orion, and I roll my body closer. Orion's hand moves down between her legs, cupping her from the front.

"Orion," she breathes.

"Mmm, there's my slut this morning," he whispers in her ear, grinding his cock into her ass from behind.

She grins as we stare at each other. I scoot even closer and press my lips to hers, devouring her, because my need is painful right now. I cup her breast, massaging and pinching her nipple, pebbled from desire. Orion lifts her knee, opening her thighs, and pushes her forward onto my cock. A growl leaves my throat as I'm met with the arousal between her legs, and I slide inside her perfectly.

Orion pinches her nipples as he continues to grind against her ass and I fuck her with the same rhythm. I'm not gonna last long. My thrusts pick up speed. She fits me perfectly, like a tight glove that needs stretching, and I think I'll explode in less than a minute. Orion's fingers slide down her belly and go straight for her swollen clit. Her rhythm speeds up, taking me with her as she begins to chase her high. Even though Orion and I have her pinned between us, she's bucking and riding my cock brutally, like an animal, and her whimpers, *oh sweet Jesus mama*, her whimpers are what takes me over the edge. I ram into her five, six more times and growl as I spill my seed inside her. Her whole body rocks and shudders in response.

I know it's Orion's turn and I pull out of her, kissing her as he pulls her hips to him and slides inside. He starts fucking her from behind, grunting as he goes.

"You're ready to be filled with more cum, slut?"

"Yes," she responds as I suck on her neck.

He moves faster. "Wasn't one enough?"

"One is never enough." She turns her head to Orion. "I need more." He continues to thrust as she talks. "In my cunt, every hour of every day," she moans. "Yours."

Orion mounts her as I pull back and give them space to finish like I have. He begins to pound into her body, and her moans turn staccato against the mattress.

Maisy loves Orion's violent side and he takes her with him. The moans become grunts and growls from both, their passion rocking the whole bed on its base. *Fucking awesome!*

Soon after, having reached orgasm, they still. They go from being loud, bucking broncos to meek dolphins in the sea. *Fucking Maisy. She does that to us.*

"Sweetheart, I hope you never get enough of us," I murmur.

"Fuck off, Logan! Don't give her ideas!" Orion lifts his head and pulls out of her, looking annoyed. He sits up, propping a pillow behind him and pulling Maisy back into his arms. "Come here, darling. Don't listen to Logan. You'll always have enough of us. Because this is it. You're stuck with us." He pulls her in for a kiss.

Maisy laughs sweetly against his mouth. "You're silly. Both of you."

"Of course, unless we find out you're double-crossing us, then... *Fuck.* I don't wanna think about it."

Orion got too serious too quick. Killing the moment.

Maisy wrinkles her nose. "How could I be double-crossing you?"

"We know you're smart, Maisy. So don't start."

"We're gonna have to kill her," I tease, hoping to lighten the mood Orion just created.

"You would?" she breathes, half-smiling, half-curious.

"I doubt it." I kiss her. "Don't worry, sweetheart. Orion's just being... Orion."

"Coffee, anyone?" Kai enters with a tray holding a coffeepot and four cups.

"Please! We need three coffees in here, pronto!" I shout.

Maisy regards Orion, probably wondering if he's serious about what he said, and he yields, kissing her on the lips. She finds a place in the crook of his arm and stays there while Kai hands her a coffee.

Once all of us have a cup in our hands, Kai sits on the chair opposite the bed and we drink in silence. There's so much happening that each of us seems lost in our own thoughts.

Maisy chooses to speak first because, well, she's Maisy.

"I want to go to see Rosey today," she says in a rush.

All of us look at each other for a beat and instantly know the answer.

"Absolutely not!" Orion roars.

"Why would you wanna see her?" Kai asks.

"You need to ask?" she replies hotly. "How about because that animal downstairs *bred* my sister, made her have four children, and took them away from her?"

"You told her she was dead to you. What d'you think she'll do when she sees you?" I ask her.

Maisy shrugs. She hasn't thought that far ahead.

I answer for her. "She'll try to kill you."

"Not if I tell her I know where her kids are."

Orion's getting angrier by the second. "We don't do that! We use that as leverage!"

"It doesn't work like that, Maisy," Kai tells her. "It's never tit for tat. We took Milan from them. Who, may I add, will be dead soon."

"Not yet, he's not," she replies pointedly.

"About that." Orion takes over. "Explain how your shooting skills got so much better."

"I knew you'd ask me that."

"It would be strange if we didn't."

"Well, after Milan... after he raped us, my sister was held there, while I was allowed to go back home from time to time," she begins. "One of my neighbors had a shooting range in his yard. I asked him, and he helped me learn. I practiced whenever I could. Milan found out somehow, and threatened to kill Rosey if he ever saw me so much as holding a gun. I didn't want to risk it, as I've seen Milan kill people over trivial shit like that. I never held a gun again until that day at Gianini's. But then I had to dodge bullets as well as shoot. And I was still afraid of Milan. But this time, I knew he was with you in the van. I also needed to see if I could do it."

Orion nods. "That's the change I see in you. You're different now that we got Milan."

"Milan threatened my very existence, as well as those close to me. With him being gone, I... I can breathe again."

Kai nods. "I noticed that too, Maisy."

"Can I have a gun, please?" she asks Orion innocently. Like a kid asking for chocolate.

Kai laughs. I do too. We both tilt our heads at Orion, waiting on his response. He notices us staring at him and frowns, clearing his throat. Trying to remain authoritative.

"Not now, Maisy. Now, about Rosey. I think it's a bad idea, and we don't want you to go. However, since you never listen to what we say, I'm gonna ask: what are your intentions, and how do you plan to do this? Because you should always have a foolproof plan before you set out doing something like this by yourself, or with other people."

"I *do* have a plan."

"We're listening."

"I'm gonna take a cab."

"If you show up alone, they'll kill you."

"Not if I tell her why I'm there."

"You tell her, they'll kill you."

"I don't think so. They kept me in that cell for so long and nobody tried to hurt me. Maybe Rosey told them not to. Which means she won't hurt me. She won't. I know it."

Orion huffs. "Okay, let's say you get inside. What d'you expect to happen?"

"I'll tell her Milan's dead, and that I know where her kids are."

"And then? You play happy families? We don't know who's taken over from Milan yet. They'll be the one deciding what you're allowed to tell her."

"Or, once she finds out, she'll kill you," I point out.

"She won't, for God's sake. You've got to trust me. My gut feeling tells me she won't kill me."

"Why not?" Kai asks.

"Because I'm her sister. And I'll help her find her children." Maisy smiles. "I'm an aunt."

"Stop it," Orion snaps. "No. Don't go with the plan of being an aunt to her kids. You'll lose."

"I won't."

"Maisy, we live this life. We know. Maybe you know Rosey, but we know the mobsters surrounding her. I mean, Milan was using her to breed. We do that to those who are only used for making babies. Even if you tell her who has her kids, she won't be able to do anything about it."

"Are you saying my sister doesn't have a say over there?"

"I don't know. I just don't."

Maisy looks impatient. "Look, Orion, I'm going. Who knows, maybe she'll appreciate me telling her, and we'll make up."

"That's not how it'll go."

"I know I told her she was dead to me, but I have a chance to save her children. And if she doesn't appreciate that, well, I don't know, I'll leave."

"No, you won't," Orion barks. "She won't let you."

"Why wouldn't she?"

"Fuck knows, Maisy! Fuck knows! You're not going there!"

"I hate to say this, but you know I'm going," she insists. "And trust me, this doesn't come easy for me. I usually wouldn't tell you. I'd just do what I think is right."

"How about this, how about we come with you?" I interject. The conversation was going round in circles. "But you can't tell her that Milan's alive, unless you need to use that in your favor. We spread the news of his death just so we could draw out the snitches. And so far, we've seen nothing."

"Okay," she concedes. "But you're gonna wait for me outside."

"Sure. Kai, Orion, do we agree? We wait for her outside?"

"I'm not trusting the Slavs," Orion rages, his loathing for them palpable. "I *never* trusted the Slavs. They'll try and fuck you up when you least expect it. I'd rather kill them all. They don't deserve to live."

"Fucking Slavs, you're right," Kai agrees. "Nothing's ever straightforward with them. I don't remember a single interaction when they haven't tried to screw us over. They're the scum of the earth." He spits into his coffee cup.

"Yeah. You ask me, I'd skin them alive, one by one. Fucking filthy cocksuckers, each and every one," I say.

"I get it, you hate them," Maisy says, "but my sister's not a Slav. She's just an innocent bystander. And if I can, I'll get her to come back here, with me."

"Not this again. Didn't you hear me?!" Orion yells in frustration. "They won't let go of someone who made four babies for them just like that! Maisy, *wake up!*"

I try to calm him. "Okay, Orion. Fine. Let's just go there and see for ourselves."

"For fuck's sake!" He gets up and storms out, stark naked.

"I'm going to take a shower." Maisy climbs off the bed too. "Let's all get ready. I want to leave by noon, please."

CHAPTER 15

KAI

Sometimes, I want to punch Orion and tell him to chill the fuck out. He's an expert at killing the mood. But I know better than that. He is where he is because of his sixth sense. I mean, fuck, even I know it's not good for Maisy to see Rosey, but she's so stubborn. Just like him. At least now she's telling us what she wants to do. Not like before, doing it by herself.

I quickly grab a shower and get dressed. I'm not like the other two; I need a pair of jeans and a black shirt, and I brought plenty over when we came back with Maisy. This is where I set up my office, and where my people come to see me now. Only when needed, of course. I sometimes go back to my club, but the plan is to slowly get our families used to one another.

Orion's men downstairs are still wary of me, but maybe that's because they've seen me in the boxing ring and know I'm a wild card.

I enter the kitchen and find one of them dropping off a small package. The same guy who saw me naked yesterday.

"Um, for Orion," he tells me, and turns hastily to leave.

"Hey, I think we can be on first-name terms, now you've seen me naked," I laugh. "I'm Kai."

He stops, and grins. "Martin."

"Good to meet ya, Martin."

"Likewise. Um, that's for Orion," he reiterates, pointing at the package.

"Sure, I'll let him know."

After he leaves, I pour myself another cup of coffee and sit at the table. The package in front of me has Orion's name on the front and on the side are the sender's details. It's the hospital Marina worked at. And there it is, her name.

"What?" I mutter to myself.

Orion and Logan enter at the same time and head for the coffeepot. Both of them are dressed like they're ready for a board meeting, not a potential fight. Although come to think of it, they do fight with their suits on, so whatever.

"Orion. You have a package." I catch his eye. "From Marina."

We all exchange glances. Marina was killed in Milan's basement. About two weeks ago.

"Fuck. She managed to... Right. Okay. Not right now. I need to focus."

"What is it?" If this is the last thing she did before she died, I want to know.

"You can open it when we're back. If we come back alive," Orion says.

Maisy walks in dressed in the most perfect black dress I've ever seen: three-quarter sleeves, knee-length, with pockets marked in white thread and a full skirt that flares over her hips so sexily, I just want to lift it and fuck her. "Of course we'll come back alive," she says. "Why wouldn't we?"

Orion's still irritated. "Maisy! What planet d'you live on?"

"For fuck's sake, sweetheart." Logan takes the soft approach with some light admonishment. "We told you. You're entering the wolf's lair today. You can't have that nonchalant attitude."

"Well, how do you want me to be?" She puts on her black ankle boots, and looks up.

"When with the Slavs, just think of it as a setup, and you'll always have a way out." He kisses her. "Okay?"

"Don't worry, baby girl." I kiss her neck from behind as I help her into her coat. The three of us already have ours on. "We got your back." My cock's bursting in my pants. I didn't have a chance to get off this morning. I can't fucking wait to have her on my own.

Orion groans. "Let's go. The sooner we get there, the sooner we'll be back."

We all walk out and head straight to the car waiting for us in the driveway. Orion must've organized this. The four of us climb into the back. Maisy sits between Logan and Orion and I take the seat facing them, behind the driver.

Orion presses the intercom button next to his seat. "Emilio, just get us there as soon as possible."

Emilio nods in the rear-view mirror.

"What's your plan, Maisy?" I ask. I want to be sure she has a plan of action. "With the Slavs, you must have a plan B."

"I don't have one," she says.

"Do you think we're gonna need backup?" Logan asks Orion. "If things go south, I want us to be prepared. They don't have that many men in the house, but we need to be ready."

"How soon do you think you can get your men there?"

"Ten minutes, tops," Logan replies.

Orion nods, then looks at Maisy. "A plan. Now."

Maisy shrugs. "I'll walk up. Tell her I have information on her children's whereabouts. And then I expect her to invite me in."

"And then?"

"Then I'll get inside, tell her where her kids are, and that'll be that."

"Okay. What do you do if she tries to kill you?" he asks her.

"Um–"

"Bang. You're dead."

She frowns. "What *do* I do?"

"If there's a possibility of you getting killed, tell her Milan's alive," I say. "That's your only get-out-of-jail card. Do not forget to use it if needed."

She nods.

"Make sure you yell. You want plenty of people to hear you," Logan continues.

"And if she says she wants to see him?"

"Then we'll fucking bring him," I say.

"Then that's my plan."

CHAPTER 16

MAISY

After an hour or so of driving, I see we're approaching the house. That beige, two-story house atop a hill. Ugly. Dreadful. Reminds me I don't want to be here, but I'm here for Rosey. Again trying to save her.

It's a residential street and there's not much happening, so we're immediately seen as we park on the opposite side of the road, at a distance from the house.

I never would've come near this place again, knowing it's the Slav headquarters, had it not been for Rosey. I've done so much for her that I know this is the final call. Then, it will be down to her.

"They don't know we're coming, right?" I ask the others. Our windows are tinted and we watch the entrance, where three men are standing around and smoking. They all have guns tucked in their waistbands, clearly visible. They nod to each other and look over at our car.

"Now they do." Kai narrows his eyes, watching them closely.

"Fucking Bobby," Logan curses. "That's him, at the door. The snitch who blasted my knee. Well, that's perfect. He's dying today."

"No, he's not. Logan, we came here for something else." I'm quick to remind him this will not be a shootout.

"Maisy, I don't like this whole setup," Kai warns.

"You can always change your mind, darling." Orion is last to speak. His voice is filled with unease.

I shake my head. "All this time, everything I did in my life was for her. This is the last time. Wish me luck."

"Break a leg," I hear Kai murmuring as I exit the vehicle.

The moment I'm on the street, each of the three men at the entrance place a hand on their gun. One of them is on his cell, calling someone.

I take a good look at the house, hoping Rosey will be watching me from one of the windows, and take a step to cross the street.

"Maisy, look out!" Orion yells as a bus whooshes past me, missing me by an inch. *Fuck.* I glance nervously back at my boys. *"That was close,"* I mouth.

Orion shakes his head, clearly annoyed. Kai smirks, while Logan, well, I can't see Logan's face. Probably mad, too.

This time, I look both ways before I cross the street. By the time I get to the other side, there are quite a few people staring at me from the house. The men at the door have their guns aimed at me, and the front door opens slowly. Rosey appears in the doorway, standing in wait for me.

There's no going back now. She won't harm me. She can't. We're sisters. Twins.

I focus on Rosey. She's looking much better than the last time I saw her. Her hair's shoulder-length, shorter than mine. The brown maxi dress she's wearing has a red knitted scarf over it, covering her shoulders. She looks like a grown woman.

Behind her, a man with bushy hair and eyebrows and scars on his face stands on lookout. Rosey and I eyeball each other as I walk inside.

She nods at Orion's car. "I hope you told them to leave."

"I didn't."

She rolls her eyes, and gives an order to someone behind me. "Close the door."

The door closes, and this is it. I'm here, with my sister. Alone, like I wanted. Well, no Milan. But every other Slav on this earth.

"Come." She takes the lead walking ahead of me, and I follow. Four men follow me in turn.

She leads me through the house, down a corridor, and finally takes me to an office. *Milan's.* It's jampacked with boxes. Either she's been looking through them, or they've been here like this for a long time. She goes around the large desk and sits down, then points to the space in front of it. "Make yourself comfortable. Sit."

I look around the cramped space for a chair, and upon spotting one, move a few boxes aside and pull it out. I unbutton my coat before I finally manage to sit down, yet still my legs are squashed among the boxes. I glance at one, and instantly I recognize it. My mind never let me forget it. I attempt to cross my legs and as I do, I manage to tip the lid off. Lucky for me, no one bats an eyelid and Rosey just nods at me.

"What made you change your mind about coming over?" she asks.

"I found out stuff about you that... that I couldn't digest."

"Like?"

"Um, what they've done to you."

She laughs mockingly. "Haha! What *have* they done to me?"

"They raped you, Rosey." I have to get through to her, so she can see that it's wrong. But the way she acts, it's as if she has Stockholm Syndrome.

"Um, no. Milan raped me, *us*, actually, when we were twelve. No one else raped me."

"I know you have four children."

"He told you that? Ha! Of course he did!" She laughs, and the men behind me join in. "What a weak, spineless little asshole he turned out to be!"

"Well, do you?"

"I do."

"I know where they are."

She arches an eyebrow. "Is that a threat?"

"What? No!" I protest. "Milan said he took your children from you. I'm here to tell you I know where they are. I want to help you, Rosey. I'm your sister."

She lifts her chin. "Do you know that I'm head of the Slavs now?"

I shake my head. "That can't be. You're lying."

"And *you* want to help *me?*" she laughs.

"Um, don't you want to know where your children are?"

She leaps to her feet and bangs her fist on the desk, making me jump. "I fucking *know* where my children are. The moment we heard Milan was dead, they were brought back to me." She sits back down. "The Irish mafia in DC know our power."

"Rosey… what happened to you?" My voice is barely audible. She seems like miles away from the sister I once had.

"Nothing. I was like this all my life. And now that Milan's gone, I've never been more certain of who I am. This is where I belong, Maisy. This is my home. These people you see? They're *my* people."

"That's not true. And you know it."

She looks at me, and for a split second, I see *my* Rosey, her eyes shrouded in that sadness I left her with. "Even if we didn't want it," she says quietly, "we were always going to end up here, you and I."

"No, we weren't. We make our own destiny. Remember what Mom used to say?"

"Pfft. *Mom*." She looks through the window, into the distance. "We belonged to Milan even before we were born."

While her back's turned, I glance down to where the open box is. It's full of random papers but just as I remember, I see that newspaper clipping at the top, the one with 'Rebecca Trellis' in the headline. That's all I remember seeing back then, her name. Now, I can see the full headline.

Four generations of bystanders killed in a shootout on Good Friday! Rebecca Trellis, 12, the only survivor of a family of over 40 members, is in a critical condition.

The box is literally next to my leg. I lean down and scratch my shin, and with the other hand I take the clipping, scrunch it up, and put it in my pocket, just as

Rosey looks round. I freeze, my heart nearly exploding from the tension.

"Stay here, Maisy, with me." Her voice is full of love, excitement, wonder. It seems she didn't see me, and nobody behind me did either. "You're supposed to be by my side, not over there with our enemies."

"Tell me about your children. Will I get to see them one day?" Until my thumping heart calms down I can't concentrate, and I definitely don't want to talk about anything else but her.

Rosey stands up, comes around the desk, and sits on the edge of it. "Out!" she snaps at the men behind me, and they obey. I hear the door closing as I watch her. She smiles, that beautiful, carefree smile she has. "They're the best thing that ever happened to me. Sure, you'll meet them. They'll be happy to find out they have an aunt."

"You mean you haven't told them?"

"Oh, Maisy, I barely see them. Once I'd given birth, within the first twelve weeks they'd be taken away from me. That, and only that, broke me. Nothing else in this life could be harder." Her eyes tear up.

"Why would they do that?"

She shrugs. "Milan's orders."

"Tell me their names."

"Maxim, my firstborn." She smiles. "Then Luca, Mila, and Damien. You met Damien. They let me choose their names." She looks proud of that fact.

They 'let' her choose their names? I could kill every Slav myself for what they've done to her.

"And their father?" I've got to try to make her see she doesn't belong here. To get her to come back with me. To stop this nonsense altogether. Orion, Logan, and Kai will protect her, too. And her kids. We haven't explicitly talked about it, but I know they will.

"I don't know who their father is. It could be anyone." The tone of her voice changes, and she stands up again, her face taking on that rough, guarded expression. Like we've done enough talking in a sweet, sisterly way.

"Why's that?"

She goes to the window and leans against the sill, sighing. "Maisy, come on. Enough with the questions. I know what you're doing. You're smarter than me, but that doesn't mean I'm stupid."

"Did you say you're now head of the Slavs? How come?" I ask, changing the subject. Yes, I *am* smarter. I can get her to talk longer, even if she doesn't want to.

"Milan had it in his will. If something was to happen to him, I'm to be in charge."

I can't hide my surprise. "You?! And everyone's fine with it?"

She shrugs. "I don't question orders like you do."

"I don't get it."

"What don't you get?" She raises her voice. "You and I were promised to Milan when Mom had us in her womb! Milan told me the truth!"

My volume rises to match hers. "He's a liar! You know he is!"

"Why would he lie? Why would he say that Goran Slavinovich, the head of the Slav family, is our father? And that before he died, he made Milan promise to take us at age twelve and do with us as he saw fit?"

Wh-what? A jumble of blurred, long-ago conversation has just stirred in my memory. I came across that name while working for Milan, and recently, at Orion's but... No. *No.* "What are you talking about, Rosey? Our father was just an ordinary man, who..." I'm drawing a blank, I don't even know what words to use any longer, because I refuse to remember, to connect the dots. "He was... He was no one." I'm losing power with every breath I take.

"Wrong. Our father was Goran Slavinovich. The head of the Slavs, who died in a drive-by shootout when Mom was five months pregnant with us. He fathered two daughters. *And they will bear as many Slavs as the family needs.* Hence I'm fucked by everyone, all the time. If you consider yourself a Slav, you have a right to fuck me. And for the past five years, that's all I've been doing. While you've been out there having a great life, I was here, having children." Her tone is bitter.

I shake my head, refusing to believe what I'm hearing. I'm not his daughter. "No. This has Milan's stench all over it. Don't believe them!"

"Maisy, Milan's will was read in front of everyone. That's why they made me head of the Slavs until my firstborn turns eighteen. There was a DNA certificate included in the paperwork. That's the reason no one dared object. Everyone was shocked."

"And you?"

"I knew already. Milan told me when he took Maxim. He said it was for the good of the Slavs. I didn't get a say, anyway."

I'm speechless. I need to get my thoughts in order. To see if there really was something that I missed. I couldn't have. *No.*

"You were too smart for Milan. He couldn't tame you. So when they brought you here half-dead, riddled with bullets, I was the one that suggested you were sent to Riyadh. He agreed because he thought if anyone could tame you, it would be the Arabs. I secretly hoped you'd run away and never return here. You see, I was the one looking after you, Maisy. But here you are. Back where you belong. I guess you can't run away from your destiny."

I try to stand up, but it's difficult with my world collapsing before my eyes. Everything I have has been literally taken from me at this very moment. I've been sticking around for Rosey, wanting to save her, but she's pulled me down with her. Now, even I can't be saved. In a heart-stopping collision, and in a split second, she's altered my life forever. And the trail of devastation I'm going to leave in my wake is illuminated in my head, and I don't want it. *No!*

"Maisy, stay. Together, we're stronger. I know half the Slavs already want to take me down, but with you by my side, we can run New York."

My world is spinning; I look at her, but none of what she's talking about makes sense.

"Plus, you're the firstborn. This, here, is your life. We were made to rule."

The door suddenly opens, jolting us both back into the here and now. She may have thought she was convincing me to stay, but I know I was falling deep into the abyss of a world that won't accept me any longer.

"Rosey–" One of her men goes to say something, but never gets the chance. She pulls a gun on him and shoots him between the eyes.

"Asshole. Next time, knock." Two other men run in, but seeing the fate of their comrade, they stop, looking petrified of what she'll do next. "Take him out," she orders.

They pull him legs-first out of the office, leaving a bloody trail on the floor. They close the door again.

I'm still in shock, and Rosey tugs on my hand. "Come on."

She just killed a man who did nothing to her. I can only stare at her, thunderstruck.

"Don't look at me like that. You have to show them who's boss, from the beginning. That's what Milan used to say. He did something right – he groomed me to become the best Slav possible. Milan believed in me."

"Are you fucking crazy?" I rise to my feet and raise my voice, pulling my hand from hers. I feel like I might throw up. I have to leave. This is not what I came here for. I want nothing to do with her. She's not my sister, not my family. As far as I'm concerned, we're not related. "All this is a lie. A lie! Why would you do that, Rosey? I dedicated my life to you, to *saving* you, and this is how you pay me back? By believing everything they tell you?" I back away and yank open the door. "I'm out of here!"

"Boss, we have a problem out front," one of her men says as I shoot out of the office and run towards the front door.

"Hold her!" she orders, pointing at me. "What kind of problem?"

I'm grabbed from behind. I kick and bite to get myself free, but the men holding me are stronger.

"We're under fire. It's the Delgados, Cartes, and Vitalis. Again."

"Fucking idiots! Didn't they learn their lesson? Kill them!" she barks.

"No! No! Don't kill them! They have Milan! Milan's alive!" I yell. "Milan's *alive!*"

My words echo around the corridor.

Everyone stops and exchanges glances. This is their opportunity to overthrow Rosey. I wouldn't want her to be head of anything. It's not that she can't do it — it's that she has so much anger and resentment inside her, she'll be doing too great a job.

Just at the right time, the front door bursts open and it's them, Orion, Logan, and Kai coming to my rescue, yet again. What have I done to deserve such men to love me? They brought reinforcements: three other men I don't know are with them, all of them pointing their guns at Rosey. There are dead people on the ground behind them. One of them's Bobby. Logan was right. He did die today.

"Let me go. Let-me-*go!*" I yell, thrashing about while everyone stands frozen in place. I count seven Slavs, including Rosey.

"You heard her." Orion nods at the men holding me and cocks his gun.

One of them squeezes my arm harder and I squeal. "Where's Milan?" he demands.

"We'll deliver him tonight!" Logan roars.

Everyone's looking at Rosey now, and finally she nods. They release me and I run into Orion's arms.

"Don't forget our conversation, Maisy," she says, and I'm reminded of what hell felt like only minutes ago.

"Let's go. I don't wanna stay here a moment longer." I pull on Orion's arm as he walks backward with me. The rest of our men follow us. I want out of here. I want nothing to do with her. Or with what I heard. I run for the exit, the others close behind.

They must never find out. I don't want to lie to them, but if I do and they find out, they'll reject me. Or finally kill me. I don't doubt for one moment that they won't do that, once they find out I'm a Slav. *No. I can't be. It can't be true. I'm* not *a fucking Slav.*

"Kill them all. They don't deserve to live." Orion said that this morning. I remember it clearly.

I recall Kai spitting in his coffee. *"They're the scum of the earth."*

"Skin them alive, one by one. Fucking filthy cocksuckers." Logan's exact words.

And me? What about me? What will they think of me?

Another fucking secret to keep.

I've had enough of them. Rebecca made me promise, and she was just another lost soul, like I was. Every day I heard what they were doing to her. I heard her being raped, tortured, electrocuted. If only I didn't go in, if only my brain told me to walk away and not get involved, then all this, meeting them, wouldn't have happened. But I did, stupidly, and now I'm tangled up in this world in more ways than I can understand.

The seven of us walk back out of the house and down the driveway. Nobody fires at us, but they follow as we leave.

Logan's mistrustful, as always. "Something's off."

Yes, something's off, Logan! I want to yell. *My blood is tainted. You'll hate me.*

Just when I think we're far enough away, and I've made it, Rosey's voice curdles my blood.

"If only our father could see you now, Maisy!" she calls out, making sure she's heard by all.

"Shut up! Shut *up!* I don't wanna talk to you ever again!" I shout back.

"No? What about my children? You said you wanted to meet them. They'd love to meet their famous auntie. The firstborn daughter of the great Goran Slavinovich."

"Stop it! Stop it! Stop it! Stop it! Stop it!" I shriek, losing control at the mention of his name, so hysterical that Orion pulls me into his chest and tries to calm me.

Eventually, I stop screaming. I dare not move. But I know everyone heard Rosey. That was the point. Orion pushes me away from him. I know why, and all three of them are staring at me now.

Orion's voice is dangerously calm. "Is that true? Is Goran Slavinovich your father?"

My eyes well up. Tears roll down my cheeks and I shrug helplessly. "That's what she says. But she *must* be lying. Milan would say anything to get what he wants." I glance back at Rosey, who's grinning maliciously at me.

Logan turns to Orion. "It makes sense if it's true. And why Milan wouldn't kill Maisy. Why he needed her. They bred her sister, took her children away to prepare them. All this time. Huh... The last twenty years have been preparation for a bigger, better Slav mafia."

"Fucking Slavs," Kai mutters under his breath.

Orion turns his back to me, shutting me out of the conversation.

"What are we doing with her?" I hear Kai asking.

I turn to the street, looking at our getaway car. *What are we doing with her? Her?! What am I, an unknown person?*

"We have no other option," Logan says quietly.

My vision is blurred, my tears running in rivers. But there's nothing that would rid me of the ugly, toxic blood running through my veins. One moment I'm delivering on a promise I made and the next, I'm at the center of the most horrendous story, my world turned upside down.

"Then it's settled," Orion tells them, and turns back to me.

Logan nods at the three men with us, who enter the car next to ours and drive off. But Rosey is not finished, apparently. And I can't scream loud enough to drown out her words. I'm dead. *I'm no one.*

"You can run, Maisy, all your life. But you can't run away from yourself. Eventually, the Slavs will find you and bring you here. Where you belong."

"I'm not a Slav!" I cry out. I'm helpless to defend myself against the lies they're feeding her. She's become this heartless, cruel, brutal person I don't know anymore.

"You're a firstborn Slav and you need to claim your place here, next to me."

I start sobbing and turn to Orion. "Will you... Will you take me home? Please?"

He eyes me coldly. "A firstborn Slav."

The final stab in my heart. If Orion, Logan, and Kai don't want me, and they won't – why would they? – then what is there for me here?

I see another bus speeding up the hill, and maybe that's all I need.

A chance for everything to end.

Without thinking about anything else, I take a step closer to the street and wait for the right moment. Just as the bus rushes up, I close my eyes and bravely take a step.

Instead of going forward, I feel myself being pulled back sharply.

"What the *fuck*, Maisy?!"

Orion has pulled me back. He's gripping me by the upper arm and the three of them are all staring at me in disgust, shock. Like I've let them down.

"I... I don't want to be this. I'm not a Slav." I continue to sob. "They ruined my life. All of them. They ruined Rosey's life."

"And you wanna make their lives easier, by dying?" Kai scolds. "Come on, let's get in the car. I have a feeling they'll start shooting any second now."

Orion's astonished. "You'd actually jump in front of a bus? I never thought that of you."

"Well, you don't know me." I try to shake my arm out of his grip but he's holding me tight. "Let me go."

"Do *not* let her get away," Logan warns as we cross the street. He comes to my other side, grabbing the other arm.

"Hey, let me go!" I try again to wrench myself free of their clutches, but they ignore me. We reach the car, and Orion gets in. I'm thrown inside, and Logan follows. Kai's already in, sitting opposite us.

"Take us home, Emilio."

We pull away. I peer at everyone from under my lashes, but they're ignoring me. Everyone's in their own world. Thinking, deliberating, planning.

"How much am I worth? Have you calculated that already?"

Orion shoots me a murderous look, then turns to look out the window.

"Have you thought about breeding me, too?" I continue.

"What the fuck are you talking about, Maisy?" Logan snaps.

"Get me pregnant!" I plead. "I'm willing to give the Slavs hell."

"No! That can never happen now." Kai retorts with a grimace.

I know it's a hard thing to stomach. I couldn't bear to fuck a Slav, either.

"Absolutely not a chance!" Logan scoffs.

"It'll help you win," I insist.

"D'you even hear how you sound, Maisy?"

"I do. And I hate everything about myself. This, this will make me feel good."

Orion shakes his head at me. *Disappointed? No. Saddened.*

I try again. "Get me–"

"Shut the fuck *up*, Maisy! I don't wanna hear you talk anymore," he orders. "Breeding you. Ugh. Children with a Slav. Like hell."

I take my cue and remain silent for the rest of the trip. I'm back to square one with them.

The moment we arrive back at Orion's, the four of us enter the house and find the men who are supposed to be with Milan in the basement are waiting for us in the kitchen.

"Milan's dead, boss."

"Fucking bitch," Logan growls. I know this is directed at me; I shot Milan yesterday. Logan was hoping to find out more about his mother from him.

"Martin, take Milan to his house in Central Valley," Orion commands. "When you dump him in the driveway, shoot him."

"Sure, boss."

Orion, Kai, and Logan lead me out of the kitchen, and somehow, I know the three of them are taking me to my room. *To make sure I go there? To keep me prisoner?*

We reach the door and they stop as I enter. I get into my large bed. Alone. Without anyone. Cast away.

The door closes and the key is turned in the lock.

This is it.

End of Book 2

ABOUT THE AUTHOR

Alexandra loves writing love stories, drinking Champagne and of course, wearing high heels.

Most days she is glued to her trusty laptop, creating magic, but on an odd occasion you'd find her on her social media accounts, connecting with her readers. Feel free to (virtually) follow her.

www.alexandraiff.com/links